PRIDE

THE DAMNING BOOK 5

KATIE MAY

EXPRESSO PUBLISHING, LLC

To Tiny Dick Hunter. May your life be full of tiny dicks and misery until the day you die, you crusty tampon.

CONTENTS

Recap of previous books — vii

1. Z — 1
2. Z — 11
3. Devlin — 19
4. Dair — 27
5. Z — 39
6. Jax — 49
7. Ryland — 57
8. Z — 73
9. Ryland — 83
10. Z — 95
11. Devlin — 103
12. Z — 115
13. Killian — 125
14. Z — 133
15. Bash — 141
16. Z — 153
17. Z — 163
18. Z — 171
19. Z — 193
20. Lupe — 209
21. Killian — 217
22. Z — 227
23. Jax — 235
24. Z — 245
25. Z — 253
26. Z — 265
27. Dair — 275

28. Killian   281
    Epilogue   289

    Afterword   297
    Acknowledgments   299
    About the Author   301
    Also by Katie May   303

When Z wins the Damning—a competition that pits the best assassins against each other—her world is overturned. Suddenly, she's forced to be the assassin for the exact kings she wishes to kill.

Fortunately, she has the seven princes to help her with the tasks ahead, each prince one of the seven supernatural species descended from the Seven Deadly Sins... and her fated mates. There's a prophecy surrounding the seven princes that states they'll either save the world or destroy it. They despise their parents and their inhumane treatment of humans.

At the end of the first book, Z is poisoned by a competitor of the Damning named Zack at the order of Aaliyah. Her mates are completely unaware that she's been poisoned...and that the poison is slowly killing her.

The kings assign seven tasks, seven games, Z has to complete to prove her loyalty. Despite her hatred for them, a spell administered by the mage king prohibits her from harming any member of the royal family.

She completes the first task, assigned by the mermaid king. In the process, Dair kills his evil older brother, Tavvy, who attempted to rape and kill Z. Just before he dies, Tavvy tells Dair that he and the rest of the Z's mates weren't born—they appeared out of thin air.

Meanwhile, a mysterious female named Aaliyah is sending extinct supernatural creatures after Z, including a gorgon, kraken, and fae. She instructs her monsters not to kill Z but to bring her to Aaliyah alive.

At the end of book two, Z discovers that Jax, her vampire mate, has gone missing.

The kings assign Z her next task—find Jax and return him to the capital in five days. If she fails, she dies. If she succeeds, the kings will have a special reward waiting for her. The kings force Axel, their former assassin, and T, a member of the Alphabet Resistance who has been taken prisoner, to accompany them.

While in the Vampire Kingdom, the inn they are staying at is lit on fire and Z is kidnapped and brought to the Bloody Carnival—a macabre event where vampires and other nightmares prey on humans. She meets a young boy, Miles, who she instantly feels protective of.

During a confrontation at the Bloody Carnival, Miles is killed, a fact that devastates Z. Axel agrees to search for Miles's younger sister while Z and the other freed humans bury the bodies.

The gang discovers that Aaliyah has been keeping Jax prisoner. Through her connection with Jax, Z knows he's been forced to feed on blood regularly, losing himself to the bloodlust and madness.

Aaliyah arrives with her pet gargoyles and Jax. She

tells the group that she's Z's sister and a demon. A fight ensues. During the battle, Jax is stabbed and killed. Aaliyah disappears before anyone can stop her. Z, in her grief, pours white light into Jax, bringing him back to life. In the process, the poison coursing through Z's system catches up to her and she collapses.

Meanwhile, Axel finds Miles's sister and discovers she's the first nightmare-human hybrid to exist.

T reveals to have been the one to give Z's location up to the human traffickers at the Bloody Carnival in exchange for S's—his brother and Z's ex-boyfriend—soul.

At the end of book three, S is alive and well and demanding to know Z's whereabouts.

In book four, Z struggles to survive the poison coursing through her bloodstream and her mates are desperate to find a cure. When Z's condition worsens, the men must separate in order to save her life—Devlin and Lupe return to their fathers while the others decide to visit Bash's eccentric grandfather, Paco.

While at Paco's cottage, the group discovers that the spell to save Z's life will only work once she's dead.

Z is visited in her dreams by Aaliyah, who tells Z she's an angel named Gabrielle. Aaliyah reveals that she herself is a demon who was once in love with the Seven Heavenly Virtues before she murdered them on behalf of her sister. Z begins to suspect that the monsters attacking her have been brought through a portal that leads to hell.

At the capital, Lupe and Devlin discover that Ryland's father—the shadow king—is a spy for the resistance. The other kings throw him into the dungeons for his crimes.

Meanwhile, an army of humans—led by the ex-assassin Axel—arrives at Paco's house and claims to be followers of Z.

Z proves herself to the humans when she saves a group of them from a trafficking ring. In the process of doing so, Z succumbs to the poison. She passes away, but her mates are able to save her life and rid her body of the poison once and for all.

Lupe and Devlin, however, do not know that Z survived and feel their mating bonds break. Lupe goes feral, and Devlin leaves the capital to get revenge on Aaliyah.

Z and her mates return to the capital and discover that she is now engaged to Axel as a reward for finding Jax and bringing him home.

CHARACTERS:

Z — Member of the Alphabet Resistance that advocates for human rights, assassin, mate to the seven princes, and winner of the Damning. She was poisoned at the end of book one but saved at the end of book four. Currently, she's engaged to Axel.

Dair — Z's mate, mermaid, and descended from Envy. Like all mermaids, he's forced to live as a mermaid for twelve hours a day and a human the other twelve. His father constantly cuts his legs off, grows them back, and then cuts them off again each night. Paco provided him with a potion that will allow him to walk, though he only has a little bit of it left now.

Devlin — Z's mate, genie, and descended from Greed. He trapped S's soul inside of his magic lamp until it was freed by T in book three. He was Z's childhood sweetheart. At the end of book four, he left the capital in order to avenge Z and murder Aaliyah.

Killian — Z's mate, incubus, and descended from Lust. As a child, he was forced to watch his father rape and kill his nanny. Currently a virgin.

Lupe — Z's mate, shifter, and descended from Wrath. His father implemented the first human concentration camp. He prefers to fight with words rather than violence. At the end of book four, he lost himself to his wrath after feeling Z die.

Ryland — Z's mate, shadow, and descended from Pride. He hides his face in his shadows to hide his hideous facial scarring. He was the first to know all of the princes were mates with Z. His father was thrown into the dungeons at the end of book four after being revealed as a spy for the resistance.

Jax — Z's mate, vampire, and descended from Gluttony. He's facing madness because he refuses to drink human blood and is only coherent around Z. Currently, he's engaged to Atta. He was kidnapped by Aaliyah at the end of book two but was rescued in book three.

Bash — Z's mate, mage, and descended from Sloth. He initially distrusted the mate bond and what he perceived as a lack of free will, so he struggled with his affections for Z. However, they finally confessed their love to each other in book four.

Atta — Shifter and descended from Wrath. She's Lupe's younger sister and the mate to Mali but is currently engaged to Jax.

Mali — Vampire and descended from Gluttony. She's Z's best friend who unwittingly betrayed her, leading to the death of the mage, Diego. Mate to Zack (now dead) and Atta.

Diego — Mage and descended from Sloth. Z's best friend and mate to HH. He was murdered by Zack protecting Z after Mali betrayed them.

T — Z's friend from the Alphabet Resistance and brother of S. He traded Z to the Bloody Carnival in exchange for his brother's soul.

S — Z's deceased ex-boyfriend and T's brother who was killed by shifters. It's discovered that Devlin had his soul inside of his lamp until he lost it. T made a deal with human traffickers to retrieve his soul, thus bringing him back to life.

B — Leader of the Alphabet Resistance.

A — Z's former mentor before he died.

Aaliyah — Main antagonist of the series who wants to capture Z for unknown reasons. She revealed herself to be Z's sister and a demon at the end of book three. She confessed that she was once the lover of the Seven Heavenly Virtues before she killed them.

Zack — Mage and evil assassin who killed Diego and poisoned Z. He was Mali's mate, but now he's dead.

Axel — Shadow and ex-assassin of the kingdoms. He's currently engaged to Z at the urging of the kings.

Slippy - A kraken Aaliyah sent after Z and her mates in book two. Slippy is now Z's beloved pet.

ONE

Z

I stared at my reflection in the full-length mirror, trying to ignore the way my heart twisted into a dozen, intricate knots. No amount of tugging would be able to unravel the emotions circulating inside of my chest.

It felt like weeks since the kings "rewarded" me Axel as a fiancé—or maybe *he* was rewarded *me*—but I knew it to be only days. Days stuck as a virtual prisoner inside the opulent capital building, with its stark-white walls, floor-to-ceiling windows, and bustling staff. Days planning, waiting, and praying for the opportunity to strike and finally end this once and for all.

My hands curled into fists by my sides, even as my expression remained serene and almost pleasant. I was a damn good actress, and the woman fitting me for my wedding gown bought every lie that spilled from my mouth like poisoned honey.

I had already removed the puffy, white garment and now stood in my underclothes, watching the woman—

Ester—hurry to and fro, murmuring under her breath about needing to adjust the bust size. I didn't know if that was a compliment or an insult, but I'd take it. I loved my tits.

"Will the dress be ready in time for my wedding in a few days?" I questioned with a saccharine-sweet grin.

Ester was an older, robust woman with brown hair braided away from her wrinkled face and compassionate green eyes. I believed she was a shifter, though her gentle countenance was at direct odds with what I knew about most of the species descended from Wrath.

Except for my sweet Lupe, of course.

At the thought of my shifter mate, the knots in my stomach and chest tightened exponentially until it felt like I was choking. Still, I pushed the emotions down. Shoved them into a steel box reinforced with iron chains and then buried them six feet under. No amount of digging would be able to uncover them.

"It should," Ester assured me. "I'll have to make a few minor alterations..." She pursed her lips as she studied the length of my body before nodding once. "But yes. I hope to have it ready for you soon. However, I believe you're done for the day."

I took her words for what they were—a dismissal. Though why she would be dismissing me when this was my room remained a mystery.

With another fake-ass smile, I stepped off the raised podium and grabbed a gossamer robe hanging off the back of a chair. I pulled it on over the underclothes and knotted it tight.

"Thank you again, Ester," I told her. My cheeks

ached from how large my smile was, but I didn't dare let it waver, not even a fraction of an inch.

For all I knew, Ester reported every interaction with me directly back to the kings. The last thing I wanted—or needed—was for them to know how unsettled I was by the "reward" they gifted me for completing the vampire king's task and saving his son, my vampire mate, Jax.

How did everything in my life go to shit so quickly? One second, everything was great. Amazing, actually...if you considered being poisoned and almost dying amazing. I, however, preferred dying a painful death to *this*.

Lupe, locked in the capital's dungeons out of his mind with wrath.

Devlin, on a mission to murder my sadistic sister, thinking I'd succumbed to the poison she had one of her minions inject me with.

And me...about to marry a man I'd once trusted like a brother while my other mates were forced to watch. No, not just watch. Their asshole fathers were encouraging them to "pursue other options," despite knowing they were my fated mates.

All in all, I wasn't a happy camper. I was actually a very murdery, slightly stabby, and completely unhinged one.

Ester fretted around the room a few seconds longer— checking over her measurements, grabbing the pale white fabric where she had placed it on the couch, and then cleaning up all of her supplies. By the time she finally left, I was exhausted, though I was pretty sure my face had frozen in the demented smile I was forced to wear all evening.

"Is she finally gone?"

I didn't bother to lift my head and greet my mage mate. I was pretty sure I had collapsed at some point during this ordeal, though I couldn't remember when. All I knew was that I was sprawled on the couch, my head dangling over one end and my feet hanging off the other.

"Most women are so excited for their wedding day," I deadpanned as he moved to sit opposite me on the sofa. He lifted my feet and placed them in his lap. A second later, the soft pads of his thumbs dug into the soles of my tender feet, eliciting a low moan from me. "Fuck, keep doing that. Just like that."

"You keep using that tone with me, baby, and you'll be begging me for a completely different reason," he said with a distinct smirk in his voice.

"You're a pervert, but I love you," I all but moaned, my lashes fluttering shut at the sheer pleasure of his magic fingers. Pun unintended.

Since mages were descended from Sloth, they were often lazy, negligent, and forgetful. Bash used to be like that months ago...until I whipped him into shape. Yeah, I was taking credit for it. Sue me. He was still a dick, but he was my dick—as in, I claimed ownership of his delicious cock. No other girl was allowed to even think about it, let alone sample it.

Since confessing his feelings for me, Bash had become extremely attentive and touchy-feely, as if he thought he had to make up for all of the times he was an ass to me. And let me be very clear about one thing—he *was* an ass to me. Multiple times. Hell, I didn't think I could even count just how many times. Maybe in the hundreds?

I knew why he did it, though, which made it easier to forgive him. It was a defense mechanism because he feared what having a mate would mean for him and his brothers. It was only after he got to know me—and consequently fell in love with me—did he change his stance on fated mates.

"You're moaning like I have my fingers buried in your pussy, not on your stinky feet," he mused with a snort of derision, proving that all the love in the world couldn't completely alter his personality.

"First of all, my feet are *not* stinky." I lightly kicked at him to emphasize my point, and his dark chuckle flooded the bedroom. "And second of all, your fingers have to be good for something, because they obviously aren't at giving me orgasms."

Was it smart to tease my most...volatile, angry mate? Probably not. Would I continue to do so until the day I died? Most definitely.

"Why, you little..." Abruptly, he threw his body on top of mine until the hard planes of his chest crushed my soft curves. His hands tightened around my wrists like iron vises and held them above my head.

My eyes fluttered open, immediately greeted by his handsome face. Everything about Bash was a literal work of art. His chiseled, sharp features once made him appear cruel and haughty but now emphasized the soft curve of his pink lips and the ash-blond of his hair. Brilliant green eyes ensnared my own, leaving me helpless to look away.

Not that I wanted to. I could lose myself in the intensity of those verdant orbs for the rest of my life.

"Hi," I whispered with a demure grin.

Who the fuck was I kidding? There wasn't a demure bone in my body. But it was fun to pretend, if only for a moment.

His own smile was predatory. Dangerous. *Hungry.* Licks of fire ate a pathway along the length of my spine.

"What's this I hear about *not* being able to get you off with my fingers? Who was it that made you orgasm seven times last night?"

"That was with your tongue," I countered as his fingers fumbled with the tie securing the robe around me. "Not your fingers."

"I know what you're doing." He narrowed his eyes at me, though his nimble fingers didn't leave the silk fabric. He tugged it apart roughly until the translucent material of my chemise was bared to him.

"And what is that?" My chest heaved, heat cascading through my veins and burning me up inside. All I wanted to do was fork my fingers through his blond hair and tug his lips down to mine.

Apparently, he had other plans for me. For us.

His soft lips caressed the underside of my jaw before trailing downwards, peppering kisses along the column of my throat. I arched upwards instinctively to grant him better access, acutely aware of the wicked smile touching my skin.

"Being a brat," he finally answered as he pulled down the neckline of my dress, freeing my right breast. His lips found my pebbled nipple, and he sucked it into his mouth, his teeth grazing the sensitive nub. "You want my fingers in your sweet little pussy again, don't you, baby?"

As he spoke, his fingers inched down my flat tummy until they were able to push up the bottom of the lacy gown—

"Bash! Z!" Our names were immediately succeeded by the poignant clap of shoes against the floor. And then... "Holy meatball!"

I shoved Bash off of me as if he were toxic, and my mage prince tumbled onto the floor with a low groan. I sat up immediately, not even caring that the lacy fabric of the dress was bunched around my calves and my breast was still hanging out of the top. It wasn't anything that Killian, my sweet incubus mate, hadn't seen already.

Still, he stared at my body as if he didn't know quite what to do, quite what to say. His lips parted on a breathless exhale as his gaze devoured me from head to toe.

Killian was hot. There were no ifs, ands, or buts about it. If Bash resembled the stereotypical princely, aristocratic look, then Killian was every woman's wet dream. He believed his appeal to only be a product of his incubus allure, but I knew that not to be true. It was *him* intricately. Garnet hair highlighted in brown and gold framed a face so sharp, you could cut glass on it. The rest of his body was just as delicious—broad shoulders leading down to a tapered waist, numerous tattoos on his biceps and chest, a defined six-pack most women dreamed they could lick, and plush, kissable lips.

But it was his eyes that reeled you in, that made you discombobulated with no way to differentiate up from down. They were by far the most expressive, open, *inno-*

cent eyes I'd ever encountered before. Killian viewed the world through rose-tinted glasses, and I never wanted that to change. Where some found his innocence amusing or infuriating, I found it endearing. Beautiful. He was that single flower blooming amidst miles upon miles of snow, poking through the white blanket and providing much-needed color to a monochromatic world.

"Were you able to do it?" I asked urgently, grappling with the strings of my robe.

"Errr..." Killian didn't pull his gaze away from my tit. Honestly, you would think he had never seen one before.

"Kill." I snapped my fingers impatiently in front of his face until his head snapped up and his eyes met mine.

He blinked rapidly, as if coming out of a daze, and made a noncommittal noise in the back of his throat.

"Killian, focus," Bash drawled, pulling himself to his feet and dusting himself off with a pointed glare in my direction.

Once my body was completely covered by the robe, Killian seemed to come back to himself. He gave his head a brisk, rueful shake, color pluming in his cheeks, and then said, "Yes. I got permission. It took some convincing, because our fathers...well..." He sheepishly scratched at the back of his neck.

"They're assholes who like to see us suffer?" Bash filled in, his voice heated.

Killian's blush deepened at Bash's candid statement. "Y-yes."

His stutter always became more pronounced when he was anxious, and I imagined he felt that tenfold. If the last few days had been a lot for me, it was nothing compared to what my mates were going through. Devlin thought I was dead, Lupe was out of his mind, Dair was back in the home of his abuser, Ryland's father was in prison, Jax was struggling with his mental health, and Killian and Bash? They felt helpless, unable to offer an easy solution to help their brothers. To help me.

"But we can do it? We can go down to the dungeons?" I could barely breathe through the tightening, tugging sensation in my throat. It felt as if garden shears were pinching my skin, digging in deep enough to draw blood.

"Yes." Killian nodded once, though his face had gone oddly pale. "But, Z..." He glanced desperately at Bash, once again waiting for the mage prince to fill in the blanks.

Bash didn't fail to deliver. "There's no telling what Lupe will do when he sees you. He may still not recognize you. You need to prepare for that," he told me with a grim frown.

Lupe.

My sweet, protective bear shifter.

When he felt the mate bond sever, when he felt me die, it was too much for him. He lost himself to his sin, to his wrath, and had since been locked away until he could regain control of himself. I had only been to see him once —days ago, when I first arrived—and he hadn't even remembered me. His bear had paced the small cage restlessly, pawing at anyone who got too close. I thought speaking to him would dampen his rage, would spark recognition in his amber eyes.

I was wrong.

He'd stared at me as if he didn't know what I was to him and what he was to me. The vitriol spewing from those golden orbs had been a slap to the face. What made it worse was the fact that the kings deemed it too "unsafe" for me to visit and had since refused to allow me access to the dungeons.

Fucking kings.

But I was determined to get my shifter mate back...no matter the cost.

TWO

Z

The dungeons smelled like piss.

Not the most eloquent description, but certainly the most accurate one. The stale, pungent scent immediately assaulted my senses as I descended into the belly of the beast—or the capital, as the case may be. Though at this point, I was beginning to believe they were one and the same.

My pulse hammered in nervous anticipation, and my grip around Bash's hand tightened until I feared my fingers would leave a permanent bruise on his naturally fair skin. If he noticed—or cared—he didn't show it, leading me forward down a long hall lit by lanterns interspersed evenly for the first few feet. The farther away from the main entrance we got, however, the darker the room became until it felt like I was trudging through a pool of waist-high tar. Only Bash's hand in mine and Killian's palm on the small of my back reminded me that I wasn't alone.

And I wouldn't be alone again as long as they were with me.

The feeling that thought evoked—a light, buoyant sensation that reminded me of swallowing bubbles—momentarily eclipsed the overwhelming terror devouring me. I had no idea what tomorrow would bring, but I knew I could get through it if I had my mates.

Cheesiness aside, it stood to reason that I needed to actually *get* my mates back if I wanted this perceived happily ever after. We had to rid the world of their sadistic parents—and hopefully remove the manacles said sadistic parents placed around their sons—find Devlin, or at least find a way to contact him before he could do something stupid, and save Lupe from himself.

Easy peasy.

"How bad is he?" Bash murmured, and at first, I thought he was directing the question at me. But when I turned towards him, his gaze was fixed pointedly at the corner of the room, where the shadows coalesced into a single being.

Ryland, my shadow mate.

As I watched, the darkness around him parted until his features were visible through the sparse candlelight flickering intermittently.

I remembered when Ryland used to hide in the shadows. He still did, but not nearly as often. And never with me.

His face was mottled by puckered pink, red, and white scars. They distorted his cheeks and eyes, cut through his lips, and traveled down the length of his neck. The whittled skin only proved to me time and time again how strong he truly was, how much he had endured. And how much he would continue to endure.

Even though I knew he trusted me implicitly, he still hadn't shared how he received those particular scars. For the longest time, I'd assumed they were inflicted by his father, the shadow king, but now...

Against my will, my gaze drifted to the lone cell Ryland was hovering in front of. A figure sat inside, his gaunt body and haggard face nearly unrecognizable.

The shadow king had once been regal, though without any of the arrogance the other kings seemed to exhibit in spades. Now, he was merely a shell of himself, his clothes hanging off his thin form in tatters. I couldn't help but swallow heavily while staring at his hunched body, my heart twisting into knots.

It was revealed that the shadow king had been working with the Alphabet Resistance for years. All this time...

Why hadn't B, the leader of the human resistance and my friend, told me? I had entered the Damning believing myself to be completely alone only to discover I had an ally on the inside. I knew, logically, that the shadow king couldn't risk revealing his identity to me, but it still felt like information I needed to know.

I would have to talk to the shadow king, and soon. He might have information for me, for us, that would help us end this mess once and for all. I still didn't know where the Alphabet Resistance went after they abandoned their last base of operations, but according to Toby, a human man I met at Paco's, they were still alive. I'd assumed they were dead or gravely injured, but now...

Now, I had hope.

But the shadow king—and by extension, the Alphabet Resistance—could wait. For one, I didn't trust that the other kings weren't listening in, dissecting every move I made and every conversation I had. For two, despite the shadow king's current predicament, he was still a nightmare. He was the man human parents would tell stories about in order to scare naughty children into staying in their beds instead of sneaking out at night. It had been conditioned inside of me to fear the kings and everything they represented, and I couldn't throw away those misgivings in a span of days. And finally, I had more pressing matters to attend to.

Like my shifter mate.

"He tried to bite my head off," Ryland said, dragging my attention back to the conversation at hand. His lips pursed into a determined line as he flicked his gaze in the direction of Lupe's cell. "He's not well."

"Of course he's not well," I snapped, though we all knew my ire wasn't directed at him. "He thought I died." I swore my heart shattered at that exact moment, every piece cutting me up like minute pieces of glass.

"We'll get him back, Z," Killian vowed from behind. He leaned forward and planted a chaste kiss on my cheek. Heat migrated from where his lips touched my skin, igniting a thousand miniature bonfires inside of my body.

"We damn well better." I tried to emulate a confidence I didn't truly feel as I pulled away from my mates and ventured swiftly down the tiny hall. Cages lined either side of the walkway, but most of them were empty.

Put your big-girl panties on, Z. You need to face him.

Why did it sound more appealing to stick my hand in a tub of acid, gouge out my eyes, and then roll around in rusty nails for shits and giggles?

Maybe it was because I would rather deal with a million immeasurable agonies than have one of my mates face even one. They had already been through so much in their lives, and I feared they would reach the point of no return. The point where the weight of the world descended on them and crushed their spines. That fear... It *burned* me.

I wouldn't be able to live if something happened to my men.

The last cage—as far away from the main entrance as physically possible—was occupied. My heart climbed up my throat and made a nice, cozy home there at the sight of my mate pacing the small confines.

His brown, furry head swiveled this way and that, his amber eyes first focusing on the iron bars of his cell and then on the destroyed mattress against the left wall of his cage. Feathers littered the tiny, dirty room, along with...

"My dress," I whispered, stunned.

My purple dress—the one I wore the day Zack killed my friend Diego—sat in the corner of the room, the only thing even remotely intact. It almost seemed as if Lupe had been sleeping on it, though I didn't dare analyze what that meant. Did a part of him recognize me? Recognize my scent? That was the only reasonable explanation, and it stabbed at my brain like a flaming sword.

There's still hope.

"Lupe?" I pressed a hand to the bar of the cage, and

my mate's huge bear head swiveled in my direction, locking on me. His golden eyes flared like coins crafted out of solid gold. "Lupe? It's me. It's Z—"

A roar ripped through the dungeon, causing every hair on my arms to spike at attention.

"Maybe you should back up," Bash cautioned, materializing at my side and grabbing my arm gently.

Lupe didn't seem to like that.

He swung his head in the mage's direction and pulled his lips away from his teeth. Another grating snarl erupted from the beast as he pawed at the ground.

"Maybe *you* should back up," I countered, eyeing my shifter mate warily. All I wanted to see was *something*. A spark of recognition, perhaps? Familiarity? Love?

That *something* continued to elude me as his golden eyes flitted from my face to Bash's and back again.

Ignoring Bash at my side, Ryland and Killian behind me, and the shadow king a few cells over...

I focused on my mate. Only my mate. Fear gnawed at me, tightening my muscles, even as the rest of the world dimmed to a dull, monochromatic shade of gray.

"Lupe, it's me. It's Z," I repeated, keeping my hand pressed to the iron bars. "Please come back to me. I...I need you." My voice broke, but I refused to stop. I needed to be vulnerable with my men if I hoped to have them be vulnerable with me in return. Even after all this time, I still struggled to open up to them, to let them in the way they deserved. "I need you to come back. Dair... He's back with his father, and we all know how that'll end. Jax is who the fuck knows where. And Devlin..." I shook my head rapidly, as if trying to dispel an errant thought.

Fuck. Devlin. Even thinking of my genie mate threatened to send me careening off the edge of a steep ravine. "He's going after Aaliyah. By himself. Alone. He's going... He's going to get himself killed, so I need you to come back, okay? I need you to be the voice of reason and tell me everything will be okay. I just... I need my mate back. I love you, Lupe. Please."

Tears cascaded down my cheeks, but I didn't lift a hand to brush them away. I kept my palm fixed firmly to the cell as I waited, waited, waited.

I prayed Lupe would hear me, would answer. I hated being weak around anyone, even my mates, but just then, I didn't feel it. I felt *strong*, as if the love coursing through my veins like magma gave me immeasurable strength. And hell, maybe it did. Maybe the fact that I had finally opened up to my men allowed me to transcend or whatever the fuck that term was.

A part of me assumed that Lupe would immediately shift back, open his huge arms, and then pull me into his embrace, where not even the fiercest of storms could hurt me.

But he didn't shift back.

He didn't open his huge arms.

He didn't embrace me.

He simply...growled, the noise so chilling, I felt it in the marrow of my bones.

And for the first time since I learned of Lupe's condition, I feared I was too late to save him.

I feared I'd already lost.

THREE

DEVLIN

There was nothing particularly remarkable about Chaz Lenny. He was neither thin nor fat, neither handsome nor ugly, neither tall nor short. He was just...there, with slightly graying hair, a large, bulbous nose, and a noticeable cleft on his chin. Insignificant. Forgettable.

He fidgeted with his mug of ale as he stared at me over the wooden tabletop. Nervous energy rippled off of him in palpable waves. Mine, in contrast, was icy cold. Unforgiving. I had one mission and one mission alone—find Aaliyah and end her miserable excuse of a life.

It was because of *her* I lost the person I loved most in the world. She took—

I shoved the thought away. If I were to think about the woman I lost, I would go fucking insane and murder everyone in this shitty pub.

But fuck, if I didn't feel as if someone had reached into my body and ripped out my spleen. The pain... It was excruciating. I didn't know how anyone survived it. I didn't know how anyone *could* survive it. Why would they want to? It took every ounce of willpower within me to sit at this damn booth and not throw myself off of the nearest cliff.

My mate was dead.

And the only thing left to do was avenge her.

I knew my brothers were dealing with a similar grief to mine, and maybe it was selfish, but I couldn't deal with theirs on top of my own. Was I allowed to be self-centered just this once? To put my needs before theirs? Maybe. Maybe not. But none of that mattered anymore. *Nothing* mattered in this world that had been forsaken by God himself.

"Do you have what I need?" I demanded in a low voice, glancing inconspicuously around the smelly pub Chaz had instructed me to meet him at.

Just like him, the pub was forgettable and utterly unremarkable. The combined scents of stale beer, dried blood, and spiced meats barraged my senses, even though we sat as far away from the crowd as physically possible, in a booth coalesced in darkness.

"Yes." Chaz nodded once, fidgeting uncomfortably on the wooden booth across from me.

Chaz was a shadow and had once been employed by my father to spy on his enemies. He did this for years before gaining enough money to retire, though he still took on the odd job here and there. I didn't trust Chaz for shit, but then again, I didn't *need* to trust him. I just needed information.

And if there was one thing he was good for, it was that.

"Spit it out." I spoke through heavily clenched teeth, once again allowing my gaze to roam over the room, cataloging everything in sight. Women in modest brown dresses hurried in and out of the kitchen serving the patrons bread, meat, cheese, and ale. In the far corner, a few genies were talking and laughing, jostling one another and speaking obnoxiously loud.

Not a single person was aware that their prince was in their midst.

Hell, not even Chaz knew the truth. He simply believed that a wealthy noble had hired him to do some surveillance. And with my cloak pulled taut over my head, shadowing my face, it was impossible for him to know differently.

Today, I wasn't Devlin Genie. I was simply...Lin.

My throat closed up, tightening exponentially by the second, when I thought about the first time I used that name. When I met a young human girl named Susan in a bakery...

But she wasn't Susan, just as I wasn't Lin. She was Z, my fated mate and the love of my life.

Until Aaliyah took her from me.

My hand curled into a white-knuckled fist that I hid beneath the table. The last thing I needed was Chaz to believe my anger was directed at him and get antsy and leave.

"There is a girl like you described," Chaz began cautiously, his fingers tap, tap, tapping away at his glass mug. "Red hair. Beautiful. Insane." He chuckled darkly. "My type of girl, am I right?" When I remained as still as a statue, only my violet eyes peering out through the fabric of the hood, his laughter tapered off and he cleared his throat twice. "There have also been rumors..."

"Don't leave me in suspense, Chazel," I gritted out, purposely using his full name.

His eyes narrowed, turning to slits, but he relented and continued without any argument. Perhaps he could see how close I was to my breaking point, how tenuous my grip on sanity truly was. "There have been rumors about...monsters around this young woman's property. I don't really know how to explain it, and nothing I heard makes sense—"

"Don't bother." I waved my hand in the air dismissively, my mind reeling from this new information. Nothing he said surprised me, and I didn't need him to attempt to rationalize something he knew very little about. I already knew that Aaliyah was somehow reincarnating extinct supernatural creatures, though the question was how. And why.

But I supposed that didn't matter. Once I killed the bitch, she wouldn't be able to resurrect herself, let alone a fucking cyclops or whatever she had up her sleeve.

"And where exactly is she?" I demanded, placing my elbows on the table and leaning forward so I wouldn't miss a single word. I felt like a dog with a bone, only this bone was a one-hundred-and-twenty-pound female I would see dead by my hand. Only when her blood stained the ground would I feel even a semblance of peace.

Z...

My heart thrashed, rioted, as it always seemed to do when I thought of my love. I could picture her now, sitting across from me at the table with a tiny crease between her brows as her eyes flashed with irritation.

"What the fuck is taking so long?" she would say to Chaz with a haughty sneer. "We need a location, not a five-thousand-word essay."

My lips twitched into the makings of a tentative smile before I masked it.

"The shifter kingdom," Chaz said at last. "Near the shifter's palace. Do you know Lake Meade?"

"I'm familiar," I gritted out, conjuring up an image of the landscape in my head.

"It's right by there," he finished. "I can draw you a map—"

"I know where to go." I shoved away from the table and stood.

Yes, I was familiar with Lake Meade. I went swimming there with my brothers when we were younger. Dair was particularly fond of that lake, though all of my good memories of the shifter kingdom were tarnished by the bad ones—like the human work camps Lupe's father implemented after his wife was murdered. Even thinking about them made my hands shake by my sides and a cold, insidious fury light a fire in my veins.

Chaz cleared his throat obnoxiously from behind me. "And payment?"

Oh. Right. Pathetic men and their pathetic need to exploit the desperate. And that was what I was—desperate. How could I not be, when my only motivation to live was shrouded in bloodlust and violence? In vengeance and suffering?

As I dug into my pocket for a few gold coins, Chaz

continued, "If you don't have the money with you, I could always...have a wish." His voice dripped with avarice, wanton need, desire.

There was nothing more powerful than a wish from a genie, and if I had more time, I might've taken him up on it. What most nightmares and humans didn't realize, however, was that a wish from a genie was a tricky thing, full of thousands of conditions the wisher couldn't possibly uphold. The end result? Their soul.

I hadn't ever partaken in the practice of stealing souls—excluding one soul in particular—but I was damn tired of being good. Maybe I would allow Chaz to make that wish, and when the time came to collect...

Z's face manifested in my mind's eye, her lips parted and her blonde hair flowing around her angelic face. The expression in her eyes cut me to the bone. It flayed away my skin until I was a broken and bleeding man falling to my knees at her feet, begging for even a scrap of her affection.

She would be horrified by the direction of my thoughts. Sickened. That knowledge alone gave me the strength to shove the gold coins into Chaz's hand and close his fingers around them.

"Keep the change," I all but snarled, hating myself for even considering his offer. Hating myself for hungering for his soul.

"Hey, Lin?" Chaz's voice once again reached me before I could take a single step out of the pub. It was subdued this time, nearly lost in the incessant chatter from the bar's patrons, but I heard it as if he'd been screaming.

"Yeah?"

"This woman... She seems pretty damn dangerous, even for a nightmare. I've heard that she killed a lot of people, and um... It just seems like a suicide mission, you know?" He stumbled over those words helplessly, as if he didn't quite understand why he was giving me this warning.

But I appreciated it nonetheless, even if I wouldn't heed it.

"I know," I responded dismissively, finally steeling my spine and stalking towards the front door. "I don't expect to make it back alive."

And to be quite frank, I didn't plan to.

I didn't want to live in a world without Z in it. So I'd do what I needed to do, and if the price of that action was my death, then so be it. Perhaps it would be the universe's way of righting its wrong and reuniting me with my mate. Either way, I didn't expect to make it home alive.

Z, I'll see you soon. I'm so sorry.

And with that encouraging thought reverberating through my head, I stepped outside and prepared to face my destiny.

FOUR

DAIR

I ducked beneath the water and opened my eyes to the ethereal oasis hidden just beneath the surface—stringy seaweed billowing in the current, schools of brightly colored fishes, and clumps of wet clay and dirt. Rippling waves caressed my skin as I cut through the lake in sure, unhurried strokes.

The last few days proved to be a lesson in hiding and evading, both of which I'd grown pretty damn good at. I'd learned to listen to the barely audible thump of footsteps in the hall outside of my room, the swoosh of a door opening, the ragged sound of my father's heavy breathing a second before he sought me out. And...I hid. I didn't know if that made me a coward or the smartest man alive, but I was more determined than ever to free myself of his influence. Of his anger.

For the first time in my life, I felt whole, and it was a heady, intoxicating sensation, one I could get used to. Thanks to the elixir Paco, Bash's eccentric grandpa, provided me, I no longer needed to be pushed around in a wheelchair.

How long would this newfound freedom last? How long until my father attempted to reclaim what little power he had over me by cutting off my legs again?

The thought caused a glacial, insidious fear to crawl up my spine. It settled uncomfortably on the back of my neck like an itch I couldn't scratch no matter how hard I tried.

My stomach churned violently, threatening to banish the contents of the lunch I ate a few hours prior, but I managed to keep it down and continue my swim.

With every stroke of my arms through the tranquil water, a little bit of the tension tugging at my muscles abated.

I would no longer be a slave to my father.

I wouldn't let him destroy me a second longer.

I was stronger than he'd ever be.

Taking a deep, haggard breath, I forced all thoughts of my father to a back pocket of my mind and focused on what truly mattered—Lupe and Devlin. We had to come up with a way to save my brothers, and soon. I could feel the solution sitting on the tip of my tongue, just waiting for me to devour it, but the answer constantly eluded me. It trickled through my fingers just like the water I swam through.

Didn't Aaliyah have the power to exacerbate nightmares' sins? If that were true...then shouldn't Z be able to do the opposite? That is, if Aaliyah was telling the truth about being Z's sister.

I turned this theory around and around in my mind,

analyzing every side of it and struggling to correlate it with everything that had happened.

How would Z even go about doing that, for starters? She was able to bring Jax back from the brim, but was it simply because she was his mate? Did it have something to do with that strange, glowing light that emanated from her hands when she brought him back from the dead?

Question after question piled up on top of each other inside of my mind until I feared the tower would topple over and bury me under its immense weight. My chest suddenly felt too tight.

Fuck, why were the answers consistently eluding me? Why couldn't I just say, "I have an idea," and have that be the end of it? Maybe it was because those positions—the thinker, the leader, the innovator—belonged to Devlin and Lupe. Devlin took control whenever we were in a situation and wouldn't stop until he came up with a solution to get us out of it. And Lupe would study each and every obstacle extensively until he deciphered the best way for us to overcome it.

I missed the two of them with an intensity that physically ached. It felt as if my heart was growing in a steadily shrinking vise. How much more could I take, could *we* take, before the organ exploded completely?

"What did that water ever do to you?" a familiar voice retorted from somewhere above the surface of the lake, the noise slightly distorted with my head still underwater. "It looks as if you're attempting to beat the shit out of it with well-placed karate chops."

I breached the surface and drew in a long, strangled breath.

Z sat on the edge of the lake, dangling her feet in the water's icy depths. In her hands was a familiar, grotesque, gray monster. Slippy. She leisurely stroked the kraken's back as she regarded me with way too astute eyes that always seemed to see everything—even the parts of me I so desperately wanted to hide. That keen, penetrating gaze of hers cut through flesh and bone in a matter of seconds, and I felt almost naked beneath the power of her stare.

Still, I didn't allow that to stop me from swimming towards her, my tail thumping against the water and sending waves undulating in every direction.

Something akin to hunger materialized in her eyes as her gaze flitted over my broad, golden chest and the water clinging to it. I tried to bite down on my growing smile even as a dozen tiny fires lit in my sternum.

"Like what you see?" I joked, swimming until I was in front of her, my fingers skimming her ankles where they rested in the water.

"You know I do, you beautiful, golden god," she retorted with a snort.

"Is that supposed to offend me?" I quirked an eyebrow at her. "Because if it is, then you really need to work on your insults."

The first genuine smile I saw so far touched her pink lips before it immediately evaporated, swallowed by her dour mood. I didn't need to be a genius like Lupe to understand the emotions ricocheting through her.

"He didn't recognize you, did he?" I guessed, though I didn't know why I did. It was obvious for the entire world to see that the shifter we both loved was still a beast, a monster, a mindless animal grieving his mate.

The frown carved into her face was weary and grim, the crack in her mask more visible than I could ever remember it being. Her shoulders seemed to deflate as if a heavy rain washed away all of her strength, and it broke my heart to see. Z was always so full of light, drawing me in like a moth to a flame, but I never feared I would get burned to ash. I knew the heat she emitted was a beautiful, pure thing capable of cauterizing all of the wounds inflicted on me over the years. But now, that light was dimming like a weight rested on her soul that I couldn't remove.

It hurt—it fucking broke me—to know that there was nothing I could do about it.

"Why didn't he remember me, Dair?" Her voice shook, though I could tell she was trying to remain strong, to hold herself together. I wanted to remind her that I was here for her and she didn't need to always be a badass around me, but I knew everyone processed their emotions differently. And she was talking, which was a start, especially for someone as strong-willed as her. "He stared at me with...with *disdain*."

"He's not himself, Z," I consoled, my fingers digging into the skin of her ankles as I gave them a massage. "Remember that. He's not the Lupe we know and love. He's wrath embodied."

"I just..." She exhaled shakily, and I swore I felt her weariness seep into my skin and bones at that one sound. "I just need him to be okay. I need *both* of them to be okay."

"They will be," I assured her, though I wasn't sure if my promise was a lie or not. But if there was one thing I knew with unwavering certainty, it was that Devlin and Lupe loved Z more than life itself. Both would fight tooth and nail to come back to her. We just needed to give them a push to move them in the right direction, find a way to reach them and tell them she was still alive. "They're strong."

"Too strong," she mumbled with a wry, self-deprecating tilt of her lips. I wondered what she was thinking about just then to have such an expression on her face. Perhaps she was comparing them to herself? To her own impulsiveness?

"Yes." I gave her ankles a reassuring squeeze before releasing her. "Too strong."

I didn't just mean my brothers.

Z was the strongest woman I knew. Hell, she was the strongest *person* I knew. If anyone could get through all of this shit and still remain in one piece, it was her. She *would* get through this—I knew that without a shadow of doubt—and she would emerge on the other side a better person because of it all.

"So..." Z bit down on her lower lip as she continued to pet her kraken. I swore the damn thing was cooing as his single, milky eye stared vacantly ahead. The fucker was probably trying to steal my mate from me and declare himself the king of the water in her eyes. And knowing how in love with the creature she was, he probably had already accomplished that. "Is this where you've been hiding out?"

There were a million questions piled into that nonchalant inquiry.

"Z...sweetheart..." I once again wrapped my fingers around her ankles before inching them upwards, resting them on her creamy calves. "Don't worry about me."

"But—"

"I haven't been alone with my dad once since I arrived here," I assured her. "And I don't plan to be, either. Believe it or not, I'm not completely helpless." I flashed her a tiny smile to assuage my harsh words.

Her own expression softened. She reached forward with her free hand to cup my cheek. "I know that, Dair. Trust me, I know that. You're fucking incredible."

"Is this about your promise to list one thing a day that reminds me how amazing I am?" I teased, even as my heart gave a painful thump inside of my chest. Fuck. The things this woman did to me, the way she made me feel...

I was floating by simply being in her presence. How did I ever get so damn lucky to have her love me, flaws and all? Baggage and all? She was the only woman in the world—the only person in the world—who didn't look at me and see a fuckup as a prince. She saw the man I strived to be, the one who endured unspeakable agonies but still emerged stronger than ever before. I loved that she never looked down on me, never considered me lesser or weaker than her other mates.

"Well, you *are* amazing." A mischievous grin curled up her lips as her hand left my cheek and traveled down my neck to my shoulder. Goose bumps pebbled on my skin where she touched me, eliciting a soft moan from deep within my throat. "And handsome. And funny. And smart—"

"Keep going," I teased, "I don't think my head is big enough yet."

She cocked her own head to the side contemplatively. "Nah. I think it's perfectly proportionate to the rest of you."

"Big and thick?"

"You have a big and thick head?" Her smile broadened.

"I have a big and thick head down below, if that's what you mean. But you already know all about that, don't you, sweetheart?" I leaned forward to claim her lips in a slow, tender kiss, infusing all of my love and admiration for her into it.

She softened against me immediately, and a tiny mewl escaped her. I reveled in that sweet noise, in her pomegranate scent.

Pulling away, albeit reluctantly, I gave her calves a squeeze. "Now, why don't you find a way to release some of this restless energy riding you."

Her eyes flared, the heat in them traveling straight to my cock and setting it on fire. It was a damn shame I was in my mermaid form.

"I like the sound of that..." Her fingernails turned into tiny claws that she dug into my shoulders hard enough to make me bleed.

"You should..."

"Yes?"

"Find Killian and teach him how to fight like you promised," I finished, chuckling softly as the fire in her eyes instantly evaporated. An honest-to-God pout tugged at her lips as she frowned at me.

"But—"

I leaned forward to nip her lips once more, savoring her decadent flavor. I wanted—no, I *needed* more of her. I needed everything she had to offer, but now wasn't the time. My curse required me to be in water at least twelve hours every day, and since I didn't know what to expect next, I was determined to spend as much time as possible in the lake outside the capital before we began our next adventure...whatever the hell that might be.

"Go, my love." I reached forward to take Slippy from her arms. The little guy immediately began to wiggle and twist, attempting to break free, but I held on tight. "I'll be here."

She still seemed hesitant, but that familiar flare of exuberance and excitement I'd come to love about her made a reappearance in her blue gaze. She practically vibrated with unrestrained energy—an energy that threatened to zap at anyone and everyone who came too close.

That's my girl.

"Will you be okay by yourself?"

I chuckled. "I will. I promise. Go kick Killian's ass for me and tell me how it went."

"All right." She moved to stand and brushed at her pants, removing excess dust and sand that had gotten stuck to the fabric. "If you're sure."

"Not at all." I gave her the same slow once-over she gave me, making sure to make my expression purposely lecherous. "Your ass is looking amazing in those pants."

She threw her head back in laughter—which was exactly what I hoped for when I made that comment in the first place.

"Well, this ass already got rejected once today—"

"I didn't reject you," I interrupted, wanting to make that distinction very, *very* clear. "I want to pound said ass until you can't walk or think straight."

"—so I suppose it's fitting that you'll watch it walk away instead," she finished with a teasing grin.

"Oh man." I snapped my fingers and frowned. "What a shame. Having to look at that beauty is the worst possible fate you could give a man. Damn. I hate my life." I kept my expression completely impassive, eliciting another laugh from those perfect lips of hers. I loved making her smile. I swore once this was all over, that would be my sole purpose in life—to make her laugh and smile every day until the grass died beneath my feet and the sun fell from the sky.

"I love you, Dair," she said gently.

Warmth exploded in my belly at those words, words I knew I didn't deserve but strived to all the same.

"I love you, too, my world, my light, my love—"

"Oh, stop it!" She bent down to splash water at my face. "So cheesy."

"Hey!" I protectively curled my body around Slippy, who continued to wiggle in my arms, giving me the evil 'what the fuck are you doing?' eye. "You got water on Slippy."

"Oh well. He'll live, just like you will, you big baby. Now, I'm going to beat the shit out of my incubus mate. Oh! Maybe I could convince Bash to join." She tilted her head to the side and placed a finger to her lips in mock contemplation. "I haven't kicked Bash-hole's asshole in way too long."

This time, it was my turn to laugh, the last few knots in my stomach loosening, the tension draining from my body in a tidal wave of emotion. She was always able to do that—to dispel some of the restless energy coursing through my body and replace it with something pure and magical.

"I really do love you, Z," I told her, wanting her to know the truth of those words, to feel it in the marrow of her bones.

"And I really love you, too, Dair," she promised, and I could've sworn she sounded almost...shy. Which was ridiculous, because Z was the furthest thing from shy imaginable.

Still, her vulnerability tugged at something in my chest, something that beat solely for her and her alone.

And as I watched her walk away—staring intently at her ass, just as I'd promised—I felt significantly lighter than I had in years. At first, I couldn't put my finger on the elusive emotion buoying me up, but as I released Slippy and began to make laps in the lake once more, I realized what it was.

Hope.

I just prayed that it wouldn't fade.

FIVE

Z

"Harder!" I bellowed, sweat dripping down my skin. "I need you to pound into me, Killian."

"I'm trying!" my incubus mate insisted weakly. He, too, was coated in a fine layer of sweat that highlighted his colorful tattoos and made his hair glimmer like garnet gemstones.

"Not hard enough," I scoffed.

A touch of indignation entered his voice. "I'm plenty hard, thank you very much. I mean..." His stutter became more pronounced as he fumbled over his next words. "I'm tr-trying really hard."

Dair was right.

I loved a good deep-dicking just as much as the next girl, but there was nothing quite like beating the shit out of your sexy-as-hell mate in the training room to put you in a good mood.

"Again." I held a hand out to a disgruntled Killian, and he blew out a heavy, exasperated breath before reluctantly taking the proffered limb and allowing me to pull him to his feet.

We'd been working on these maneuvers for over an hour now, and my body was beginning to protest all of the fighting. I was sore in places I'd never been sore before and had more knots in my neck than I could remember having.

Maybe it would be a good idea to take a break and have Killian massage out my sore muscles...

As soon as that thought solidified, the incubus prince released an honest-to-fuck roar and lunged at me. I stealthily stepped to the side, and he careened forward with a surprised shout, landing face-first on the mat. I moved until I was standing over him, my feet on either side of his hips.

"Break?" I suggested, my gaze dipping to his delectable ass accentuated through the thin cotton shorts I'd instructed him to wear.

"No," he huffed out, moving into a push-up position that now had my gaze rising to his back muscles. Fuck, he really was sexy. "I need to get better."

I took a few steps away from him before pivoting on my heel.

"You're not going to get better if you overwork yourself," I pointed out even as my body naturally drifted into a defensive stance. "You have the strength and agility to be a great fighter, Kill, but it'll take time for you to learn all of the techniques."

It was the same lesson I'd been attempting to drill into his head since we'd first begun. For some reason, Killian believed he needed to be an expert fighter right off the bat. No amount of convincing from me could change his mind.

"I don't want to be the weak link anymore," he'd insisted when we'd first begun training.

I hadn't argued, mainly because I knew what being a liability felt like. When I had the poison coursing through my veins, when I was pale and on my deathbed, my mates were forced to go to extreme measures to save my life. I'd never felt more vulnerable, more *useless*, than I did then. They'd never said as much, but I knew.

I knew.

How could I fault Killian for feeling the same way? He wanted to better himself, and I loved him for that.

Even if all I wanted to do was pull down his tight shorts and ride his dick until we were dripping in sweat for an entirely different reason.

Hormones were such a bitch.

"Your balance is all off," I said, watching Killian amble unsteadily to his feet. I jerked my chin towards his right foot. "You're favoring your right side more than your left. You need to have your balance centered."

"Centered bentered," he muttered like a petulant child.

I reined in my snort. "I said we could have a break…"

"No break," he grunted out, and then he charged.

We trained for another hour until I felt the last of the chaotic, restless energy dispel from my body. I talked Killian through each movement, each scenario, and he absorbed everything with the astute intensity I'd come to expect from all incubi. Halfway through our lesson, I heard the door to the training room open and the pad of footsteps on the wooden tiles. My eyes collided with Jax's, but he simply offered me a dip of his chin in acknowledgment, encouraging me to continue.

"So about that break?" Killian huffed out after I threw him to the mat for the...one hundredth time? I'd honestly stopped counting after fifty.

Extending my hand yet again, I hefted him to his feet and then threw my arms around his neck, fingering his soft red hair. His sweaty body slammed into my own, but it didn't gross me out or disgust me the way it would most girls. If anything, it turned me on, a sensation I felt in the center of my belly, rippling through my veins like a forest fire.

"I'm proud of you. You know that, right?" I whispered, pushing up on my tiptoes to press my lips to the corner of his mouth.

He shuddered delicately, something I felt reverberate through my entire body. His spicy, natural scent surrounded me, and all I wanted to do was inhale deeply. But considering the fact that might've looked a little too weird, I restrained myself.

Oh, who was I kidding? Sniffing might be the tamest thing I'd done with these men.

"One of these days, I'm going to be able to kick your ass," Killian told me seriously. As soon as the words left his lips, his cheeks turned bright pink and horror flared in his eyes. "N-not your ass! Never your ass! I wouldn't hurt you. Ever! I meant... Oh fuck!" He reached a hand between us to slap his forehead, and amusement bubbled up inside of me seeing him so flustered.

Laughing lightly, I wrapped my fingers around his

wrist and lowered his hand so he was able to settle it on my waist. His fingers flexed, ruffling the fabric of my shirt, and licks of fire danced on my skin when his pinkie unintentionally touched my bare hip. He inhaled sharply but didn't pull away.

"I'll let you kick my ass in the bedroom. How about that?" I teased, my eyes greedily lapping up every bare inch of skin exposed.

He truly was handsome, made even more beautiful by the knowledge he was mine. And I'd make sure to treasure the gift that was Killian Incubus until the day I died. Which hopefully wouldn't be for many, many more years. I had too much to live for to bite the bullet this early in my life, and one of those things was poking against my stomach at our close proximity.

"I'm going to shower." His nose wrinkled adorably, tugging at his red brows. "I'm probably stinky."

"You smell like spice and daisies," I countered with an eye roll. "So unfair."

"How is that unfair?" He blinked innocently down at me.

Oh, you sweet, adorable man...

"Because your incubus powers make it impossible for you to smell awful. Unlike me and my wretched scent." I grabbed the neckline of my shirt and brought it to my nose, dramatically gagging at the stench.

Killian rolled his eyes, though his lips twitched upwards in the makings of a smile. "You smell...interesting."

"I'll smell even better after a shower..." I allowed my words to trail off suggestively, punctuating the innuendo with a waggle of my eyebrows. Honestly, I didn't usually need to spell it out so clearly, but Killian was a special case.

The tiny furrow between his brows deepened.

How could Killian be a walking, talking contradiction? The boyish smile currently adorning his face made him look innocent, but his chiseled jawline, strong cheekbones, broad shoulders, and abundant tattoos suggested he was anything but. And yet...

"Then why don't you go shower?"

Dear God.

"If only I had someone to shower with..." I sighed dramatically, my hands still looped around Killian's neck and my gaze at eye level with his defined pecs. Fuck, even his nipples were fucking perfect, which was *so* not fair.

"You need someone to shower with?" Killian stared at me like he didn't understand a single thought in my head. "Do you, like, need...help? Is it a, um, girl thing?"

I really was going to have to lay it out in simple terms, wasn't I?

Before I could suggest that he scoop me in his arms, drag me into his shower, and fuck me until I saw stars, a second pair of arms curled around me from behind. I immediately released Killian and took a step backwards until I was flush against a strong, solid chest.

Jax.

He lowered his face, his nose touching the side of my throat and his breath ruffling the few strands of blonde hair that had come loose from my ponytail.

"You smell good," he murmured against my skin.

I threw my hands up in the air with a scoff. "What is

with you guys attempting to stroke my ego when I know I smell like a sweaty ball sack?"

Killian tentatively lifted a hand in the air and waved it back and forth to commandeer my attention. "I didn't stroke your ego. I never actually said you *didn't* smell bad. But I don't really know what a sweaty ball sack smells like, so I can't compare." He smiled at me like a besotted puppy, seemingly *proud* that he hadn't reassured me I didn't stink.

"Hey!" I jokingly kicked at him, but he neatly dodged my assault. "Good reflexes," I praised, unable to stop the swell of pride inside of me.

He puffed out his chest and nodded seriously. "I've been practicing."

"Run along and shower," Jax said to him, keeping his face pressed to my neck. "I want to talk to Z." In a lower voice, the words meant only for me, he added, "I need a reprieve from the voices."

My heart immediately constricted in my chest, and I raised my hand to rub at his hands where they touched my chest. "How bad are they today?"

"Silent now," he whispered. He punctuated those words with a chaste kiss to my cheek, one that had butter-flies taking flight in my stomach,

I still couldn't imagine what Jax was going through. My poor, sweet vampire.

After he accidentally killed his childhood friend, he swore off drinking blood. However, since he was descended from Gluttony, he was unable to stop without dire consequences...consequences he was still forced to deal with to this day.

Every second he went without blood shattered another piece of his mind. Years and years had gone by without a single droplet of blood entering his mouth, and he lost himself to the madness, his life characterized by voices and images that didn't really exist. When he was kidnapped by Aaliyah, the exact opposite happened—he was fed too *much* blood and had come to crave it even more. And then, the bitch killed him, and I used my strange powers to bring him back from the dead.

Everything that happened... Well, I doubted Jax would ever be the same. His mind was irreparably shattered, but that didn't make him broken. I saw the distinction, and I just prayed that he would, too, one day.

"I heard from a little birdy that you were teaching Kill how to fight?" he murmured in my ear, nipping my lobe.

I watched the incubus's retreating back as he grabbed a towel from a nearby bench and wiped down his sweaty muscles.

Good lord. I wanted to do bad, bad things to that man...

"Which little birdy was that? Super-stalker extraordinaire Ryland? Bash-hole? Dair?"

His lips created a fiery pathway from my ear to my neck, stopping when he reached my collarbone. "I want to try training as well."

"You want to fight?" That honestly surprised me, though no more than Killian wishing to learn, I supposed. I was beginning to believe none of my mates wanted to be left on the sidelines in the battles to come—and I had a feeling there would be numerous ones.

"I want to train our minds." He spun me around in his embrace, and my breath caught as his green eyes ensnared my own. His light brown hair flopped across his forehead, in desperate need of a cut, but he didn't lift a finger to push the unruly strands away.

And then his words registered, and all thoughts of hair and haircuts evaporated like smoke.

"Wait... Our minds?"

"*Your* mind, to be more precise." His grip tightened on my shoulders as he pulled me closer, resting his forehead against my own. "When I was...lost"—he meant when he was kidnapped by that bitch Aaliyah, but you know, semantics—"you were able to visit me in my dreams. I think we should try reaching Devlin that way—"

"I tried doing that," I interrupted. "It didn't work."

A slow smile curled up his lips, one that I desperately wanted to kiss, to claim, to devour.

But then he spoke again, and it felt like I'd just been stabbed with a frosted-over sword.

"That's where I come in. You have the power to do it, Z, and I won't let you stop until you bring my brother home."

SIX

JAX

I'd grown used to the voices in my head. Their ceaseless, incessant chatter. Their cruel words, sharper than any blade I could ever wield. And then the images... I couldn't forget the images. Sometimes, they were mere flickers—there and gone before I could focus fully on what they were—but other times...

Other times, the entire world seemed to warp and distort until I didn't know where I ended and the madness began. The walls would drip deep, garnet-colored blood, and I would watch helplessly as it pooled around me. Soon, I was drowning in it, unable to breach the surface and take a lungful of sweet, fresh air.

But when Z was near, the voices were never quite as loud, never quite as persistent. They were a dull murmur I was able to shove to a dark corner of my mind, where they collected cobwebs and dust bunnies, never to see the light of day again.

I kept my arms around Z's waist as I moved us across the mats to the corner of the room, where weapons hung from the wall and ceiling in a macabre display. But instead of releasing her, I simply moved to the ground, pulling her onto my lap in the process. The squeal she made was honestly adorable, and I had to hide my smile in the crook of her neck as I positioned her legs so they were slung over one of my thighs.

"How, exactly, do you plan to train me to enter Devlin's dreams?" Z asked, only somewhat scathingly, which I called an improvement. She tended to argue over things she thought were idiotic before eventually conceding, usually with a long, drawn-out sigh.

"No idea." I shrugged my shoulders, though I still didn't release her. I liked the way she felt in my arms too much to let her go. "But I'm the best one to help you with matters of the mind, don't you think?"

I felt her stiffen in my arms, though I couldn't see the expression on her face. However, knowing what I did about the blonde bombshell, her pink lips would be pursed and a tiny bit of indignation would've seeped into her striking blue gaze.

"Why do you say that?"

My lips caressed the shell of her ear. "Because I'm insane," I whispered on a breathy exhale, and her own breath sharpened, heaving her chest in shallow spurts.

"Don't say that," she murmured, but her words were laced with heat. Fire. Passion. I loved that I could conjure that reaction from her, that my mere presence could send her pulse racing.

"It's the truth." As if to punctuate my point, the wall directly in front of us began to weep blood. It sluiced downwards in rivulets before rushing in every direction.

It wouldn't be too long before the entire floor was covered in the disgusting liquid.

Of course, I was the only one who could see it, could hear the way it cried for me, for us.

"I'm willing to do anything to get Devlin back," she said, oblivious to my internal turmoil. I supposed that was for the best. Sometimes, it was hard for me to differentiate what was an illusion and what was reality, but I was getting better at it. Like that figure in the corner of the room? The one with serrated teeth, a single blinking eye, and jaundiced skin pulled too tight over his bones? That was definitely an illusion.

But the woman in my arms, with her pomegranate scent, golden-blonde hair, and rosy cheeks? I prayed to all that was holy that she was real. That I was truly holding her in my arms.

Sometimes, I believed Z was nothing but an illusion my broken brain conjured up in an attempt to provide a respite to all of the shit I had to deal with on a daily basis. But then she would touch me, kiss me, run her soft lips across my skin, and the doubt would fade like a tornado ripping through my mind and destroying everything negative in a fatal blast of wind. I knew innately that she was real, that she was mine. Nothing else mattered.

"We *will* get Devlin back." I cleared my throat, attempting to come back to myself. I squeezed my eyelids shut, and when I reopened them, the bloody walls and grotesque monster had disappeared. "Now, do you know how you were able to contact me when I was with Aaliyah?"

I had to give her credit. She didn't immediately

answer with, "I just slept," like I expected her to. She actually considered my question and the implications behind it. Where was she? What was she feeling just before we were tugged into the same dream-slash-vision? Did she travel to me or did I travel to her? Did it have anything to do with the poison in her veins, or was it simply our connection as mates?

I rested my chin on her shoulder and stared at her profile with hooded eyes, momentarily dumbstruck by her beauty. When would I ever get used to seeing her? Holding her? Loving her? I doubted the marvel would ever fade.

"Honestly, it was nothing super climactic," she confessed, blowing out a heavy breath. "If I remember correctly...I fell unconscious because of the poison and then—" She broke off and tilted her head slightly. "Or maybe I just fell asleep? Fuck, I don't remember. Every- thing that happened has been..." A dry, humorless laugh fled her, though it was devoid of any real humor. "It has been insane. But honestly? I can't remember how it happened. At all."

"Maybe that's the point?" I suggested. "To not over- think things?"

"So I have to go to sleep without consciously thinking of Devlin?" she asked dubiously, and I knew just from her tone of voice that that would be impossible. It was one thing I loved about her—the way she was able to care about all of us equally. Most women in our society would be ecstatic that they had five of their mates still with them, but not Z. Never Z. She wouldn't be satisfied until all seven of us were back where we belonged.

With her.

"Close your eyes," I instructed softly. I kept my eyes fixed firmly on her even as her lashes fluttered shut, feathering against her high cheekbones. She wiggled in my arms, as if uncomfortable with being left in the dark, but didn't reopen them. "I want you to focus on Devlin."

"I thought you just said to not think about him," she interjected, that familiar bite of steel re-entering her tone.

"Hush." I slapped her thigh gently. "Do as I say."

"Bossy," she murmured, but when her expression smoothed out, her face going slack, I knew she was doing as instructed. However, her breathing was almost *too* modulated, as if she was consciously remembering to breathe in and out, and I realized she wasn't as relaxed as she claimed to be.

"Z..." I warned.

"Sorry. I'm trying. Okay. Okay. I'm thinking about him."

I watched as her muscles relaxed, almost as if a heavy rainfall had washed away all of her tension. With her eyes shut and her features serene, she looked like a completely different person. I was so used to seeing an ornery, almost combative glint in her eyes that it was eerie to see it hidden away behind dark lashes. I had to quell the irresistible urge to kiss her once more, choosing instead to focus on the task at hand.

It was hard, though, and not just because I had the love of my life in my arms.

The monster was back. And this time, he brought a friend.

I tried to ignore the two figures lurking in the corner

of the room opposite us, but it was nearly impossible. While the first one was tall and lanky, the second one would've only reached my hip if I'd been standing. However, his entire body seemed to be crafted out of nothing but shadows—pure, unrelenting darkness that swirled and spasmed the longer I looked at it. Red eyes stared back at me, slitted like a reptile's.

A large boulder settled in my stomach, and I swallowed convulsively, focusing once more on Z.

"Think about Devlin," I whispered to her as all around us, the walls began to bleed once more. Only this time, the blood drip, drip, dripping down was dark black interspersed with patches of...yellow? What the fuck? "Think about your connection to Devlin. About your love for him. When did you first meet him? How did you feel when you first set eyes on him? How did it feel when you discovered he went after Aaliyah?"

I continued to offer prompts for her to focus on, even as the two monsters took a single step in our direction. Their eyes—the two red orbs and the single black one— seemed to home in on us. Cold, icy dread skittered down my spine like an infestation of beetles, but I pushed the fear away, the trepidation.

They aren't real.

They aren't real.

Z is real.

I repeated that mantra in my head again and again and again—

"I think..." Z's nose wrinkled as she shifted in my arms, her hand dropping so it rested on my thigh. Her nails dug into me through the fabric of my trousers, but the bite of pain was just enough to dispel the illusions shredding apart my brain. The monsters, the bloody walls... They all vanished in the time it took me to blink.

When my eyes reopened, they landed on Z, who had shifted in my lap to face me completely.

A frown tugged at her eyebrows and mouth. "It didn't work," she whispered despondently, and her pain flayed apart my soul.

"I'm sorry," I said sincerely, trying to tamp down my own pang of disappointment. I was just as desperate as she was to get Devlin back.

"It's not your fault. I—"

Whatever she was about to say was interrupted by the door to the training room being pushed open. An unfamiliar servant stood in the entryway, her hands fiddling with the apron of her skirt. She cleared her throat multiple times though never looked directly at us, where we still sat tangled together on the ground.

"Excuse me, Prince Jax. Z." She dipped her chin respectfully and cleared her throat once more. "The kings have requested your presence in the formal dining hall in an hour's time."

"For what?" Z asked, even as my heart leapt into my throat and stuck there.

Dread sank its teeth into me.

The servant's eyes flitted to Z's face before immediately lowering, color pluming in her pasty cheeks. "For your engagement dinner, of course, Assassin Z. Didn't they tell you?"

SEVEN

RYLAND

uck the kings.

Fuck them to the deepest pit of hell where they belong.

Fuck their pompous assholes and their pompous dicks and—

Wait. No fucking their asses or their dicks.

I clenched my hand around my butter knife as I sat at the large, oval table between Dair and Killian. Jax sat on the other side of Kill, while Bash was positioned next to Dair.

Our fathers claimed the chairs on the opposite side of the table. Well, *their* fathers. Mine still rotted away in the dungeon beneath the capital.

And then there was Z...

She wore a peach-colored dress that did wonders for her porcelain complexion. Her blonde curls were tamed into an elegant bun that rested on the nape of her neck, a few strands cascading down her cheeks. She looked fucking radiant, ethereal, and that only infuriated me further.

Because on her other side, smiling diplomatically at the kings, was goddamn Axel.

Fucking Axel.

Why did we believe we could trust that slimy fucker? Perhaps we were all just idiots with our heads so far up our asses, our visions became obscured by shit. Lots and lots of shit. Horse shit. Pig shit. Bullshit. Was there really a difference?

Silence had descended almost as soon as we were all seated, broken only by the clank of silverware against the plates as we dug into the feast provided for us. I didn't taste a single thing. I could've been eating razor blades, vomit, or chicken for all I knew.

Intense, all-consuming jealousy burned a hole in my stomach as I watched the ex-assassin fawn over *my* mate —filling her plate with food, pouring water into her glass, asking if she needed anything. It was nauseating.

"So..." The shifter king's low, growly voice grated on my nerves and made me ground my teeth together. He casually cut off a portion of his meat and speared it with his fork. "I'm assuming you two are excited for your upcoming nuptials?"

I choked on the potato I'd been attempting to chew, and beside me, Killian spat out his water. Jax had to pat him on the back so he could breathe again.

But Z's smile didn't falter, didn't even twitch, as she addressed the almighty douchebags in front of her. "I think you know exactly how I feel about it, Your Highnesses."

"What I think the two of them will be most excited about is the honeymoon," the incubus king interjected with a wink in my girl's direction. His voice dripped with twisted delight. "I think I'm going to enjoy it too."

"Ahhh." The vampire king reclined back in his chair and rested his steepled hands on his flat stomach. "I nearly forgot about that tradition."

Yeah. I was going to call bullshit on there being some mysterious tradition, though I had no idea what the fuck they were going on about.

But if their smiling, enigmatic eyes were any indication, I didn't *want* to know.

Z's expression remained placid as she asked, "What do you mean?"

"Well..." The mage king yawned, his eyelids drooping as he struggled to remain awake.

The mermaid king quickly took over. "If an assassin gets married while under service to the kings, it's tradition for the kings and princes to witness the...consummation of the marriage."

Wait...what?

What?!

My heart pounded in my ears, barely audible over the sluicing of blood that seemed to have congregated in my head.

What the fuck?

"I never heard of that rule before, Father," Bash gritted out, and I watched his hand curl into a white-knuckled fist on the table.

The kings' smiles broadened almost as one, something eerie to see.

Were they really suggesting...?

Were they really suggesting for us to watch Z have sex with another man?

I didn't know if I wanted to gag, cry, or ram my sword through their hearts. Anger slid through my veins like poison, caustic and bitter. I felt like the reaper of fucking death, and if they'd touched me, they'd fall dead at my feet.

I swore I saw Z's smile wilt for a fraction of a second, but she smoothed it out before anyone could catch on. Even the pride I felt towards my girl for keeping her composure couldn't eclipse the rage burning like magma through my body.

My form flickered in response to my agitation. The shadows that rippled across my skin reminded me of waves made entirely out of ink.

"Calm down," Dair whispered to me out of the corner of his mouth.

"Why can't we just kill them?" I murmured back, because I honestly didn't understand why we couldn't just shove a few swords into their hearts. I really, really wanted to stab them.

Dair didn't dignify my question with a response, choosing instead to focus on Z and Axel, who had both recovered from their shock much quicker than we had.

"Oh. That's an interesting tradition," Z said cordially. "I would very much like to know more information about it."

"You don't trust your kings?" The genie king's voice was taunting.

This time when Z smiled, it looked more like a baring of teeth. "That wasn't what I meant, Your Excellency."

I wondered how much vomit came up her throat saying that. Probably the same amount that had been burning mine since the kings first brought up this "tradition."

"We would be honored to have you witness such a... sacred moment between husband and wife," Axel said proudly, and I swore the fucker puffed out his chest and flexed his biceps for good measure.

And then he did something that had me seeing red, had my tenuous control dissipating entirely.

He leaned forward and kissed Z's cheek.

It was a chaste kiss, the barest brush of lips against her creamy white skin, but it was enough to speckle my vision with red and black dots. My shadows writhed, crawling across the table and inching towards the fucker who thought he could put his lips on—

"Leave the room," Dair hissed in my ear, his hand clamping down on my shoulder. "*Now*, brother."

The shifter king's cruel chuckle rolled over me as I struggled to regain control of my emotions, to reel in my shadows. "You have a temper like your father, boy," he told me. No one could miss the malicious threat in those words.

He wanted to remind me where my father currently was and what would happen to me if I crossed him.

This was nothing but a game to the kings. They knew Z was our mate, yet they insisted on this sham of a marriage. They wouldn't stop moving us across the boards until all of the pawns and knights were dead and only the king remained.

But what they failed to remember was we had a goddamn queen on our side, and if she wanted to flip the board on its head, then she wouldn't hesitate to do so.

With the shadows coalesced around me like a second skin, I jumped to my feet and stormed out of the dining room, not even caring when my shoulders bumped into a servant carrying a tray of hot fudge cake, causing the dessert to fall to the floor.

Fuck the kings.

Fuck this game.

Fuck it all.

"Ryland!" Z's voice drifted to me as I used my shadows to propel me up the stairs and to the floor above.

"Shouldn't you be back there with your fiancé?" I called down to her scathingly.

"Oh, grow the fuck up," she snapped, and her ire only seemed to exacerbate the rage ripping me apart at the seams.

One second, I was a level above her, and the next, I was directly in front of her face, my shadows cocooning around the two of us until we were in a world of my own making. A world separate from that of the kings and fucking Axel.

"Don't push me today, little dove. I'm not in the mood."

She scoffed derisively and flicked a strand of blonde hair over her shoulder. "And you think I am? Seriously?"

"You didn't seem to protest too hard when his lips

touched your skin," I bit out, knowing I was misdirecting my anger but not giving a single damn at the moment.

She pushed out her lips in a mocking pout. "Awww. Is poor Ryland jealous that another man kissed my cheek?"

"Don't mock me."

"Then stop giving me something to mock," she retorted without pause. "You're acting like I *asked* for this." She folded her arms over her chest, the gesture doing more to reveal her vulnerability over this entire situation than any words would've been able to.

All at once, the hurt, the anger, the jealousy... They all whooshed out of me. My shoulders deflated as something akin to shame prickled the back of my neck.

"I know you didn't ask for it." It hurt to get the words out. My anger was a living, breathing entity crawling inside of my body and searching for an outlet. "But it doesn't make it any easier to deal with."

"I know," she said simply, blinking her huge blue eyes up at me.

"You're not his." I felt the need to reiterate that point, to drill it into her skull.

"I know."

"You're mine. *Ours.*" My chest heaved, though it still felt like I couldn't take in air. Were my lungs broken? Or did Z somehow siphon all of the oxygen out of the room? My bet was on the latter.

"I know." She took a single step towards me and stared up at me through her fringe of onyx lashes.

My stomach tangled into a dozen tiny knots as I held

her stare, waiting with bated breath. What I was waiting for, I had no idea, but it felt electric.

"Show me."

My breathing hitched. "What?"

"Show me that I'm yours. That no one will ever take me from you."

There was a note of pleading in her voice, something I'd never heard from her before. It had my cock hardening instantly.

Z wouldn't give up control for just anyone. She was too meticulous about it. Giving up control meant she trusted me implicitly, and the knowledge set my veins on fire. I *wanted* her to trust me, to know that I always had her best interests at heart. She should never, *ever* fear me, should never be wary of me.

She wanted me to prove to her that she was with me, with us, and that the kings wouldn't win.

What my little dove wanted, my little dove got.

I didn't care that we were in the middle of the hallway and that anyone could see us. I didn't care that she was engaged to another man. I didn't care about any of that shit.

All that mattered was her and alleviating that fear I could see poking through the apathetic barrier she attempted to erect around herself.

I wasn't going to hold myself back. Not now. Not ever.

Z was mine, and it was about time the entire goddamn world realized it.

With a growl, I spun her around so her back was to my chest, my hard cock poking into her ass through my trousers and her dress. I wrapped one hand around her throat, applying just enough pressure to remind her who owned her, and settled my other hand on her belly.

"You're mine, little dove," I whispered in her ear, trailing my hand down her toned stomach so I could rub her pussy through the skirt of her dress. "I don't want Axel touching you."

"Ryland…"

"Tell me who you belong to." I bit down on her earlobe even as my free hand continued to rub over her pussy.

"Don't be a dumbass." Some of her familiar sass returned as she wiggled in my arms, rubbing her ass against my erection. "You know the answer to that."

"I need to hear you say it again."

Before she could get a word in, I released her and gave her a light shove. She stumbled forward a few steps before immediately righting herself, her eyes flaring with indignation. Offering her a challenging smirk, I sent my shadows forward like slithering snakes until they gripped her dress. And then, they tugged.

"Ryland!" she hollered, furious, but my grin only broadened as the ripped fabric fluttered to the ground at her feet, revealing the white undershirt and silk panties she wore underneath.

"I'll ask you one more time. Who. Do. You. Belong. To?" I tugged her once more into my arms and gripped her pale throat. My other hand creeped downwards until I fingered the waistband of her panties.

"You, okay? How many times do I need to goddamn —" She broke off abruptly when my fingers dipped downwards and entered her tight channel, spreading around her juices.

"Your pussy certainly seems to agree," I purred, then licked up the side of her neck.

She gasped and arched backwards, jerking her hips in a clear demand for more.

But my little dove needed to learn patience. I was still riding a fine line between anger and lust, my feelings over the encounter in the dining room too raw to completely disperse, even with my fingers knuckle-deep inside of her.

"What can I say?" she panted. "My pussy likes cock."

"Not just any cock," I hissed. "Your cunt likes mine. Isn't that right, little dove? This sweet, little pussy craves the feel of my cock in it. You want me so fucking badly, you're practically soaking my fingers."

"Fuck you," she said, but there was little heat in it. Actually, there was *a lot* of heat in it, but that heat wasn't anger. Not at all.

I chuckled as I continued to piston my fingers in and out of her tight hole. "Your cunt is mine, Z. Mine and my brothers'. We won't share you with anyone else."

"I'm not a fucking toy to be passed around," she exclaimed angrily...though that anger quickly tapered off, replaced by a breathy moan.

"No," I agreed instantly. "You're Z."

I tilted her head back and claimed her lips in a searing, possessive kiss. It was the type of kiss that broke apart worlds, discovered lost galaxies, and dried up oceans. It was earth-shattering and soul-crushing all at once. I wanted to drown myself in Z—in her larger-than-life presence, in her enticing scent, in her anger and her love.

I planted open-mouthed kisses down her neck and to her shoulder as her hands reached behind her and grabbed my hips, forcing my body to meld to hers.

"You like that, little dove? You like my fingers in your pussy?" I shoved her tank top strap down to get more access to her bare skin. Goose bumps pebbled everywhere my lips connected, and as her hips gyrated against my own, I swore I was seconds from coming in my pants like a damn teenager.

"Fuck," she bit out as my shadows once more converged on her perfect body and tugged at her tank top. In seconds, it fell to the ground beside her ripped dress. "Ryland, someone could see us—"

"Let them see," I murmured against her neck. "I want them to know *exactly* who you belong to. And it's not some small-dicked assassin."

"Fuck no," she agreed as she began to rub my dick through my pants.

My lips slanted over hers as I added another finger to the two already inside of her.

"You like that, don't you, you little slut?" I purred. "Fuck, I can feel how wet you are for me."

"God, yes," she praised as I continued to kiss her skin. Her cheek. Her neck. Her shoulder. Her lips. Anywhere I could reach, I kissed, nibbled, *devoured.* She moaned encouragingly as her hips moved faster and faster and faster—

My thumb reached upwards to thrum her clit, and she convulsed around my fingers as she came with a sharp yell. I prayed the entire capital heard that noise, that they knew who caused it.

But I wasn't done with her yet, and she knew it.

Roughly, I grabbed her tits and gave them a squeeze before spinning her around. I guided her with one hand on the back of her neck until her palms touched the wall and she was able to arch her back so prettily. From this angle, I could see the evidence of her arousal dripping down her thighs, and it only heightened my own desire. My *need*.

"Fuck, little dove. *Fuck*."

I wasted no time pulling my shirt over my head, but I didn't immediately remove my pants. Instead, I rubbed my bulge through the rough fabric as my eyes devoured the perfect sight before me.

She turned to stare at me over her shoulder, her blue eyes hooded and wild with need, but I simply bit down on my lip as I took her in.

"I don't know what part of you I like more," I confessed as I curled my body around hers and grabbed both of her tits in my hands, giving them a squeeze. "You have the most perfect breasts. So big. So incredible. God, I could play with them for hours. I love your little pink nipples too." To emphasize my point, I gave the tiny nubs a sharp tug. Stepping back, I allowed my right hand to run down the curve of her spine before stopping at her ass. She immediately wiggled impatiently, wordlessly demanding more, and I complied with a wicked smile. I slapped my palm down on first one ass cheek and then the other, watching the flesh jiggle. "But your ass... You have a fucking gorgeous ass too." I ended my exploration with a single finger running down the length of her pink pussy lips. "But we can't forget about your pussy. I don't know if I've ever seen one more perfect."

She growled sharply at me. "I don't want to think about you seeing *any* pussy besides mine, Ryland."

I bit down on my lip to hide my smirk. "Is my little dove feeling possessive tonight?"

"Pot, meet kettle," she hissed.

"Touché." With a mischievous grin, I called on my shadows to obscure me from view.

Her eyes widened, a shout of protest on her lips, but before she could demand an explanation, I dropped to my knees and pressed my lips to her pussy.

She tasted decadent—the forbidden fruit in the Garden of Eden I knew I shouldn't try but kept coming back for more. Flavors exploded on my tongue as I used my fingers to hold her pussy apart so I could reach even deeper inside of her.

With my free hand, I finally gave into the impulse to release my cock from the confines of my pants and stroke myself in tandem to my tongue fucking her sweet pussy.

"Ryland," she cried, her legs trembling as she struggled to keep herself upright.

"Don't remove your hands from the wall," I warned her, momentarily pulling my lips away from her sweet nectar.

She whined at the loss of contact but did as instructed. Satisfied she wouldn't drop her arms, I dug my face back into her pussy.

"God, I love the way you taste," I moaned against her skin as I began performing figure eights with my tongue.

Inarticulate praises left her lips as I showed her

exactly who she belonged to. And I hadn't even used my cock yet.

As if she could read my mind…

"I want your cock, Ryland," she all but begged, her hips continuing to jerk against my face, fucking herself on my tongue.

I chuckled. "Say please."

"Fuck you."

"Close enough."

I removed my pants the rest of the way and then kicked them aside, finally allowing the shadows around me to drop once more. It was almost funny how, once upon a time, I used to hide from her. Now, I wanted her to *see* me, to see the pleasure she was able to draw out of me. I wanted her to know that I belonged to her just as much—if not more—than she belonged to me and the others. Her name had been indelibly tattooed on my heart, and I knew it would never be removed.

I marveled at the contrast in our skin tones—me, as dark as night, and her, as pale as the moon in the sky—as I rubbed my cock back and forth across her pussy lips, lubing myself up with her juices.

"Are you ready for me, little dove?" I asked as I placed my fingers on her hips, holding myself still. I wanted nothing more than to ram into her until we both saw stars, but I would never take more from her than she was willing to give me.

"Fuck me, Ryland. Show me I'm yours."

"No." I shook my head as I lined my head up with her entrance. "I'm *yours*."

And with that, I thrusted inside of her.

I fucked her like a man possessed. Hell, maybe I was. All I knew was that I loved her, she loved me, and some assholes were trying to ruin that for us. The world was crumbling down around us, but tonight... Tonight, none of that mattered.

"Yes! Ryland, yes!" she cried as I fucked her ruthlessly, savagely.

The tiny noises she made made my orgasm sharpen and heighten. I was fast reaching the point of no return, and I knew the only option was to have her fall with me.

I grabbed a fistful of her hair and hoisted her upright, until her sweaty body connected with my own. Tilting her face towards mine, I claimed another toe-curling kiss from her. She pried my lips apart with hers, her tongue darting in as her hips continued to move with mine.

"Fuck, Z," I whispered against her lips as I reached around our bodies to rub at her clit.

"Oh god," she moaned on a breathless whisper, arching into me farther.

"Come for me, little dove. Let me feel you around my cock."

Warmth blazed through me as her pussy walls tightened around my cock, gripping it like a vise. I tried to hold on, tried to fend off my own orgasm, but it hit me like a train. My body exploded into a million ribbons of ecstasy as my balls tightened and my cock jerked inside of her.

"Holy fuck," she murmured, panting heavily as she came down from her post-orgasmic high. "Holy fuck."

"You said that already," I murmured, struggling to

regain control of my own erratic breathing. But she was right. Holy. Fuck.

"Maybe I need to get you jealous more often," she teased breathlessly, and I reached down to slap at her pussy, causing it to clench around my half-erect dick.

"Not funny."

"It's sort of funny." This time when she kissed me, it was slow and exploratory, a meshing of souls finding each other after centuries apart. I could feel it in the hollow of my bones. "But you don't ever have to worry, Ryland. I'm yours. I may be with the others, too, but—"

"You belong to all of us, just as we belong to you," I agreed. "We're a team."

"A team." She nodded sagely, even as a wicked glint manifested in her blue eyes. "And since I'm such a team player, I wouldn't be opposed to playing another round of the game..."

"That was a horrible sports pun," I pointed out even as I began to fuck her slowly once more.

"Oh, shut up and fuck me again," she huffed out.

And I did.

Five more times, to be precise—and probably five more times than that fucker, Axel, would've been able to.

But then again, who was counting?

EIGHT

Z

I had to give Axel credit. He certainly had bigger balls than any of us expected.

By the time we finally made it up to Ryland's bedchambers—his shirt haphazardly thrown over my shoulders to conceal my body from any wayward eyes—we found the ex-assassin leaning against the wall opposite the door. Ryland's jovial mood diminished almost instantly, though I wasn't surprised. He always had a nasty temper, though it was often hidden behind his dry, witty veneer.

"What the fuck are you doing here?" he growled out, attempting to push me behind him. His shadows flickered in and out of existence as they collected around his muscular body.

I instinctively placed my palm on his lower back and began to rub soothing circles into his bare skin, hoping to get him to calm down.

"I was hoping I could talk to Z," Axel replied nonchalantly, seemingly unconcerned that Ryland looked seconds away from pouncing on him and ripping off his head. Then again, nothing seemed to perturb the dark-haired assassin with the piercing stare. I was pretty sure he had a few screws loose, but I wouldn't dare say that to his face.

"I'm mad at you," I decided to input unhelpfully from over Ryland's shoulder. When Axel's grin simply widened, I narrowed my eyes. "You blindsided me, and I don't like being left in the dark."

He waved a hand in the air as if to dismiss my words. "Are you mad about the whole wedding thing, little sister?"

My nose wrinkled instinctively. "Don't call me 'little sister' when we're engaged to be married. It's gross."

He rolled his eyes before grabbing a knife out of his thigh sheath and cleaning his fingernails with it. If I ever needed proof that he was a psychopath, then this was it. What fucker just casually performed a manicure on himself with a five-foot blade?

Axel, that was who.

"Fortunately for you and your little mates, I'm not interested in you like that." His voice dripped with derision and maybe even a little disgust too.

"Rude," I retorted haughtily.

He shrugged his shoulders as if he gave zero damns. Then again, he probably did. "Grow a penis, and then we'll talk."

"No thanks. I like my hole a little too much to say goodbye to it," I quipped.

"I like your hole too," Ryland murmured, and I knew

exactly what he was thinking about. Namely—pounding into said hole as I screamed his name and promised to be the mother of his babies. I was probably going to renege on that last promise—my uterus was very much closed for business, thank you very much—but that didn't change the fact that he literally made me forget my own name.

"Hole, smole, tole," Axel mocked before planting his pleading eyes on me. "Now, can we talk? Please?"

Ryland looked ready to argue—he literally puffed up like some sort of blowfish and took a threatening step forward—but I hurried to move around him and block his path.

"Ryland, let me talk to Axel for just a moment, okay?"

His eyes flared with defiance—frosty blue orbs that shone through the thick shadows—but whatever he saw on my face drooped his shoulders, his muscles relaxing. He might not trust Axel, but he trusted me.

He huffed out a harsh breath.

"Stay where I can see you," he relented, and though his words were addressed to me, the glare on his face was directed at Axel. The muscle in his jaw bunched up as his fists clenched at his sides.

"Deal." I gave Ryland a quick peck on the lips before turning to face Axel.

The crazy bastard was grinning maniacally while shaving off his nails and humming an old nursery rhyme under his breath.

"That's gross," I pointed out, nodding towards his clipped nails as I sauntered forward.

Axel laughed giddily before sliding the knife back into the sheath.

"That's life," he countered with a shit-eating grin, and I figured I probably shouldn't contradict him.

We moved a few steps down the hall until we were far enough away that Ryland couldn't overhear our conversation but close enough we were still in his line of sight. And from the scowl tugging down his lips, he wasn't happy about it.

I sent my shadow mate a flirty finger wave to assure him I was okay, but that only made his frown grimmer.

"You better hurry and tell me whatever you want to tell me, because my mate looks seconds away from stabbing you in the ball sack," I pointed out casually.

Axel immediately moved his hands to cover his private parts, a look of horror on his face.

"Why would he do that?" He sounded genuinely bemused, as if he couldn't quite understand Ryland's resentment towards him.

"Hmmm." I pretended to contemplate it before drawling out sarcastically, "Maybe because you're engaged to his mate, kissed her in front of him, and just now demanded that she speak to you without him. But that's just a guess."

His brows furrowed. "That's a pretty shitty guess." He shook his head rapidly as if trying to clear it of everything I'd just said and then added, "But I do want to apologize to you, Z."

I folded my arms over my chest and gave him a glare. "I trusted you, Axel, and you broke my trust."

"I know." His head lowered in shame, a surprisingly humbling thing to see on the terrifying assassin.

There was a reason he was nicknamed the Butcher, after all, and it wasn't just because he liked machetes. Well...maybe it was, in part, because he liked machetes, but it was also because he liked to slaughter people with them and string their bodies up afterwards. Did I mention he was a teeny tiny bit of a psychopath?

"Please tell me you didn't know about the arranged marriage before the kings announced it," I all but pleaded, remembering all of the times we'd spent together.

I honestly thought I could trust him. But how much of it was a lie? Did he report everything I said and did back to the kings? Did he tell them about the human army who found me at Paco's house...and were still camped out there?

"I knew," Axel admitted on a breathy exhale, and my heart shattered inside of my chest, slicing at everything it came into contact with. He must have seen the defeat on my face, because he quickly forged ahead with a half-assed explanation. "They mentioned it to me before, but what could I say? Are you suggesting I rebel?" He sounded almost scandalized, which I found fucking hilarious, considering the fact he was a member of an army trying to overthrow the kings.

And at the same time...

I understood.

He was doing the exact same thing I was—going along with the kings' schemes because he feared the consequences of disobeying. Could I really fault him for that? No, I couldn't, so there was no point in holding on to my anger when I knew he was nothing but a pawn in this fucked-up game, the same as me.

"Of course not," I scoffed. "I rather like your head on your shoulders."

"Words of a bewitched fiancée." He released a dreamy sigh, and I snorted and shoved at his shoulder.

"I was always told that fantasies and dreams are sometimes the only two things that can get you through reality. But me and you? That's not even happening in your fantasies, shadow man."

"Ehh." He shrugged a negligent shoulder. "Agree to disagree."

"You don't even like women."

"Very true." Leaning forward, he gave my nose a playful boop. "I suppose you're right. Even if I wanted to, we can't be in a romantic...entanglement, as the kids these days would say. It would make Mary jealous."

What in the fucking world...?

"Mary?" I could feel the crease between my brows deepen. "As in, Mary-Lynette?" A boulder-sized lump settled in my chest as I stared at him in horror. "She's a child."

"I'm talking about my machete." He blinked owlishly down at me. "What the fuck were you droning on about?" Before I could even dignify any of that with a response, he continued on cagedly, "That's actually one of the things I would like to discuss with you."

"Your machete?"

"Mary-Lynette."

Our eyes met, and a bolt of ice slashed through me.

Where before, his amusement was evident in the tilt of his lips and the twinkle in his eyes, just then, he appeared somber. It was a drastic change, one that hinted at the severity of the situation...whatever that might be. His eyes shone like flinty chips in the darkness of the hall.

"What about her?" It took monumental effort to school my expression, though I knew both Axel and Ryland could see how tense I was by the stiffening of my shoulders.

Mary-Lynette was Miles's little sister, and after he died, I vowed to look after her. Axel, surprisingly, took her under his wing—err, his machete-holding arm. He had mentioned before that he wanted to discuss her with me...

"I want...no, I *need* to tell you everything, little sister. I need you to trust me." Axel's eyes emanated nothing but sincerity, but I was still cautious, and rightfully so. He had been the kings' assassin for five years until I took over for him. During that time, he'd committed unspeakable acts, all in the name of protecting the kingdom and kings. How many of those people had been innocent? How many of them had been humans like me fighting back against a system that wanted to clip our wings and cage us?

We were a dying breed, but we emerged from the ashes stronger than ever before. *Weapons* were forged in fire, after all. And that was what humans were becoming, what we were forced to become after being mistreated and stepped on by the nightmares in power for so damn long.

Shackled by oppression but forged in righteous anger.

"Tell me everything, Axel," I gritted out. "Why you've helped us time and time again. Why you didn't tell me about this damn marriage. What you meant when you claimed Mary-Lynette was special—"

"Patience, little sister." He leaned forward to give me a patronizing pat on the shoulder. At least, it felt that way, mainly because he was the size of a fucking boulder compared to my five-foot-nothing slender frame.

"Axel..." I warned on a growl. Anxiety burrowed in my chest as I held his dark stare.

"Would you like to know my tragic backstory first? How my parents never loved me, my father beat me black and blue, and my mother eventually sold me off for profit?" he asked, his insouciant voice belying the tension radiating from his body.

This time, my voice was softer, almost soothing. "Axel, I'm sorry—"

"Or how I was saved by a lovely human couple who raised me as their own until they were brutally murdered by rogue shifters?" he continued, still in that lazy, negligent drawl of his. "Or how I joined the resistance shortly after, won the Damning, and became the kingdom's newest assassin...while remaining a spy for the humans?"

Axel...a spy? For the resistance? My brain struggled to wrap around his nonchalant words.

"I don't—"

"Or maybe you want to discuss the anomaly that is Mary-Lynette... What's her last name? I suppose it doesn't matter. I call her Spitfire. Has a nice ring to it, wouldn't you say? Anyway, do you want to discuss the fact that Mary-Lynette is half human and half mage—"

His words stabbed at my brain like a blazing sword. I physically staggered back a step as if my heart had been punctured by it. The surrounding coldness of the hall seeped deeper into my bones, until I feared I would pass out from frostbite.

"What...?" Stars danced along my vision before the whole world disappeared. My breathing became a ragged sound, distant through the thrumming of blood in my ears. "What did you say?"

"I decided to call her Spitfire, because she has—"

"No. No. The part about her..." I swallowed heavily.

How could that be? What he was suggesting was impossible.

His expression turned somber. "It's the truth. She's half human and half mage, the first of her kind."

"Humans and nightmares can't reproduce." I shook my head in denial. "It's impossible."

"I'd planned to talk to the shadow king about all of this, but as you can see..." He forked his fingers through his buzzed black hair.

The shadow king. The fucking shadow king.

Why did every string to this mystery seem to lead directly back to him?

From over my shoulder, Ryland exclaimed, "What exactly does my father have to do with all this? I know the other kings claim that he was a spy for the Alphabet Resistance, but..."

I startled when he first spoke, having not heard him approach, but Axel met the shadow prince's gaze with an impassive stare of his own.

Immediately, I leaned against his chest, soaking in the comfort his presence offered me.

"You need to speak to him yourself, boy," Axel told him, and Ryland noticeably bristled at being referred to as a boy. The ex-assassin then lowered his gaze to me. "You too, Z. You guys want answers? The dungeons will be the place to start."

RYLAND

How did I go from having some of the best sex of my life to standing outside the grungy cell my father had been kept prisoner in? Was it karma? Fate? Bad luck?

I'd been down here numerous times in the last few days to visit Daddy Dearest, but I'd never spoken to him. I'd simply...watched.

I would stand in the shadows as he paced the small expanse of his cell, running a hand through his tightly coiled black hair. He never cried or shouted or did any of the million things I would've expected a man in his position to do. A part of him seemed to have accepted his fall from grace.

And it broke my heart.

I'd hated the bastard for years now, but for all the wrong reasons. I hated him because I felt like I needed to, because I thought he was inherently evil. I hated him because I *didn't* hate him, and that confused me greatly. All of the other princes had malicious parents who did unspeakable things to them, but not my father. He was flighty, yes, and easily distractible, but he wasn't cruel or evil, despite what I sometimes believed. Despite what my perceptions of the kings *led* me to believe.

He never raised a hand to me, even as I called him every vulgar name I could think of. He never yelled or screamed or cursed me out. He simply offered me an indulgent smile that always made my blood curdle and then proceeded to tell a long, drawn-out story about one of the many artifacts he'd collected on his travels.

Now, I wondered if those "travels" weren't actually secret spy shit for the resistance.

A low chuckle got lodged in my throat at the thought —my dad, the feared shadow king, a spy. It was almost laughable, despite the fact I knew it to be true. We were shadows, after all, designed to blend into the darkness with a flick of our wrists.

How had I misjudged my father for so long?

Now, I stood before him, not as a man or a prince, but as a child who desperately wanted to understand his father's actions. The haggard face staring back at me wore a striking resemblance to the man I loved and despised in equal measure, but those eyes... They were all *wrong*. Dad's eyes sparkled with jovial glee when he told one of his awful jokes and twinkled when he was about to cause trouble. Now, they were dull, almost as if the striking gold had been rubbed out of his irises to be replaced by gray.

Words failed me as I stared into the stranger's face. My brain seemed to have jammed, repeating question after question, each one tripping over one another in their haste to be asked.

Who are you?

That single question settled on the tip of my tongue, burning the flesh like a corrosive acid.

"Your Highness—" Z began from the left of me, taking a tentative step forward until her hands could touch the bars of the cell.

My father coughed, and when he pulled his hand away from his mouth, I saw a little bit of blood on his fingers.

"At this point, I ain't no king, child," he said, though not unkindly. For the first time since we'd entered the dungeons, a familiar light returned to my dad's striking gold eyes. "Call me Seth."

Z's mask remained in place, an impeccable wall no one could hope to breach.

"Seth," she agreed, albeit reluctantly. "There's a lot we need to discuss."

"And here isn't the place to do it," he countered almost immediately. In a lower voice, one I had to strain to hear, he added, "The kings have eyes and ears everywhere."

"Don't worry about that," Z assured him. She grasped two bars of the cell and stuck her face between them. "Bash put a spell on us...to make it so we won't be overheard."

Dad still seemed hesitant, but he eventually nodded. I didn't quite know if it was a nod of agreement or resignation.

"I guess the first thing we want to ask is... Is it true?"

Trust Z not to beat around the proverbial bush. "Do you truly work for the Alphabet Resistance?"

Dad kept his eyes on Z. Now that I thought about it, he hadn't looked away from her once since we entered the dungeons.

That lump in my throat turned into a boulder, one that made swallowing virtually impossible.

Was he ashamed of *me*? Or himself?

My heartbeat echoed in my skull as I struggled to read the expression on his face.

"I do..." He paused. "*Did.* I *did* work for the resistance."

"Why?" I couldn't help but demand, stalking forward until I was shoulder to shoulder with Z. He couldn't look away from me now. I wouldn't *let* him.

The sigh he released was weary—the sort of sound you made when the weight of the world was crushing your spine, when it hurt to stay on your feet, when you wanted nothing more but to collapse beneath the pressure of it all. My heartbeat increased from a trot to a gallop as I willed him to look at me, to meet my gaze.

He didn't.

Pain exploded inside of me as he dropped his gaze to his bare feet, focusing on his torn-off nails—a macabre display of blood and skin.

"I used to believe that what we were doing was right, that we were just keeping the order the way nature intended." His voice was a hushed murmur, a breath of air. It coiled around my throat like a noose and tightened with every consecutive word that left his lips. "The kings and I... I thought we were doing the right thing."

Z's lips pursed, though she didn't look away from him, her eyes burning a hole into his forehead.

"What changed?"

"I met a woman." His gaze slid to me for a fraction of a second before lowering once more. "And no, I don't mean like *that*. The genies and shadows had gotten into a small...ruffle over a territory dispute. I had gone to check in on our troops and was attacked. I thought I was a goner when Camille found me." A wistful sigh fled his lips as his eyes squeezed shut. "She was kind. Witty. She didn't hesitate to help me, even knowing I was a nightmare." He chuckled humorlessly. "I wonder if she would've been so inclined to patch me up if she knew I was the king... Anyway, she saved me, and I knew I was to be indebted to her. I was a prideful man and hated that prospect, so I made a promise to her—no harm would come to her while she was under my protection. And for years, it worked. We developed a friendship of sorts. I would check in on her over the years, and she would tell me about her life and family. But then one day..."

Silence stretched and thickened, each second of it laced with an agony I couldn't quite comprehend.

"Yes?" Z pressed, when it became apparent he wasn't going to continue on his own.

"I came to her home to find her bruised, bloody, and naked, surrounded by vampires. Somehow, the vampire king discovered what she was to me—a friend—and sent his men to her home to teach me a lesson about mingling with humans. They ripped her apart in front of me." His eyes had gone distant, faraway, reliving a memory that brought him immense pain. He blinked away tears as he attempted to refocus on Z.

"So that was when you decided to help the humans?" she asked dubiously, and I couldn't even blame her for her trepidation. The kings were notorious for being cold-hearted snakes. I doubted even the death of his friend was enough to steer him in the right direction.

Dad shook his head. "No, but it made me look at the world differently. Every human we killed...tortured... maimed... I thought of Camille. How many of these humans were just like her—sweet, caring, generous, selfless, funny?" His chin jerked in my direction, but even then, he *still* didn't look at me. "And that was also around the time I began noticing strange things about my son."

My eye twitched. "What about me?"

He swallowed convulsively. "You weren't like the other nightmares. You and your friends... You valued human life. I saw you make friends with the human servants, chat with the humans on the street. Fall in love with one." At that, his gaze flicked to Z once more before lowering.

"So you joined the resistance *after* I met Z?" My voice betrayed my incredulity.

"No." He shook his head again. "I joined it when the Alphabet Resistance attacked one of the work camps in the Shifter Kingdom, almost five years ago."

Five years?

My father had been a part of the resistance for *five fucking years?*

I didn't know if my mind was spinning from the onslaught of information or the lack of it. Either way, I felt dizzy, and my legs trembled as I struggled to remain upright.

"What happened?" Z asked, because apparently, I was incapable of speech. I was incapable of anything, really, except tugging at the copious shadows in the dungeon and wrapping them around myself like a cloak of comfort.

"We... The kings and I...went to one of the camps. We had heard the resistance was attempting to free the humans there." He rubbed his hand down his face as if fighting off fatigue...or maybe just fighting off the memories. "What I saw... I wouldn't wish that treatment on anyone, even my worst enemies. I was *horrified*. Disgusted. Ashamed."

"How did you get in contact with the resistance?" Z fired off. Where my brain had imploded from this news, turning into nothing but smoke and flames, Z's remained sharp and alert, twisting apart his story and searching for discrepancies.

"I met a shifter...Tonio...who worked for the resistance. It took some convincing, but I was able to gain his trust enough for him to arrange a meeting with B."

B. That was the leader of the resistance and Z's mentor.

My mind supplied me that information, even as it continued to burn. Burn. Burn. Burn.

"And B trusted you?" Z cocked an eyebrow skeptically, and Dad broke into laughter.

"Fuck no. He actually tried to kill me." He continued to chuckle at the memory before clearing his throat and turning serious once more. "But he changed his tune pretty quickly when I began to supply him with information."

"What type of information?" I interjected.

Dad shrugged. "Everything I could. Where the kings planned to hit. How. Why. Human cities that were going to be attacked. A whole bunch of other things."

"You're the one who warned them about the latest attack? The one who told them to run?" Z breathed.

"I did." He nodded solemnly. "And I know where they are now, as well."

"You can find them?" Z practically melded her body against the iron bars in her desperation to get closer. Her eyes were wild in her face, frantic with need and desire to find and save her old friends.

"I can." Quick as lightning, Dad lunged forward and grabbed Z's wrist, pulling her practically inside of the cell.

She released a startled cry of surprise.

"Let her go!" I bellowed, prepared to cut off my own father's hand if that was what it took. I wouldn't let him hurt her.

But he was already speaking, ignoring me entirely. "You need to promise me, Z, that you'll end this. That you'll stop the kings. Whatever it takes."

"I—"

"Promise me." His eyes ensnared hers, and I was stunned by the intensity emanating from them. The desperation—the same desperation reflected in Z's. "Promise me."

"I promise," Z replied weakly. And then, in a louder, strident voice, she repeated, "I promise."

She didn't tack on what she was promising, but I knew it was only because of the spell prohibiting her from doing so. When she agreed to become the kingdom's assassin, she drank a potion that made it so she *needed* to protect the kings from all harm—even from herself.

My father nodded once and released her.

I immediately crowded in behind her, making sure she was truly okay, that my father hadn't hurt her.

"I'm fine," she assured me softly before focusing on the shadow king and hardening her voice. "Tell me where they are."

"My kingdom," he answered without preamble or fanfare. "I brought them there myself."

"Your castle?" I asked, incredulous.

"A series of caves in a mountain range," he elaborated, though I noted his face had taken on an unnatural pale tint. He looked almost...pained.

My heart rate spiked with fear and trepidation.

"Where is this mountain range?" Z asked slowly, her eyes narrowing.

"Through the Forest of Monsters and Beasts," he whispered at last, and every organ in my body froze, the breath of winter itself kissing my spine.

Z went very still. "You're joking."

"It was the only way to protect them. I was able to use my shadows to provide us a safe passage through the forest. Ryland should be able to as well." His gaze dipped to his dirty feet before lifting once more. "Z, I should tell you... When I last talked to B, he mentioned he had a way of...ending things. For good."

"Ending things," Z parroted suspiciously, but I knew what my father hadn't said.

If he had told her that B found a way to stop the kings, it might trigger Z's curse and send her into attack mode. We had to be very, very careful about the way we talked about these things. Z mentioned a few days prior that she was able to think bad thoughts about the king—something she hadn't been able to do before she died—but we didn't know if the curse was broken or if it had merely been altered. And we definitely weren't going to test it out until we had more information.

"I see," I murmured, even as Z's brow wrinkled with confusion.

Finally—fucking *finally*—my father shifted his gaze to land on me.

I didn't know what to do with the tears welling in his eyes, with the downward slant of his lips, with the bruises poking through the collar of his dirty tunic. This despondent, disheveled man wasn't my father. At least, not the father I remembered.

But maybe...

Maybe I never knew my dad after all.

"I'm so sorry I didn't tell you the truth sooner," he whispered, a single tear cascading down his cheek. "You would've understood."

"Yeah." I hated that my voice came out bitter. Scathing. "I would've."

A tentative smile pulled up his cracked lips as he closed the distance between us and placed his hands above mine on the bars. "I truly am proud of you, Ry. You're going to make a great king someday. The man you've become..." He cleared his throat doggedly, as if fighting off some strong emotion. "I'm in awe."

Were there dust bunnies in here, or were my allergies just acting up?

I sniffled and cleared my throat, straightening to my full height.

"I'm going to be the king you and the others never were," I said, because it was true. The shadow king working for the resistance didn't negate years of mistreatment and torture under his rule. It didn't change the fact that he continued to watch humans go through hell for *years* without lifting a hand to stop it using the power he already wielded as a king.

A part of it might've been hopelessness—maybe he thought he had no choice in the matter—but I knew a larger part of it was cowardice.

He hid in the shadows because he was afraid, and that was something I couldn't condone.

"You will," he agreed, seemingly without thought. "You all will."

"And if it makes any of this better...I'm proud of you, too, Dad. You did horrible things, but you made the right decision when you joined the resistance. When you decided to help the humans."

Another teardrop slid down his cheek.

As one, the two of us looked away from each other, shuffling from foot to foot uneasily. My throat felt too tight, my heart too large, my skin too itchy.

But then Z rested her hand on the swell of my back, and all of my discomfort faded in a sweep of gentle winds. Safety flooded me, something I didn't get to experience often.

Dad watched the two of us with a tiny smile.

"Take care of my boy, Z," he told her, affection brimming in his eyes.

She scoffed but gave me a tender look that had my heart climbing out of my chest and landing at her feet like a sacrificial offering. "If he'll let me. I don't know if you noticed, but he's pretty damn stubborn."

Dad's smile broadened. "He'll let you. After all, he showed you his face, did he not? If that's not a declaration of love from my Ryland, then I don't know what is."

TEN

Z

My head reeled from the onslaught of information as I wore a hole in the carpeting with my interminable pacing.

Bash's right eye actually began to twitch as he watched me from where he sat on the end of my bed.

"Sit your cute ass down, baby girl," he scolded. "You're going to destroy the carpet."

"I don't have any carpet," I quipped. "Clean-shaven for the win."

He rolled his eyes at me while I continued my purposeful march back and forth, back and forth, back and forth...

Jax tapped his fingers against his thighs as he leaned forward in his seat in the corner of the room. "So we need to go after the humans, correct?"

"We need..." I nervously chewed down on my thumb nail, grinding it to dust between my teeth. "We can't..."

Fuck, where did my articulation go?

Dair, as always, knew what I wanted to say. "We

can't leave Lupe behind in the dungeons. Not with our fathers."

"And what about Devlin?" Killian piped in from where he leaned against the wall, his muscular arms folded over his chest. "We need to find him."

"We're not splitting up," Bash protested vehemently, his mossy green eyes flaring hotly with unabated anger at even the idea of that.

"No," I agreed, still pacing. Still chewing on my nail. Still falling apart at the seams like a loose thread that had been plucked at. Soon, I would unravel completely. "No, we can't split up."

I refused to separate from my mates again. The last time we did that, Devlin ended up on a suicide mission to kill my evil sister and Lupe lost himself to his sin. Yeah. No thanks. I did not want another repeat of that shitstorm.

"So then what's the plan?" Ryland inquired softly, his blue eyes flashing amidst the inky darkness that surrounded him.

It was only then that I realized all eyes were on me... waiting for a decision. A direction. An answer. I both loved and loathed that they put their trust in me so irrevocably, but for the first time in forever, I didn't have a solution. My thoughts were scattered—pollen in the breeze— and no matter what I did, I couldn't grasp a single one.

"I..." Words failed me. They slipped soundlessly into the air, ironically deafening in their finality. Why couldn't I come up with a solution? Why did I have to fall apart when it actually mattered? "I don't know."

"Z." Dair flashed me a gentle smile and grabbed both

of my hands, giving them a reassuring squeeze that had goose bumps pebbling along the length of my arms. "Breathe."

"I don't know if I can." Ragged, shallow spurts of air escaped my parted lips as I struggled to maintain control of my rapidly fleeing emotions. They swirled around me like a tornado, and I feared I would be carried away at any moment, lost to the storm.

"Just breathe," he soothed, his cerulean eyes capturing mine and refusing to let them go. "Breathe."

Slowly, I worked to do as he instructed, copying the movements of his chest and modulating my erratic breathing. I thought of Lupe and Devlin and how they needed me. I couldn't save them if I lost myself to my own fears and anxiety.

It took a while, but soon, I got myself under control. My breathing evened out, and my hands stopped shaking.

"Okay," I whispered, blinking rapidly at Dair's angelic features enveloped by weariness. And then louder, "Okay." I scrubbed a hand through my disheveled blonde curls as I thought through everything we knew, everything we needed to do.

Save Lupe and Devlin.

Stop the kings.

Stop Aaliyah.

Free the humans.

But wouldn't the last three goals be easier with the help of the Alphabet Resistance, with B and my old friends? They cared about me when I had no one. They took me in and treated me like their own. And if they truly had information that could help us...

"We need to continue to try and get in touch with Devlin," I ordered, releasing the death grip I had on Dair's hands and focusing my attention first on Jax and then the others.

My vampire mate dipped his chin in acknowledgment, that unruly strand of brown hair falling forward to obscure his right eye from view.

"Afterwards, we will travel to the new resistance base with Lupe—"

"How do you propose we do that?" Bash drawled, his fingers tapping against his muscled forearm in irritation.

I knew that irritation wasn't directed at me but at the situation. He hated being sidelined, unable to help the men he considered brothers. I suspected that a part of him blamed himself, though why he would remained a mystery. Devlin and Lupe chose to depart from our group and travel back to the capital to appease their fathers. It was the only play we had at the time. None of us could've expected what would happen after.

That uneasy feeling in my gut intensified, though I tried not to let my discomfort show on my face. Turning towards Ryland, I asked, "There are cages in the dungeons that are portable, correct?"

His thin lips smashed together. "Yes."

"You aren't seriously suggesting we cage Lupe like a damn animal, are you?" Anger coated Bash's words, but the pain in his eyes was a blazing beacon to my soul. He hated this so fucking much that it was destroying him, the same as it was me.

"We don't have a choice, Bash," I told him gently. "We can't leave him here."

"Do you think our fathers will allow us to take him?" Killian interjected nervously.

My pulse thudded in a rapid rhythm against my skull. "We won't give them a choice." There was a finality in those words, one the world better heed to or face my wrath. If the kings had a problem with it, then they could take it up with me. I technically couldn't hurt them, but I would find a way if they argued with me on this.

"So we travel to the Forest of Monsters and Beasts..." Jax mused, tilting his head to the side in contemplation. "How do you suppose we cross through it?"

"The shadow king mentioned that he used his shadows to create a safe pathway," I explained, focusing my attention on Ryland. And though my next words were meant for all of them, I didn't allow my gaze to drift from my solemn shadow mate. "He said Ryland should be able to do the same."

A mirthless laugh belted from his chest as he leaned back against the wall. "I can try, but this is a lot of pressure to put on me when I have no idea what the fuck he even meant."

"Can we ask him?" Killian asked.

Ryland shook his head. "The kings are on high alert after we visited him the first time. I doubt we'll be given a second chance without one of them breathing down our necks."

Anger spread through my veins like a disease, one that wreaked havoc on my body and mind, and my nails bit into the palms of my hands hard enough to sting. "We can't let them discover the location of the resistance. If they do..."

"It won't happen," Dair reassured me, once more reclaiming my hands and giving them a gentle squeeze. "We won't let it happen."

"There's so much we need to do. So much that needs to be done in preparation." I was speaking to myself more than them at this point, but they allowed me to continue my incessant muttering without interruption. Smart men. "What if the kings assign me another task to prove my loyalty? What if they don't let me go? What if—"

"Let us worry about that," Ryland said. When I glanced up at him in surprise, he lifted one shoulder in a shrug. "The genie king needs his heir, after all. I'm sure we can convince him to allow you to search for his runaway son."

"They're probably getting a kick out of all of this," Bash muttered with a frown. "They thrive on our misery and pain."

"We can bring it up with them tonight," Dair concurred. "They'll agree, just because they want to see us run around like chickens with their heads cut off."

"But before we do any of that..." Jax pushed off the wall and stalked towards me. My heart migrated to my throat as the heat of his body seeped through my skin, setting my veins aflame. "We need to find and talk to Devlin."

The heat dissipated almost instantly. Icy tendrils of cold wrapped around me in a mockery of an embrace, and I fought down a shiver.

"We tried already," I pointed out helplessly. "Multiple times. But..." But it wouldn't hurt to try again. Devlin wouldn't give up on me if the situations were reversed, so I wouldn't give up on him. I jerked my chin up and pushed my shoulders back, emulating a confidence I didn't truly feel but wanted to desperately. "But I won't give up. We need to get in contact with Devlin as soon as possible."

Jax's grin lit a fiery pathway down my sternum.

"Good girl," he praised, and the resulting flutters in my stomach nearly made me weak-kneed. "Now, do as you did before and close your eyes and focus on Devlin. Focus on the bond connecting the two of you."

Dair immediately tried to detangle his hands from mine, but I held on firm, needing his comfort. Safety flooded me when his hands squeezed mine, something I didn't get to experience often.

I heard the poignant slap of Jax's shoes as he moved behind me, and a second later, his palm clamped down on my shoulder.

"Focus, Z. Think of your mate. Think of your love for him."

And...I did.

I envisioned Devlin's face the first time I saw him, when I pretended to be a ditzy human named Susan and he called himself Lin. I pictured all of the nights we snuck away in order to be together, his body moving over mine as his lips devoured my own. I thought of our reunion years later, the fury, hurt, and love that barraged me from every direction when I stared into his striking violet eyes. He'd left me, but it had never been because he didn't love me. He had only ever loved me *too* much.

I pulled up an image of him the last time I'd seen him —in his customary, form-fitting suit that highlighted the grooves of his muscular body. His olive skin, curly brown hair, and enticing purple eyes that glimmered like diamonds.

And...

I felt something.

It was almost as if there were a rope wrapped around my heart, and just then, it was being tugged on incessantly. All I needed to do was follow the silver cord, allow it to lead me to my mate...

Dair released my hands, and the vision I had been holding on to faded away.

Wait.

"Dair"—I didn't dare speak above a whisper, afraid to break whatever tenuous grip I had on my connection to Devlin—"hold my hand." I wiggled my right hand in his direction, and he obediently took it without a word. "Kill, grab my other hand. Bash, I need you to touch my shoulder, the one Jax isn't already touching. Ryland, touch my cheek."

All of my men went to do as instructed, and the silver bond that connected my soul to Devlin's flickered once, twice, and then illuminated so brightly, it burned my irises even with my lids shut. I grabbed the luminescent rope with both hands and tugged.

And then, I was falling, and the rest of the world ceased to exist.

ELEVEN

DEVLIN

The room I had been assigned was painfully sparse and had a pungent, undefinable odor to it that made me wrinkle my nose in distaste. Still, it was a room at a somewhat respectable inn, which was more than I could say about the majority of the town located deep within the shifter kingdom.

I chanced a glance at my reflection in the mirror and nearly winced at the man staring back at me.

My brown curls hung limp and greasy around my shoulders, and my skin had taken on an unnatural gray pallor. Even my once vibrant eyes appeared dull, the color more plum-looking than violet. I supposed it didn't matter. None of it mattered anymore.

I hadn't even worn one of my suits since I first felt the mate bond snap. What was the point?

I didn't bother undressing as I threw myself onto the uncomfortable, lumpy bed. I just wished for sleep to claim me until I reopened my eyes and could begin the next leg of my journey. Sleep...

Why did I have to partake in such a mindless, mundane thing? It was absolutely ridiculous. However, my body was beginning to protest the three days I had gone without any sleep, and I knew that if I didn't shut my eyes soon, I would collapse and never wake up. And though that wouldn't necessarily be a bad thing, I wasn't ready to embrace death and the finality of it just yet.

I had bitches to kill and a mate to avenge.

I just prayed that my dreams didn't include a certain blonde-haired temptress. I wasn't ready to see her face. I wasn't sure I would ever be.

* * *

*D*ARKNESS.

It pressed in on me from all sides, whispering words into my ears that I couldn't even begin to understand. I didn't know if the darkness was speaking some foreign language or if my mind was playing tricks on me. Either way, its words caressed my skin, seared my flesh, tumbled around in my head like loose change.

And then, from the darkness, came a voice that was both a heavenly dream and a nightmare combined. Paradise and damnation wrapped into one enticing package.

Z.

No...

I didn't want to see her, want to hear her. I didn't know how I would survive knowing that when I inevitably opened my eyes, she would be gone once more.

"Go away," I whispered, dropping my head into my hands. "GO AWAY!"

"Devlin, dammit! Where the fuck are you?" Irritation coated every word, but I didn't remove my hands from my face, content to hide there for the rest of eternity. "DEVLIN!"

Soft hands grabbed at my wrists and gave them a yank. But even as my arms dropped back to my sides, my eyes remained closed.

"Go away, go away, go away," I muttered repeatedly under my breath. All I wanted to do was wake the fuck up before I could lose myself to the dream even more, before I began to believe that this was real. Because it wasn't real.

Z was dead.

Murdered by a crazy woman who claimed to love her.

And soon, I would join her beyond the grave. If there was an afterlife, and I was beginning to believe there was one, then I would meet with Z there and we could continue our fairy-tale story as if there had never been an interruption.

"Dammit, Devlin," Z snapped in irritation. "Open your eyes."

"You're not real."

"I am real," she insisted. "And I'm getting really annoyed with you."

Fuck, my mind was truly a cruel, sadistic beast. It replicated her familiar sass to perfection.

"You're not real."

"Devlin, I know what you're thinking, what you believe, but it's wrong. I'm alive. I promise you, I'm still alive. I'm at the capital now—"

"You're not real."

She huffed out a heavy breath. "I am real, Lin." She guided my hand to her chest, where her heart beat erratically beneath the fabric of her dress. "Feel me."

"This is a dream," I whispered.

Wake up, Devlin.

Wake the fuck up.

"It is," she agreed. "But that doesn't mean it's not real. I was able to use our mate bond to find—"

"It's not real." I shook my head in adamant denial. "It's not—"

Warm lips pressed to mine, silencing my newest protest. I froze automatically, unsure if I wanted to push this illusion of Z away or kiss her back just as desperately as she was kissing me. Her soft curves molded to my body as she stood on her tiptoes to rake her fingernails through my wild curls. And then, I didn't have a choice. My body reacted to her proximity even as my mind rebelled.

I wrapped one arm around her back, tugging her even closer to me, and my other hand cupped her smooth cheek.

"You're not real," I whispered between kisses.

"You can feel the mate bond, Devlin." She began to kiss down my neck, her hands fiddling with my belt buckle. "You've just been too consumed by grief to try."

"Because I know there won't be anything there." My voice broke. "I felt it shatter, Z. I felt you die."

Horror infused that last word as memories of that fateful day played on repeat in my head. I had never felt such pain before, and I never wanted to experience it again. Z, my reason for living and breathing, my reason for surviving, was gone from this world. Her light had been extinguished, and I hadn't even been there to say goodbye.

"Focus on me, Devlin." Her tiny hand dipped into the waistband of my pants and boxers and palmed my hard cock. "Focus on our connection."

"I don't want—"

"Devlin," she hissed, applying just enough pressure to my dick to make me wince. "Do it."

My eyes snapped open, and Z's face immediately took up the entirety of my vision. My heart hammered like an anvil against my breast plate as I held her glossy blue eyes. She had an ethereal beauty about her I'd always admired, but just then, that beauty was almost too much to look at. I imagined it was like staring into the sun—one second was fine, but any longer and your eyes would get burnt.

"Devlin." She released her chokehold on my cock and began to stroke it from base to tip. "Feel me."

I knew what I would find if I allowed myself to focus on the mate bond, but I was unable to resist my mate, even if she was only an illusion.

I took a deep breath, bracing myself for the pain and emptiness of our severed connection, and opened up the bond between me and my mate.

Immediately, all of her emotions entered me in a tidal wave of feeling. Her love, her fear, her relief. She continued to stroke my dick as the cord tethering her soul to mine shone brightly between us, practically vibrating with excitement.

No...

"No, this isn't real." Venom laced my words as I took a step backwards, away from her. Away from the illusion that hurt so damn much, it felt as if my heart were breaking all over again.

She simply took a step forward, her hand never once leaving my cock. "You may think that, but when you wake up, you'll realize that this is very, very real. I'm here, Devlin. I'm alive. And I love you."

Keeping her eyes fixed on me, Z released my dick and dropped to her knees.

"Z..." I whispered breathlessly as she tugged my pants and boxers down the rest of the way. My dick sprang free, the tip already beaded with precum, and her eyes dilated when she saw it.

"I love how hard you get for me," she murmured, then leaned forward to run the pad of her tongue over the tip.

Tasting me.

Tasting my arousal.

Tasting my feelings for her.

My hips jerked forward instinctively, but when her eyes flared hotly, I worked to still my erratic movements.

"You know the rules, Devlin," she practically purred. "You can't move until I give you permission." She ran the tips of her nails along the inside of my thighs, leaving a trail of goose bumps in their wake. "I don't know how long I can stay—"

"Please don't leave me again," I all but begged as her fingers moved to my hips and then my ass, keeping me in place.

Her eyes softened. "Never, my love." And then she leaned forward and took my cock into her mouth.

I groaned at the feeling of her tiny pink tongue licking the vein on the underside of my dick, at the way her teeth grazed the length of me, at the way her head bobbed back and forth as she sucked me in deep.

"Fuck, baby girl..." I moaned as she released my cock with a satisfied smirk adorning her beautiful face.

"I think you still need some convincing that I'm real, wouldn't you say?" She playfully nipped at first one ball and then the next before rising to her feet. Keeping her eyes on me, bewitching me with her sultry blue gaze, she moved her hands to her back, unclasped her dress, and allowed it to pool at her feet.

Her naked body nearly sent my head into a tailspin.

Fuck. Fuck. Fuck.

I tried to remind myself that she wasn't real, that this was just a dream, but it was hard to remember that with the mate bond thrumming between us with its own electrical current and Z standing before me, looking like a wet dream come to life.

"Take your shirt off," she murmured in my ear, but even though she gave me the order, her own fingers were nimbly working through the buttons. Both of us seemed to sigh as her fingers came into contact with the hard skin of my abs and chest.

When my shirt was finally removed, we both stood before each other, sharing one breath, one soul, one heart. I couldn't demarcate where she ended and I began. But maybe there was no unraveling the bond between us. Maybe we were always supposed to be one being, born time and time again to love and die with each other.

There were no games, no foreplay.

She jumped into my arms, and I slid inside of her with one single thrust.

Our fucking was ruthless, fast, and dirty. My arms banded beneath her ass as she rode my cock, her head tilted backwards so her breasts were practically in my face. I leaned down to capture one of her nipples between my teeth, relishing the way she screamed my name into the dark abyss.

"Fuck, Devlin. Fuck!" she praised, writhing in pleasure as my fingers dug into the soft skin of her plump ass.

She almost seemed to shine amidst the darkness surrounding us, like her entire body was made of light and energy. No...like her entire body was made of flames, and those flames were dispelling the shadows pressing down on my soul.

And when she kissed me, I felt it in the marrow of my bones.

She began to fuck me even faster, and the rhythm had a storm gathering inside of me, a storm of sensations engulfing me, teasing me, breaking me. Because I knew... I knew I would wake up and discover this had been nothing but a dream, a nightmare. I knew, yet I continued to do it anyway, her lightness eddying away the darkness that had grown both around us and inside me.

My nerve endings sparked to life as she dug her fingernails into my shoulders.

"I'm going to come," she whimpered, her pussy squeezing my cock in an iron vise.

I fractured. Everything inside of me seemed to shatter, and I knew that when I came back together, when I was reformed, I would never be the same. I wasn't even sure I wanted to be.

My emotions crashed together like a maelstrom as I

held Z's gaze and tenderly brushed a strand of blonde hair behind her ear.

"Z—"

She sucked in a sharp breath. "I have to go. Fuck."

Panic lit a fire inside of my stomach. "No! Z!"

"I'm still alive, Devlin! We're heading to the Forest of Monsters and Beasts. It's a long story, but you need to meet us there. Feel the connection—"

And then she was gone, and the unbridled pain and rage that burned through my veins was enough to send me jerking upright in bed.

"Z!" I ROARED, STRUGGLING TO GET MY BREATHING under control. "No. No. No."

Pain twined like a thorny vine around my heart as I buried my face in my hands, my shoulders shaking with the effort of keeping my sobs at bay.

I knew I shouldn't have fallen asleep, but I had done so anyway. And now, my thoughts were consumed by her. By her sweet, pomegranate scent. By her sparkling blue eyes, constantly full of mischief. By her soft curves, sweet kisses, and unbreakable spirit.

What had she said to me?

To feel the bond?

I almost scoffed at how ridiculous my imagination was. Why would I want to be reminded of something that no longer existed? Of a frayed bond that had been abused more times than I cared to admit?

But...

The desperation in her eyes screamed at me to do as she'd instructed. Even if it was just an illusion…

Couldn't I honor her wishes?

You're being ridiculous, Devlin, I thought to myself, even as my heart battered against my rib cage with the force of the emotion percolating inside of me—hope. What if she was telling the truth? What if she truly *had* visited my dreams the way she had with Jax? What if…?

I focused on the bond I felt to Z—the bond I had felt sever only a few days before.

A gasp ripped free of my throat as the overwhelming sensation of Z flooded me. Her love. Her light. Her restless spirit.

Z…

Alive.

Oh god.

She was alive.

Oh god. Oh god. Oh god.

Shallow spurts of air escaped me, and I struggled to get my breathing under control. Tears danced in my eyes as the magnitude of my discovery washed over me, almost painful in its intensity.

Z was alive.

I needed to go to her.

I needed to—

"Are you done being dramatic?" a dry voice inquired from the corner of the room. "It's rather pathetic, wouldn't you agree?"

My head snapped upright, my eyes immediately homing in on the figure sitting in the corner of my room on the wooden rocking chair.

Even with half of her features obscured by shadows, I would recognize that red hair and the cruel, malicious tilt to her lips anywhere.

"Aaliyah," I rasped out.

Her grin broadened. "I heard you've been looking for me."

TWELVE

Z

My meeting with Devlin sparked a flame in me and all of my mates in the days that followed. We were more...energized, more cohesive, as we worked together to plan for our trip to the shadow kingdom.

Ryland was right—the genie king easily agreed to allow us to retrieve his son as the next task, though he did so with an indolent glint in his eyes that suggested he didn't care either way. And maybe he truly didn't. If Aaliyah were right, if the kings truly had found a way to become immortal...

A shudder worked its way through me at the thought.

There wasn't anything we could do about it now, however. We just needed to plan for the upcoming trip and pray that we could all make it back in one piece.

I was packing a bag of toiletries when someone knocked on my bedroom door. Instantly, I was on alert, the fine hairs on the back of my neck bristling at the ominous noise. If it were one of my mates coming to visit me, they would've barged right in, uncaring if I was naked or showering or sleeping. Who the fuck would knock?

I slid my dagger out of its thigh sheath and stalked forward on silent feet until I could grip the knob of the door. Then, I stealthily ducked to the side while holding my blade at the ready, aiming it at the intruder's throat.

The woman squeaked and took an automatic step backwards, her eyes wide with alarm and fear.

Oh shit.

A servant.

Human, if her mousey appearance was anything to go by.

I flashed her a guilty smile as I resheathed my dagger and attempted to casually lean against the doorframe. And I said 'attempted,' because I overestimated how far away I truly was from the wood and teetered precariously to the side, nearly falling over completely before I caught myself. I really lived up to the name of being the best assassin in all the realms.

"Can I help you?" I awkwardly placed a hand on the back of my head, stopped when I realized I looked like an idiot, and dropped it back to my side. Nailed it.

The frail human shuffled from foot to foot, her hands wringing the stiff fabric of her gray dress.

"The shifter king wishes to speak with you," she explained with a formal dip of her chin.

I stiffened instinctively, my pulse thudding against my skull as I stared into her fearful eyes.

"The shifter king?" I repeated numbly. Had I heard

her correctly? Did she mean one of the other assholes who ruled our world?

Out of all the kings, the shifter king terrified me the most. I had no idea why. The mermaid king was an abusive piece of shit who tortured the love of my life, but even he didn't instill the same terror in my heart that the shifter king did. Perhaps it was because the mermaid king's ire extended to one man and one man alone. The shifter king's? It encompassed an entire species. If he had it his way, we would all rot at his feet until the end of time. He didn't just wish to eradicate us; he wanted to enslave us. Hurt us. Destroy us.

According to Lupe, his fated mate was killed years ago by humans. He became insane once she died and started creating work camps for the humans to be transferred into. Everybody knew that if you entered the shifter kingdom as a human, you wouldn't be coming back alive. He was evil through and through, nothing but caustic poison rushing through his veins.

But despite his view on humans, he had never been openly hostile to me. It wasn't as if I believed he liked me or anything like that—the exact opposite, in fact. I imagined he hated me so much, the hatred was burning a hole in his chest, consuming him from the inside out. He wouldn't rest until my head was on a silver platter before him.

So why did he want to meet with me?

Alone?

And where the fuck were my mates when I needed them?

I wasn't a damsel in distress. I didn't necessarily need

the handsome princes to ride in on white horses and save me from the big old baddy, but if anyone could keep the kings in line, it was their sons.

I tried to swallow down the refusal sitting on the tip of my tongue and instead smiled serenely at the frightened-looking servant.

"Please. Take me to him," I said cordially, returning her nod with one of my own.

I just prayed to all that was holy that I didn't come to regret this stupid decision.

So far, the scoreboard looked a little something like this.

Z—negative five hundred and twenty two.

The kings—nine.

I hated to discover what they'd do when they reached that fatal tenth victory.

Ignoring the fear strangling me, I followed the servant girl out of my room.

WE DIDN'T MEET THE SHIFTER KING IN THE THRONE room like I expected. Instead, the trembling servant girl led me to a small office located at the end of the hall.

My heart was in my throat, though I worked to keep my expression placid. The last thing I needed the shifter king to know was that he rattled me.

Fear burrowed into my chest and made a cozy home there as I rapped my knuckles against the wooden door.

Silence, and then, "Come in." Gruff and domineering, just like I had come to expect from the cruel, malicious shifter. How could such an evil man produce a son as wonderful and sweet as Lupe?

And then I remembered Tavvy's words about the princes appearing out of thin air...

Of not being the biological sons of the kings...

I entered a dark-schemed office, the floor made out of polished black marble and the walls plated with dark beams. The desk, similarly, was crafted out of dark mahogany and took up the majority of the room.

A large, imposing man sat languidly behind the desk, watching me with keen, penetrating eyes. I swore those eyes cut through my skin, muscles, and bones until I was a bleeding mess at his feet—exactly how he preferred it.

How could one look manage to unravel me so completely?

"Your Highness," I greeted, following my words with a curtsy.

Deep grooves bracketed his eyes, but I knew they didn't stem from laughing. No, his sharp eyes were nearly black with anger and fury as he watched me exist in his personal space.

Did he intend to kill me right here and now? Get this entire thing over with by cutting off my head?

And funnily enough, I would allow him to kill me. The spell placed on me by the mage king wouldn't give me a goddamn choice. I knew it in the hollow of my bones. I might've been able to think about harming the kings now, but the curse wasn't broken. Not by a long shot. There was still an innate part of me that longed to protect the kings, to save them from any and all threats.

The thought smashed my lips together, and I struggled to rein in my temper. I focused on the amused smirk lighting up his face as he sat upright in his chair, folding his arms on the desk.

"Z, I'm happy you could come visit me today." He spoke as if I had a choice in the matter when we both knew I didn't. At least the servant girl had the brains to run as fast and as far as humanly possible after she brought me here...though I doubted her speed compared to that of a nightmare, especially a shifter.

"Of course, Your Highness. What do you need?" Curt but diplomatic. I wasn't beating around the bush any more than he was.

The steel in his eyes hardened the longer he stared at me. Well, maybe *glared* at me would be a more adequate description. I imagined he was visualizing skinning the flesh from my body and placing it on his floor as a rug. Honestly, I wouldn't put it past him. I wouldn't put it past any of the kings.

The question was... What were they waiting for? They had to know I opposed them and everything they stood for. Did they believe the spell placed on me was strong enough to keep me at bay? Keep my mates under lock and key? Or was there something else at play here?

A muscle twitched in the shifter king's jaw, commandeering my attention.

"I'm going to be blunt with you, Z." His rough, growly voice stood every hair on my arms at attention. His threat weaved through every word, the promise of violence and vengeance. "I don't trust you."

I held myself perfectly still. Hell, I didn't even dare to breathe as if the rise and fall of my chest would remind the sadistic shifter sitting across from me that I had a heart that could be ripped out of my body. Yeah. No thanks.

He licked his lower lip as he continued to watch me. Study me. Analyze every facial tic and movement. To say it unnerved me would be an understatement if I ever heard one.

It fucking *terrified* me.

"We have a rule in the shifter community when one of us goes feral," he said, pushing out his lips.

My mind immediately drifted to Lupe in the dungeons far below, and my blood went cold.

"Which is?" I couldn't make my voice rise above a whisper.

"We kill them before they can kill us." He spoke so bluntly, so nonchalantly, as if talking about the murder of one of his own kind was an everyday occurrence. It made me sick, though I refused to let that show on my face.

"Oh?"

"Unfortunately, we had the resources to contain my good-for-nothing son." His upper lip pulled away from his teeth in a snarl at the mention of Lupe, and anger curdled in my veins like poison.

He saw Lupe as beneath him because Lupe preferred to fight with his words over his fists. It infuriated me like nothing else in my life. Lupe was ten times the man—the shifter—this pathetic waste of space would ever be.

"That's fortunate," I said breathily as my heart pounded in my chest. "He's a good man, and I just pray we'll find a way to get him back."

Surprise flickered over his expression, as if he didn't

expect me to actually say something in return, before anger took over. He stood, towering over my small form at over seven feet tall, and stalked forward until he was directly in front of me. I had to crane my head back to meet his eyes, but I refused to cower, refused to be intimidated. If he wanted to kill me, I would stand on my own two feet and accept it with a smile on my face, just to piss him off.

I only knelt for my mates.

"So if you're a bad pup..." His large hand slammed down on my head, his fingers forking through my blonde curls. I imperceptibly winced at the brief stab of agony before painstakingly reforging my mask.

He wouldn't see me break.

"Yes?" I blinked innocently up at him when it became apparent he wasn't going to say anything else.

"I'm gonna have to put you down," he finished, squeezing my skull tight enough that I genuinely feared he was going to crush my brain. But then he released me and stepped back around the desk, focusing on the pile of papers in the center. "Please keep this in mind, darling Z, as you venture out into the great unknown to save our precious genie prince." Amusement rang in his voice.

"Of course, Your Highness." I dipped my chin once, my teeth gritting together so tightly, I was surprised I didn't crack a molar.

"And I'm assuming your betrothed will be joining you as well?" He glanced up from his papers with one dark brow quirked.

I bit back a snarl. "Yes, Your Highness."

"Perfect." He smiled satisfactorily and straightened

the papers on his desk. Just before I could reach the door, his voice called out, "Z?"

I waited, not dignifying his games with another response.

"Don't mention this little meeting to your mates, okay? Some secrets deserve to be between a man and his daughter-in-law."

THIRTEEN

KILLIAN

Lupe growled from the bed of the truck, and I jerked forward instinctively, hiding my wince by bringing the book I'd been reading up to my face.

We'd been driving for over five hours now, stopping only for food and bathroom breaks, and I was about ready to throw myself out of the truck. Lupe had been locked in a cage in the back, and from the ceaseless growls escaping his lips, he was not happy about that. His huge, furry, brown paws swiped at the iron bars containing him, but they had been imbued with magic from Bash. No matter how hard he attacked the cage, he wouldn't be able to break free.

I squeezed my eyelids shut, and when I reopened them, I forced myself to focus on the book highlighted by the gaudy, fluorescent bulb built into the vehicle. It was the only light we had as the sun sank down below the horizon and drew the world into a dark gray embrace.

Pulling in a staggered breath, I flipped the page in the book...and immediately went still.

Since Lupe and Devlin were indisposed at the moment, it was all on me to do all the research I could on the Forest of Monsters and Beasts. Well, maybe not entirely all on me, but since I wasn't the best fighter, I figured I could use my talents elsewhere and learn what I could.

The Forest of Monsters and Beasts? Only one word could encapsulate the limited knowledge I had gathered about it from the capital's library—hell. Yup. We were driving straight to the border of hell, and nobody seemed to care besides me. My skin crawled as I read the paragraph concerning the—boy oh boy—monsters we would be facing. Big monsters. Little monsters. Fat monsters. Skinny monsters.

I could probably write a children's book about the monsters in this forest.

"Are you sure that we actually have to go through the forest to find your people?" I directed my question at Z, who was sitting beside me on Jax's lap.

The eccentric vampire nuzzled her neck, his arms tightening around her almost imperceptibly as she shifted to face me.

Her lips flattened out. "What did you find?"

"Death. Pain. Suffering," I ticked off, turning the book so she could see one of the illustrations—a huge monster crafted entirely out of shadows, with yellow teeth and bright gold eyes rimmed with blood.

That was a whole lot of "nope" from me.

"Oh. Goodie. What else is new?" she drawled sarcastically before leaning forward to place her hand on top of mine.

Immediately, the heaviness pressing down on my chest lightened up, and I was able to focus entirely on the expansion of my lungs. Deep breath in. Deep breath out. Deep breath in. Deep breath out. Repeat. Repeat. Repeat.

"That forest has been around for centuries," Ryland exclaimed from the driver's seat. He glanced quickly over his shoulder, as if to ensure we were paying attention, before focusing on the road once more. "Legend has it, if a shadow dies and their soul is full of darkness, they'll turn into one of the beasts trapped in the forest for all of eternity." His voice took on an ominous tone that had goose bumps rippling across my skin.

"And the truth?" Z lifted an eyebrow.

"The truth? Nobody knows for sure." He shrugged. "But my father once mentioned that the kings before him had...experimented on the humans." Through the rearview mirror, pain enveloped his face. His hands tightened on the steering wheel, turning his naturally dark skin almost pasty in appearance. "He told me that the monsters roaming the forest are all products of those times."

"Experiments gone wrong?" Z's expression darkened with horror and anger. "What the fuck is wrong with some people?"

"A lot," Ryland answered curtly. Ripples of shadows skidded down his arms and then wrapped around his torso in a dark and deadly hug. "A whole fucking lot."

Silence once again reigned supreme as I focused on

the book—and the shitstorm we were diving headfirst into, complete with shitty rain and shitty lightning and shitty thunder—and Z conversed quietly with Jax, so softly I couldn't hear a single word said. The monotony of it was broken apart only by Lupe's enraged roars as he struggled against the iron bars containing him.

"How do you think the other car is doing?" Z's lips quirked upwards with amusement as she flicked her gaze towards the vehicle following directly behind us.

Grateful to be able to stop reading the Book of Pain, Misery, and Death—not its actual title, but it seemed fitting—I directed my attention towards my mate.

"Axel is probably annoying the shit out of Bash by now," I said, amused.

"All Axel would need to say is one comment about how he's engaged to Z, and Bash will lose his shit," Ryland agreed, though I couldn't help but notice that the temperature in the car lowered substantially at the thought of Z's engagement to the other man.

Jax pressed a kiss to her shoulder, as if reassuring himself that she was with him, that she wasn't married to someone who wasn't her mate.

I kind of wanted to do the same, but I held myself back.

"At least Dair is with them to play peacemaker," Z pointed out.

Ryland snorted derisively. "I wouldn't be too sure about that, little dove. Dair can be particularly possessive when it comes to you."

She rolled her pretty blue eyes and slumped farther

into Jax's arms. "I already told you guys. I have absolutely zero romantic feelings for my fiancé."

All three of us winced at her use of that term.

"W-we know that, Z," I stuttered out, giving her hand a tentative squeeze even as lances of sharp pain shot through my chest. "It's just...hard."

"Speaking of things being hard..." Z very pointedly glanced down at my cock, which had somehow turned half erect during our conversation.

Honestly, I had no idea when. The little bastard had a life of its own, and that life seemed to revolve around Z.

Was it when she first grabbed my hand? Fuck, that would be embarrassing.

"Oh shit." I fanned my cock, as if air would somehow get my boner down. "Go away," I hissed at the misbehaving dick. "Go the fuck away."

Ryland guffawed from the front seat. "Are you seriously talking to your dick right now?"

"It wouldn't be the first time," Z sang with an amused grin.

I gave her a withering stare. "Glad my misery can amuse you," I muttered petulantly, still willing my cock to turn flaccid. I tried to think of disgusting things. Aaliyah, the kings, Slippy, hairy buttholes, hairy nipples, hairy—

Z placed a hand on my thigh, her fingers splaying across the hard muscle there. The noise I made? Practically inhuman. I was pretty sure it was a combination of a grunt and a squeal, like a dying pig having sex for the very last time.

Not that I knew what that sounded like.

I didn't.

Promise.

"Z..." I gave her a pointed look and then lowered my gaze to her hand on my thigh. "Your fingers are close to my..." Heat plumed in my cheeks.

"Your dick, Killian?" Z's voice dripped with sinister amusement. "Your cock? Your penis?"

My nose wrinkled. "I hate that word."

"Dick, cock, or penis?" she teased.

"The p-word." I shuddered delicately. "It just sounds so weird and gross to me. Peeee...ness. Pee-pee-ness. Penis. Peeee. Ness."

Z smashed her lips together to contain her laughter, even as her eyes flashed with mischief. And when her fingers shifted a few inches to the side, so they caressed my rock-hard dick, I understood why.

Fuck, this woman was going to kill me.

"You're an incubus, and you can't even say the word penis?" Jax asked dryly, his arms still wrapped around Z's waist and his chin on her shoulder.

For the first time in what felt like forever, there was coherence in his mossy green gaze. He wasn't far away in some distant land none of us could see or hear. He was present, and it was all thanks to the woman in his lap.

"I can say the word just fine, thank you very much," I responded primly, jutting my chin out.

"Oh?" Z's fingers teasingly brushed my cock through the fabric of my pants a second time, and my hips jerked upwards of their own accord.

"Oh, sweet baby chicken wings," I blurted, my pulse slamming hard against my chest.

Ryland practically swiveled the truck into a ditch as he stared at me through the rearview mirror, his brows drawn together. "Did you just say...?"

I swore my cheeks were so hot, you could burn yourself on them. I wouldn't be surprised if Z got third-degree burns from touching me the way she was.

"No, I didn't say anything. You must be mistaking me with a different incubus," I rambled like a dumbass.

A breath of warm air fanned over the back of my neck a second before a feminine voice trickled towards me. "I don't want another incubus." Her lips pressed to my overheated skin. "I just want you."

"PENIS!" I blurted out, the word fleeing my lips before I could even consider the ramifications of saying it. Well, screaming it while karate-chopping the air and bucking my hips. But...semantics.

Z leaned away from me, her eyes comically wide.

Fuck. Fuck. Fuck.

Where was the confidence I had before when I bossed Z around in the bedroom? Where the fuck did that Killian go? He was such a cool fucker, while I was such a weirdo.

Did I really just shout penis at the top of my lungs like a prepubescent boy touching a booby for the first time? Yes. Yes, I did.

Z's fingernails once more scraped against the outline of my hard cock. "Yes. You do have a good penis."

"I really don't—"

Whatever I was about to say was interrupted by Ryland's shout of alarm. I had only a moment to look out the window and see a row of jagged nails sticking upwards in the middle of the street before the car careened precariously to the side.

I grabbed onto Z at the same time Jax tightened his grip, and then we were spinning, spinning, spinning, spinning. Smoke emanated from under the hood as we slammed against a tree on the side of the road. Behind us, the car carrying Axel, Jax, and Dair pulled to an abrupt halt directly before the row of nails.

"What the fuck was that?" Z exclaimed, her eyes wide as she scanned the horizon for threats.

Ryland's voice was grim, colder than ice, when he said, "We're under attack. This was a trap."

FOURTEEN

Z

Under attack?

By whom?

The kings? Aaliyah? Another one of her pet monsters?

I climbed off of Jax's lap and kicked open the door, already palming the hilt of one of my blades. Ryland disappeared into the shadows and then materialized a second later directly beside me.

I took a moment to do a quick scan of my surroundings and make sure my mates were accounted for. Killian appeared dazed, but he was walking and talking, which I considered a win. Jax climbed out of the car after me, his eyes sparking with more coherence than usual, and immediately crossed to Lupe. The large bear released a guttural roar and swiped at the air in front of him, and the tightness in my chest eased at seeing him unharmed.

Enraged? Most definitely.

But injured? No, thank God.

I waited until Bash and Dair caught up to our

makeshift huddle—and Jax finished checking on Lupe—before nodding towards the nails set up in the middle of the road.

"There. That's what crashed our car. They must've laid that down to stop our vehicles," I explained, though I didn't know why I bothered to point out the obvious. Anyone with eyes could see that.

"Are you okay?" Bash demanded, gripping my arms and spinning me to face him. His verdant green eyes frantically devoured my body from head to toe, checking me for injuries. Only when he seemed satisfied that I hadn't been injured did he release me.

"I'm okay," I assured all of my mates, spinning in a circle so I could meet each of their eyes individually. Axel stood slightly apart from our group, his gaze intent on the horizon. "And you guys?"

"We're fine. Lupe's fine as well, though he seems upset about the crash," Jax murmured, then pulled his plush lower lip between his teeth. "But am I hallucinating again, or are there people coming at us with swords?"

"What—?"

I spun around at the same time my mates did to see figures slinking out of the woods on either side of the street, each one carrying a weapon. Swords. Knives. Javelins. Axes. Machetes. Their features were taut with anger and righteous indignation as they circled us.

Humans.

Oh...fuck.

"Let the girl go," a tall, voluptuous woman with thick

brown curls demanded, moving towards the front of the group.

It was apparent from the looks of reverence and worshipful awe directed her way that she was the leader. Her bronze skin suggested she spent a lot of time outdoors, and that was only reinforced by the sinewy muscles I could see peeking through the fabric of her tank top and shorts. She was beautiful in the way that most apex predators were, practically exuding a savage lethality. She had a face designed to lure unsuspecting prey in but an expression that made it clear she wouldn't hesitate to kill if the need arose.

Normally, I would respect that, even admire it, but I didn't appreciate the fact that her glare was directed at my mates.

Two humans took a step towards the cage holding Lupe, and my massive bear shifter of a mate stood on his hind legs and roared, swiping ineffectually at the air in front of him. The humans, despite being on the opposite side of the bars, stumbled backwards as if they'd been mortally wounded, twin expressions of fear on their faces.

The woman held up a hand, signifying for everyone to remain still, and focused on us once more.

"Let the woman go, and we'll let you live." Her amber eyes locked on mine, softening significantly. Deep grooves were etched into her face—around both of her eyes and the corners of her lips. "Sweetheart, are you okay? Did they hurt you?"

Oh...fuck.

Understanding slammed into me as if I'd just been kicked in the stomach by a damn horse.

They thought my mates had kidnapped me when that couldn't be further from the truth.

I needed to de-escalate this situation, and fast...before this turned deadly. I had no doubt these humans would fight my mates if they deemed us as threats, and I also had no doubt that my mates would win. However, they would hate themselves if they hurt, let alone killed, a human trying to protect themselves.

"I'm okay!" I stepped away from my mates, ignoring their protests, and lifted both hands into the air. "I promise you that I'm okay. These are my mates—"

"Wait." A red-faced, sweaty man rushed forward, his eyes comically wide in his face as he stared at me. "That's...That's the Liberator." He grasped the brown-haired woman's shoulder and gave it a shake. "Davia, that's her."

The woman's—Davia's—lips compressed in a grim line as she studied me from head to toe. It almost reminded me of the look Bash just gave me, but without any of the anxious energy he had. Her gaze was...assessing. Critical, even, as if she were seeking out my flaws and deciding if they outweighed my good traits.

A muscle ticked in her jaw, but otherwise, her face was impassive and unreadable.

"The Liberator," she repeated dryly.

"Yes. That's what they call me." I nodded once, continuing to step closer despite my mates' growls of warning behind me. "My name is Z—"

"We know your name, Liberator," Davia interrupted.

Her gaze shifted towards my men, who hadn't moved an inch during this entire interaction despite their obvious desire to. They trusted me to handle the situation and get us out of this mess in one piece. Sparks of love for them shot off through my body, crackling down my spine. I never had anyone care for and trust me as much as they did. It was a heady, disembodied sensation that rippled through my nerve endings like fireworks.

"And these are my mates," I said, gesturing towards my men. I included Axel in the introduction as well, just because I didn't know what to call him. My fiancé who wasn't truly my fiancé? An assassin for the kings who actually worked for the resistance? "I'm sure you've heard of—"

"Yes. I've heard that the Liberator was mated to the seven princes." Davia still sounded doubtful, but I didn't know if that doubt was directed at my story or me personally. Did she not believe I was truly the so-called "Liberator"? Or did she simply not trust me?

Murmurs began to ripple through the crowd like a wave, and my name repeated over a dozen times before I zoned out the incessant chatter. Davia was obviously the leader, so she would be the one I addressed.

"We're traveling to the Forest of Monsters and Beasts," I explained stoutly, lifting my chin ever so slightly to show the woman I wouldn't be cowed by her.

She froze. "Why in the world would you want to go there?" Shock bled into her tone, momentarily eclipsing the incredulity from a few minutes earlier.

"That's none of your business," I said simply.

And it was true. I felt no reason to lie about where we

were going, especially if they intended to follow us and spy. However, I didn't need to say anything about our exact location and mission. I didn't even know if the Alphabet Resistance members were truly hidden in the mountains, but if they were, I wouldn't put them in harm's way by announcing their existence, even to other humans.

For the first time since I'd met her, a hint of a smile touched her face and her eyes glimmered like diamonds. "You're just like they said, Liberator. Smart, witty, and too brave for your own good. You do realize that no one has ever returned from the Forest of Monsters and Beasts, correct?" Her voice dripped with twisted delight and perverse pleasure.

I matched her grin with a taunting one of my own. "And you do realize that no human has ever been mated to nightmare royalty before, correct? I suppose there's a first time for everything."

Bash coughed behind me to hide his laugh, and Ryland chuckled darkly. I could feel my other mates' pride and amusement trickle down the bond connecting us.

Davia's smile grew until it practically cleaved her face in two. The anger I had seen before had all but diminished. "It's not far from here. Only a few minutes north." She nodded towards the men and women surrounding us, their weapons still drawn and their expressions decidedly cautious. "We'll escort you to the border."

"Thank you, but we don't—"

"This area is dominated by humans, Liberator,"

Davia interrupted, though not unkindly. "It's one of the only places in the entire world that outnumbers nightmares eighty to twenty. That isn't to say we're the ruling species or anything..." She forked her fingers through her dark brown hair. "But if a human were to see you guys? There's no guaranteeing that they won't attack your...*mates* on sight, especially if they recognize them as the princes." She said "mates" as if it were a dirty word and she needed to immediately wash her mouth out with soap.

I tried not to bristle at her tone, but it was hard.

And at the same time...

I understood.

I would've behaved the exact same way if I hadn't met and fallen in love with my guys. They proved to me time and time again that not all nightmares were inherently evil just like not all humans were born good. There were facets to every aspect of human nature, and the distinction between black and white had never been so blurred before.

"I understand." I nodded once, recognizing that we wouldn't have a say in this matter. I doubted Davia wanted to follow us to the border for our "protection," but I didn't dare call her out on it. She wouldn't learn anything from spying on us—at least, nothing that would be useful.

Hopefully if we showed her trust, she'd extend us the same courtesy and realize we were all on the same side, fighting the same enemies.

"Perfect." Her smile resembled that of a shark's as she turned towards the red-faced man from earlier. "Earl, bring the car around, please. Tell Tracy where we're heading."

He nodded once before running off to do her bidding. My gaze followed his retreating form into the thicket of trees...before my entire body went rigid at the sight of a figure standing at the edge of the tree line.

A very, very familiar figure with dark brown hair curling around his ears, a modelesque face constructed out of sharp cheekbones and a clean-shaven jawline, and startling brown eyes flecked with rings of gold.

"S?" I whispered, taking an automatic step towards the man who had once been the love of my life...until I saw him ripped apart by shifters. Obviously, this man wasn't S, but the resemblance between the two of them was uncanny, though this man's hair was slightly longer.

Still, seeing my ex—even a lookalike of him—seared my chest and clawed at my heartstrings.

A cluster of humans moved in front of the man who looked like S, obscuring him from view, and when they finally stepped aside, he was gone.

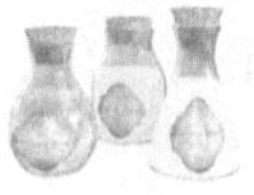

FIFTEEN

BASH

"You okay?" I nudged Z inconspicuously as we exited the cars at the edge of an immense, dark forest.

Skeletal trees ripped apart the ground and clawed at the sky like sharpened talons, melding with the gray horizon. At first glance, there wasn't anything particularly exciting about the forest, but the closer I looked into the inky blackness, the more I saw *shapes* take form. It was almost as if the sunlight couldn't breach this section of the earth, as if nothing but darkness lived within the trees, and it had somehow transformed into living, writhing creatures.

Fuck my life.

"Yeah." Z offered me a timid smile, one that didn't reach her eyes. "I just... I thought I saw someone I knew." She shook her head slowly as if to dismiss such an absurd thought, though I noticed there was still a minuscule crease between her brows I yearned to kiss away.

What the fuck?

Since when had I ever wanted to kiss goddamn *worry crinkles*? What was this girl doing to me?

Honestly, at this point, I should just cut off my balls and hand them to her to carry. Heaven only knew they didn't belong to me anymore.

"Do you need me to...?" I honestly didn't know how to finish that sentence. Did you need me to murder someone for you? Kiss away your worry crinkles? Give you a massage? Castrate myself? Hand you my balls on a silver fucking platter? The possibilities were endless.

She interlocked her fingers with mine and gave them a squeeze.

"I'm more worried about what to expect when we go in there." She jerked her chin towards the ominous Forest of Monsters and Beasts, a place I had only ever read about in storybooks. Horror novels, to be exact. Even now, staring up at the darkened tree trunks, I couldn't stop the trill of fear from skating down my spine. Yup. Didn't like that. Not at all.

I said it once, and I would say it again—fuck my life. Seriously.

Fuck it.

Icy terror swirled around in my chest like a typhoon.

"My father's right." Ryland quite literally stepped out of the shadows and manifested behind us, though his face still remained shrouded in shadows—no doubt to hide his scars from the curious humans milling around the border of the forest. "I should be able to provide us with a safe passageway through."

"Should?" Z quirked an eyebrow as she studied the forest dubiously.

"Your faith in me astounds me," Ryland responded dryly, and even though I couldn't discern any of his features, I imagined his eyes would be rolling.

"You know I didn't mean it like that." Uncaring of the cold shadows slithering around him like angry, hissing snakes, Z reached forward to capture his hand.

It was almost eerie, the way her pale flesh disappeared into the darkness of his cold embrace. I couldn't help but gape openly before I stopped being an idiot and shut my mouth.

"W-what are we going to do about Tall, Dark, and Furry?" Killian moved to join our group with Jax and Dair.

The latter had a contemplative expression on his pretty-boy face, while the former... The former was staring aimlessly in the distance, his lips pursed as if he were seeing something he didn't particularly like. When I followed the direction of his gaze, I saw nothing but humans clustered together casting furtive glances our way. I gave them the finger when I caught them looking, and they hastily lowered their gazes.

"We can't leave Lupe alone with the humans," Z whispered adamantly.

"You don't trust them?" Ryland inquired.

"I don't trust anyone but you guys," Z retorted without thought.

A warm, fuzzy feeling exploded in my chest and then expanded outwards, trickling down my arms and legs until I felt like a fucking firecracker—popping, sizzling, and burning.

Fuck her.

I didn't know if I loved or hated the feelings she evoked within me.

Okay, that was a lie. I fucking loved the way she made me feel, as if my heart was too heavy to remain in my chest.

The tightness in my throat subsided at heartfelt words, even as outwardly, my expression remained indolent and cocky. A smirk tugged up my lips. What could I say? I was nothing if not a predictable fucker, and I didn't get the nickname Bash-hole for being a saint.

"Awww. Does Z wuv her mates?" I mocked, using my best baby-talk voice.

Her eyes flared hotly a split second before she rammed her elbow into my stomach. "Shut up."

"Make me."

"I'll give your lips something to occupy their time," she bit out.

Lust lodged in my throat, hindering my witty retort, as I lazily dragged my gaze down her body.

Yes, I could definitely get behind that. It'd been too long since I had a taste of her sweet pussy and—

Killian, surprisingly, was the one who reached around Z and hit me along the back of the head. When I gaped at him, stunned, he shrugged sheepishly and scrubbed a hand down the back of his neck. Color entered his cheeks, turning them a vibrant red that clashed with his striking garnet hair.

"Your lust is through the roof, brother. It's making my..." He trailed off with another shrug.

"It's making your penis hard?" Z suggested, and his blush deepened, even as his eyes turned sharp.

What the fuck did I miss there?

"Don't use the p-word," he all but pleaded, and she threw her head back in laughter.

That laughter faded almost instantly, though, when another growl reverberated through the night air.

We all turned in the direction of Lupe's cage, where he snarled at the humans nearby, his fur bristling along the length of his spine.

The jovial mood from only moments before turned somber as we stared at the man we all loved fiercely—albeit in different ways. He might have been Z's mate, but he was our brother. It pained us to see him this way, lost to his sin.

Z's jaw bobbed, and for the longest moment, she didn't speak, simply watched.

After what felt like an eternity, she gritted out, "I don't understand why he isn't turning back. Why he doesn't recognize me. I thought the mate bond..." She huffed out a resigned breath, her entire face seeming to droop. "I thought it would be enough."

"Don't doubt his love for you, Z," Dair promised her gently, reaching forward to place a hand on her shoulder. "He's just...lost. And it's our job as his brothers—and your job as his mate—to bring him home."

"That's a beautiful sentiment, but in reality? It's much harder to accomplish." The muscles in her jaw bunched up before she shook her head. "One of us will have to stay behind with him."

"Or I could stay behind with Growly Pants over there." The masculine voice trickled towards our group a second before Axel joined us, grinning maniacally as he twirled that damn machete of his around and around like a baton.

Z shot him a glare. "Why should we trust you?"

"Have I ever given you any reason not to trust me?" he countered immediately, still grinning like the irritating asshole we all knew he was.

"Yes," I said.

"Definitely," Ryland agreed.

"You're engaged to our mate," Jax deadpanned. He blinked his eyes rapidly, finally seeming to come back to the present.

"Oh! That reminds me!" Axel practically bounced on the balls of his feet in excitement. "We need to get rings—"

Ryland disappeared in a cloud of onyx shadows. When he reappeared, it was directly in front of Axel's face with his arm drawn back. Before the punch could land on Axel's cheek, the crazy assassin moved to the side, using his own shadows to propel him behind Ryland.

"Okay, enough! Enough!" Z moved to stand between the two men, her hands darting out to touch both of their chests. Of course, in their shadow forms, she couldn't actually touch them, but it was still effective in getting them to calm the fuck down.

Axel laughed giddily as he turned tangible. "That was fun. We should do it again sometime," he said to Ryland, who immediately poofed back into existence and grabbed Z's wrist, holding it delicately between both of his hands.

"Fuck you, Axel," Ryland hissed.

"Z..." Axel waggled his eyebrows salaciously. "I think your mate is propositioning me."

The growl Z released was fierce, and I wasn't going to lie, sexy as fuck. Sparks of lust exploded in my bloodstream, crackling down my nerve endings.

"Axel, knock it off."

"But—"

"Axel!" she warned dangerously, maneuvering her body so that her much smaller frame obscured as much of Ryland's as possible.

It was fucking adorable. Who knew my girl had such a jealous, wicked streak in her?

Axel pouted but conceded with a heavy sigh, slinging his machete over his shoulder. "All right. I'll stop. But I'm being serious with my offer. I'll stay here with Lupe while the six of you go in the Forest of Death and Suffering—"

"Monsters and Beasts," Ryland corrected.

Axel ignored him. "I swear on my life that no harm will come to your little shifter mate."

"Actually,"—I took a few steps forward so I was in front of Z and Ryland, facing the crazy-ass shadow—"that sounds like a good idea."

His eyes narrowed suspiciously. "What do you have in mind, mage?"

"A spell." I gave him a smug look. "If you're as...loyal as you claim to be, then you'll be willing to perform a little blood spell with me. You promise to protect Lupe to the best of your ability, and if you fail to do so..." I pouted mockingly. "You'll die."

What. A. Shame.

A world without Axel in it? A world without him trying to marry my girl?

Oh, damn. How awful.

Said no one, ever.

Axel clapped his hands together and threw his head back in hearty laughter. "I love gambling with my life, boy. I suppose you have yourself a deal." He turned towards Z with an easygoing grin. "You hear that, little sister wife? I'm proving myself to my new...what would you call your future wife's mates? Mates-in-laws? Nah. That doesn't seem right. Brothers-in-laws?"

Z's entire face seemed to wrinkle in disgust. "Don't call me little sister wife. It's gross. If you do it again, I'll have no choice but to stab you. Painfully. In the ball sack."

"Noted." The smile on Axel's face suggested he was definitely going to do it again just to get that stabbing she'd promised. Crazy fucking psycho.

"Second,"—Z held up two fingers—"we're not getting married. We're never getting married. I would rather marry a human-sized poop than you—"

"Is that your kink? Poop?" Axel tilted his head to the side. "That's odd."

"You're odd!" Z retorted like a damn child.

But I noticed she didn't deny the whole "poop kink" thing, which was something I was totally going to tease her about later.

"It's completely okay if you like shit being placed on your—" Axel cut off abruptly at the sound of someone clearing her throat.

All of us turned towards the brown-haired human

woman from earlier—Davia or Davina or something like that—as she shuffled from foot to foot.

Z's face turned red in mortification as my grin widened. Yeah. I was definitely going to tease her about the whole "poop" thing later.

"Liberator." The woman looked only at Z, despite the six of us surrounding her.

That was okay, though. I didn't need or expect another human's attention. They still saw us as the monsters who hurt them for years and years and years. That mentality wouldn't go away just because one woman claimed we were the good guys.

We would need to prove to these humans that we had changed, that we were trying to better the world our fathers had ruined. That would take time.

"Yes, Davia." Z returned the woman's chin dip with one of her own. "How can I help you?"

"We established a perimeter to ensure no one will follow you into the forest," she said formally, like an officer speaking to the general during wartime.

And now that I thought about it...she was standing like a soldier, too, with her feet shoulder-width apart and her hands clasped behind her back.

"Thank you," Z said sincerely before huffing out a dry, humorless laugh. "Though I doubt anyone would be stupid enough to follow us in there."

"Even so, they won't be able to." The woman's lips twitched for a fraction of a second before she smashed them together. "Would you like me to send some of my people in there with you? For more protection?"

"It's okay," Z assured her quickly, and I didn't have to

be a mind reader to know what she was thinking. The forest was immensely dangerous. The last thing my girl wanted was to put more people in harm's way. Hell, if she had her choice, we wouldn't be going in there with her either. Not that she *had* a choice in the matter. I would spank her ass raw if she even suggested such nonsense. "We'll be fine."

"If you're sure..." She seemed skeptical but didn't dare contradict Z. "We'll have medics standing by when you return."

Z blanched, the movement so minute, I wouldn't be surprised if the woman had missed it.

Let us all pray that we didn't need those medics.

"Thank you, Davia. I mean it."

"Thank you, Liberator." She lowered herself into something that almost resembled a curtsey before stalking off to rejoin her troops.

As soon as she was out of earshot, Axel whistled under his breath. "Damn, little sister. You really are building an army."

Z's cheeks turned red. "I'm not."

He cocked one eyebrow at her mockingly. "So you're saying that you don't have two—maybe three, if you find the Alphabet Resistance—groups of trained fighters willing to do whatever you say, whenever you say it?" He snorted. "You're funny. Funny, funny, funny."

"I'm going to say goodbye to Lupe," Z snapped, ignoring Axel's comments.

I knew my mate well enough to know that the pressure was getting to her, that she didn't like what Axel was implying. She didn't believe herself to be a leader, but I knew a queen when I saw one. I supposed it was up to me and her other mates to fix her damn crown.

"Bash,"—she turned to face me—"perform that spell you talked about with Axel."

"Yes, General." I gave her a mocking salute, and she growled adorably before stalking towards the huge bear shifter.

"So..." Axel slung an arm casually around my shoulders, pulling me against his side like we were dear old friends. "How does this spell work? Do you need me on my back or my hands and knees? Am I taking or giving?"

I blew out a heavy breath and flicked my gaze up to the sky, praying for patience.

Perhaps the Forest of Monsters and Beasts would be a blessing compared to dealing with Axel the fucking Butcher.

Z

"We can't leave yet," I insisted, sitting on the ground in front of Lupe's cage as the aggravated bear shifter paced behind me.

Jax sat on my other side, fiddling with my fingers as he nodded thoughtfully in agreement. That was one thing I loved about my vampire mate—no words needed to be said when he was with me. We understood each other in a way that surpassed sentences or conversation, a visceral bond that connected my soul to his.

Dair was crouched down in front of us, his features sad despite the hardening of his eyes. "Ryland said we needed to leave at dark. It's when he has the most control of the shadows," he explained.

"But Devlin isn't here yet. He said..." I swallowed convulsively as a splinter of fear embedded itself in my gut. "He seemed to believe me when I said I was still alive..."

"And he might've been too far to make it here on time," Dair pointed out gently.

The sharp jawline that blessed his golden features clenched, though his irritation wasn't directed at me. He was just as afraid as I was about Devlin.

We had been waiting on the outskirts of the forest for almost two hours now, and the sun had already been claimed by the horizon. Stars speckled the night sky, though there wasn't any moon that I could spot. Still, the lighting from above was just bright enough for us to see by.

"Axel knows to keep an eye out for Devlin," Dair reminded me softly. "But we need to get to the mountain range and find the Alphabet Resistance."

I considered his words carefully, turning them over and over again in my head before finally concluding that he was right. We needed to find the Alphabet Resistance, discover what they knew, and hopefully, develop a plan of action in this war to come.

"You're right," I agreed softly. "I just thought he would be here."

My heart fractured down the middle at the thought that Devlin didn't believe me, that he was still on a suicide mission trying to track down Aaliyah. I would feel it if he were dead, just as he felt when I died, but that didn't mean he was unharmed. Bile burned my throat and tears filled my eyes, though I blinked them away and climbed unsteadily to my feet.

"He'll be here, Z," Jax assured me from my other side, his voice a low whisper. "Even if it's when we return... He'll be here."

"How can you be so sure?"

"Because it's what I would do," he confessed. The

panic trying to crawl its way up my throat was pushed back down when I met his soft green eyes. "It's what we all would do if we ever got separated from you. We'd find our way back, just like you found your way back to us."

I pulled in a sharp, staggered breath, suddenly overwhelmed with the irresistible urge to kiss him, to claim his pouty lips with my own. Before I could do that, however, Bash sauntered towards us with a forced grin on his face.

"Are we ready to be eaten by flesh-eating monsters?" he asked with feigned cheerfulness.

Dair gave Bash a scathing glare, but Bash continued to smile, completely unperturbed.

"Are we all packed up right and ready to go?" I wiped at my face quickly, praying none of them noticed the tears leaving tracks down my cheeks. How fucking embarrassing.

"Yeah," Killian exclaimed, overhearing my question as he joined our group with Ryland at his side. He jerked his chin towards his backpack. "I got food, bandages, canteens of water, knives—"

"We get it," Bash interrupted. "You're packing."

"Yes, he is," I quipped, unable to stop myself from making the joke despite my sour mood.

Bash's lips twitched upwards in the first genuine smile of the night before they flattened.

He turned towards Ryland. "How does this work?"

Ryland hovered a few inches off the ground, only his icy blue eyes visible through the cloak of shadows. "I'll use my powers to push away the darkness—and thus, the monsters. The forest is the one place the sunlight doesn't reach, so we'll be relying on the starlight to see by." He gazed up at the sky with slitted eyes.

"That doesn't make any sense," Killian piped up, waving his hand in the air erratically as if he hadn't already spoken and was waiting to be called upon. "How can starlight penetrate the forest and sunlight can't?"

"Penetrate." Bash chuckled under his breath, and both Dair and I moved as one to hit him.

I swore my mage mate had the mental maturity of a teenager.

"The forest wasn't naturally made," Ryland explained. "If my father was telling the truth, it was created centuries ago by shadows. It doesn't follow the rules of the natural world."

"Oh...how peachy," I drawled sarcastically, even as fear skated down my spine. I really, really didn't like the sound of this forest. The more I learned about it, the more I wanted to run in the opposite direction.

But I didn't run from my battles. I faced them head-on and fought like hell to emerge victorious. That reminder bolstered my resolve and made me stand even straighter.

"What else do we need to know?"

"We'll be holding hands as we enter the forest," Ryland told us, his voice growing serious and his eyes turning flinty. "Whatever happens, do not let go of each other's hands, understand?"

Killian gulped. "What would happen if we let go?"

"You'll lose yourself to the darkness and monsters," he told us bluntly, not a hint of inflection in his tone. "And then you'll probably get ripped to shreds or eaten."

"Fun," Bash deadpanned, but I swore Killian looked as if he were seconds away from passing out.

I immediately stepped towards my sweet incubus mate and took his hand in mine. "Don't worry, Kill," I whispered. "I won't let go of your hand."

He focused his relieved, glimmering eyes on me. "It's not me I'm worried about, Z." He swallowed. "What if something happened to you? What if we lost you in the forest? What if—?"

I cut off his unabated rambling with a quick kiss on the lips. "That won't happen." To the rest of my guys, I added, "We're making it out of the forest alive. All of us."

"Damn right," Bash muttered.

"Then I suppose it's time we go..." Ryland trailed off with a tight frown.

All six of us turned to stare at the forest. In the cover of night, it appeared particularly menacing. The trees resembled monsters just waiting to devour us whole. That ball of dread in my stomach grew and grew, like a snowball rolling down a hill and collecting more snow as it went.

"One moment." Swallowing down the fear that threatened to choke me, I twisted to face my bear shifter once more.

Lupe growled at me when I stepped closer to his cage, his golden eyes refracting the starlight above. Seeing him like this... It broke my heart. Shifters were known to be unstable, aggressive, and volatile because of their sin, but Lupe had always been the exact opposite. He never lifted a hand in violence unless he didn't have a choice.

His deep, raspy baritone cocooned me in safety and security instead of anger and violence.

This beast...

It wasn't Lupe, and I feared we would never get our sweet shifter back.

"I'm so sorry, Lupe," I whispered, making sure not to step too close to the cage in case he decided to swipe at me. "We'll be back as soon as we can. We don't plan to spend more than a day away. And once we return, we'll figure out how to save you."

His head twisted from side to side as he roared, and the fine strands of golden hair around my face stirred with the release of air.

"I love you," I whispered, praying that a part of him heard me, that a part of him understood my words. But when he stared at me with his huge, furry head canted to the side, I saw nothing but malice and wrath in his gaze.

Nothing but hatred.

"Z." Jax twisted me in his arms so I could rest my cheek on his pec, directly over his heart. "It's time to go, my love."

"We'll be back, right?" I asked somewhat desperately. "To save him? And find Devlin?"

Jax didn't answer as he stroked my hair, and I realized it was because he didn't *have* an answer for me. At least, not one that I would like.

But it was okay, because I had faith that this would work out. That Lupe would return to normal and we would meet up with Devlin and all of us would live out our happily ever afters.

And coming from me, the definition of a pessimist with an attitude problem, that was saying something.

"Everybody holding hands?" Ryland inquired, forcing my attention away from Jax and onto my shadow mate.

I moved to join him and the others and immediately clasped hands with Killian, just as I'd promised. Jax claimed my other hand before any of my other mates could, eliciting a grumble from Bash and a weary sigh from Dair.

Ryland stood at the front of the group, his expression taut and tension lining the muscles of his arms and shoulders. "Remember, don't let go. No matter what happens, what you feel, what you hear, what you see."

"Fuck me," Bash muttered from in front of Jax. Dair took the rear, holding Killian's other hand.

"Be careful, little sister!" Axel called. He stood in a huddle with Davia and the red-faced man, whose name I couldn't remember. When my gaze collided with his, he waved in our direction. "Don't die."

"Not planning to," I quipped back, even as my heart juddered in my chest.

And then, ever so slowly, the six of us stepped into the forest.

It was unlike anything I had ever experienced before. One second, we were surrounded by the humans, light emitting from the numerous fires dotted around their makeshift camp and the stars above. And the next, we were tossed headfirst into a sea of ink. It was endless, and it felt like I was wading through waist-high sludge.

I sucked in a lungful of air as my surroundings faded

away until I couldn't even see the trees directly in front of my face. It wasn't a gradual loss of light, like when the sun faded below the horizon. It was just...darkness, lowering itself over us all like a blanket. Anxiety began to poke at the numb barrier I'd erected around myself as I tightened my hands around Jax's and Killian's.

This darkness...

This infinite and yet infinitesimal darkness...

It washed over me in a torrent, painful in its intensity.

In the distance, something growled, the noise sending goose bumps rippling down my arms.

"Ryland..." Bash murmured.

"Shush. I'm working on it. Just keep moving."

"Fuck!" Killian screamed from behind me. "There's something touching my feet."

"Just keep moving," Ryland gritted out.

It was then that I felt it too. Something slimy and scaly was crawling over my feet, wrapping around my ankles. At first, I thought it was a snake, but then it began to growl, the noise reverberating through my body and setting my nerve endings aflame. My fight-or-flight response kicked in almost instantly, and I jerked backwards a few steps, my hands coming loose from my mates.

They tightened their grips immediately, identical curses leaving their lips.

"Fuck, Z!" Jax exclaimed.

"Sorry," I whispered.

"I almost. Have it," Ryland managed to gasp out, and then, silvery light exploded all around us, creating a pathway through the forest.

It was the strangest thing I had ever seen. On either side of us, walls of darkness remained, but the forest directly in front of us was illuminated with the light from the stars.

"The monsters shouldn't be able to touch the light," Ryland gritted out. The muscles in his neck twitched as he continued forward. "We'll be safe as long as it remains on."

"And how long can you hold the shadows back?" Bash demanded.

Ryland didn't answer, keeping his free hand raised as he parted the darkness.

Shivers danced down my spine as I tightened my grip on Killian's and Jax's hands.

It was almost eerie how the thin beam of starlight sliced cleanly through the darkness like a knife cutting through bread. Where we walked, I could see the compacted brown dirt, the stumps of cut-down trees, and the occasional branch that blew too close to my face. But outside of the single pathway, there was nothing but unending darkness—so dark, I couldn't even see the monsters roaming the forest.

But I could hear them.

Growls, hisses, anguished cries that had acid churning in my belly.

I didn't know how much farther we needed to travel, but I could tell every step we took was taking a toll on Ryland. The smooth muscles of his back rippled and dilated as he ventured another step forward, but he was beginning to slow down, shallow pants escaping his lips.

"Ryland..." Bash cautioned.

"I know," my shadow mate gritted out, but even those two words seemed to be causing him an immense amount of pain. A guttural growl vibrated his chest. "Just keep moving."

Around us, the silver light began to flicker, curling in on the edges like paper thrown into a fireplace and burning to a crisp.

"Ryland!" Bash's voice was laced with urgency and fear.

Ryland glanced over his shoulder at us, and his face leached of color. Shame and horror darkened his expression a second before wisps of shadows coiled back into him.

"Run!" he bellowed at the top of his lungs, but it was too late.

His hold on the shadows waned, and the starlit path flickered once, twice, three times before diminishing completely. In a span of seconds, we became one with the darkness again.

And then, the monsters attacked.

SEVENTEEN

Z

"Shit!" I yelled as something rammed into my stomach, forcing my hands to loosen from Jax's and Killian's.

"Z!" Killian shouted, but there was nothing he could do about it.

There was nothing anyone could do about it as my fingers slipped out of first his hand and then Jax's, and I was thrown completely onto the ground.

Fuck. Fuck. Fuck.

Panic lit a forest fire inside of my stomach, the flames wrapping around my internal organs in a heated hug, as I struggled to unsheathe one of the daggers I kept strapped to my thigh. I couldn't see the monster hovering over me, but I could taste his rancid breath in my mouth and feel the drizzle of saliva as it touched the skin of my cheek. The more I focused, the more a pair of gemstone eyes manifested in the inky darkness—a strange golden color rimmed with red. They were a stark contrast to the darkness that slammed into me from every direction.

In the distance, I could hear more shouts and growls, and I prayed my mates were able to handle themselves. I didn't even want to think about what would happen if they got injured or worse. If one of them died...

I shoved the horrible, macabre thought away and focused on taking care of the imminent threat—the beast trying to bite into my neck.

Usually with these types of kills, I would go for the jugular, but with my arms trapped by my sides by his huge paws, all I could do was swipe ineffectually at his legs. A strangled whine escaped him, and he momentarily released his grip on me. It was just enough time for me to hold my blade upright, directly over my heart. When the beast jumped on me again, I pushed upwards with all my might until my blade penetrated his meaty underbelly. At least, I hoped it was his underbelly. Either way, the scream that escaped it was nothing short of inhuman, but I didn't allow it to stop me from pushing the blade through fur, muscle, and bone, carving a pathway along the length of its stomach.

Something wet touched my cheek a second before a pile of gooey organs collapsed on top of me. I twisted my face to the side and dry-heaved, but luckily, nothing came out.

The monster gave one more pitiful cry before it dropped down onto my stomach. With a grunt of disgust, I pushed at the creature until it fell to the ground beside me and I was able to roll away from it.

I'd just barely gathered my bearings when something small landed on my head and began to stab at my face with a razor-sharp beak. I swatted at the monster, but it simply took to the air, a puff of air from its rapidly moving wings blowing back a strand of my blonde hair.

A flying monster, then.

Fuck.

I was covered in blood and guts, but I didn't hesitate as I lowered myself to a crouched position and studied the darkness for where the monster had gone. It was close. I could hear the steady beat of its wings, the noise eerily echoing my own heartbeat.

I waited with bated breath, my muscles locked tight, and then...

The winged creature dived at my face a second time, and I slashed at it with my knife. A strangled, guttural roar escaped it, but I didn't stop, stabbing at again while it struggled to remain airborne. I heard the satisfying clunk of its body hitting the ground before two more monsters converged on me. A stab here, a slice there, and a kick to what felt like the first one's bony head sent them both to the ground at my feet.

The forest was plunged in silence, so unnatural and ominous, I felt physically ill as if I'd just swallowed a barrel of acid. I strained my ears, listening intently, but couldn't hear even the chirp of crickets in the distance or the caw of birds. But then again, maybe those particular creatures didn't dare venture too close to this forest, knowing what would happen if they descended into its depths.

My breathing was a ragged, erratic sound, almost distant through the sluicing of blood reverberating between my ears.

No birds.

No crickets.

No monsters.

And no mates.

Panic nearly ate me up inside, but I forced myself to remain calm, to focus on my breathing.

Where the fuck were they? I could've sworn they were beside me during the fighting, but then...

I remembered Ryland's warning about losing yourself to the darkness, to the monsters and beasts who roamed this forest unsupervised. Was that what happened to me? To my mates?

No, I refused to believe that. Our story would not end like this. I wouldn't let it happen.

My bloody fingers drummed against my right thigh as I struggled to think through my next move. Without Ryland here to push the shadows away, I couldn't even see my hands in front of my face. There would be no way for me to find my way out of the forest alone. But maybe...

Maybe I didn't need to rely on my sight to reconnect with my mates.

My heart battered my rib cage as I squeezed my eyelids shut—despite already being cloaked in discombobulating darkness—and focused on my connection to my mates. Killian's bright, innocent soul that pushed away the darkness I had grown so accustomed to. Ryland's mischievous, mysterious one that wrapped around me in a comforting embrace, just as his shadows did. Jax's was volatile and eccentric, the type of energy you would usually feel from a shifter, but it soothed the chaos of my mind like the kiss of summer itself. I could bask in his presence until the end of time. Bash's soul was angry but loyal. Possessive and protective. He was the type of man who pushed me until I feared I would break, but when I inevitably did, I reformed stronger than ever. He saw the best in me and was never afraid to coax it out, even if I fought against him every step of the way. And finally, Dair's, reminiscent of ducking beneath ice-cold water on a one-hundred-degree day, when the sun was searing hot overhead and your skin was slick with sweat. Refreshing, comforting, and soothing.

My feet migrated in the direction I'd felt my mates before my brain could even catch up. All I knew was that I needed to find them, I needed to wrap them in my arms and make sure that they were all okay, that the monsters didn't hurt them.

I didn't know how long I walked, but it almost seemed as if the connection between all of us was palpable. Light sparked to life in the center of my chest, illuminating the forest in an ethereal, golden glow. Monsters hissed and screeched at me, but they didn't take a step in my direction, not with the piercing light emitting from my soul, dispersing the shadows around me.

After what felt like hours later, I stepped out of the forest and into a world awash with bright, midday sunlight.

I collapsed onto my knees, dimly aware that I was soaked in disgusting monster blood and guts, but I didn't have the strength to worry about that. It felt as if all of my energy had been sapped out of me, leaving me oddly bereft and empty.

"Z! Holy fuck! Z!" Hands touched me, caressed me,

lifted me up. Stark fear lined the faces of my men as they surrounded me.

"Are you okay? Whose blood is that? Is it yours?" Bash asked, alarmed.

I shook my head wordlessly, my eyes flicking back to the forest I'd just emerged from. It seemed almost... peaceful in the light of day, the trees swaying in the breeze and the long weeds lining the perimeter rustling.

"Not mine," I assured him, twisting my head to meet all of my mates' gazes individually. "It belonged to the monsters."

Killian dropped to his knees before me. "Fuck." His trembling hands ran down my hair, my shoulders, my sides, until they finally settled on my waist. "I'm so sorry, Z. I'm so, so sorry."

I placed my hands overtop of his to hopefully stop the tremor reverberating through him. "Why the fuck would you be sorry?"

His anguished eyes met mine, smoldering with an emotion I couldn't quite articulate but stabbed at my heart all the same. "Because I let go of you."

"*We* let go of you," Jax corrected, his voice subdued. He stood slightly apart from the group, his head tilted to the side. Aside from a single streak of blood on his face, he appeared to be relatively unharmed. But his forest-green eyes... They were awash with terror and horror, the two emotions swirling together in a toxic cocktail.

"I let go of you guys," I amended immediately. "How did you make it out?"

"I was able to regain control of the shadows," Ryland explained, his voice slightly shaky and his ice-blue eyes faraway and distant. "But when the light dissipated the darkness, we realized you were no longer with us."

"We thought we lost you in the damn forest, baby," Bash bit out venomously. I lifted my hand to touch his cheek before realizing it was soaked with blood. Before I could lower it, he shifted closer on his knees until he could nuzzle against my palm like an overgrown housecat. "We were just about to go in after you when Dair said he felt you approaching."

"Why the fuck would you go back into that forest of horror and fuckery?" I demanded, aghast that they would even suggest such a thing.

Bash gave me a look that suggested I was crazy. "I would rather be ripped apart by monsters than be away from you." My heart swelled at the vehemence in his words before he tacked on, "Dumbass."

Real romantic, my sweet Bash-hole.

"That's stupid," I pointed out with a scowl.

"That's love," Ryland countered.

"Now we know how Devlin and Lupe feel," Dair added under his breath.

I bit down on my lip to stop the snarl that wanted to escape.

"We need to make an agreement, okay?" I dropped my hand from Bash's cheek and claimed his hand. My other hand found Killian's and gave it a squeeze. "No running off into deadly situations, deal?"

"No deal," they replied simultaneously.

Before I could retort and remind them how idiotic they sounded, something sharp and cold pressed to my neck from behind. All of my mates froze immediately, their eyes shifting to the figure over my shoulder.

"Don't try to use your powers, mage," a familiar voice bit out, and I realized that Bash had lifted his hands and was holding them at the ready, green mist emanating from his palms. "Your powers won't work on me. I have a charm."

That gruff, raspy voice...

I gasped. "B?"

EIGHTEEN

Z

The man holding me turned to solid stone, though the pressure of the knife at my throat didn't lessen. Erratic spurts of air left his lips, caressing the skin of my neck, as he shuddered against me.

"Z? Is that you, kid?" Incredulity bled into his voice, along with another emotion I couldn't quite name. Shock, perhaps, or maybe disbelief.

Or maybe...just maybe...it was hope.

Either way, that emotion coiled around my heart like barbed wire and pressed down tightly.

"What?" I drawled sarcastically, trying not to show him how fazed I was having a dagger at my neck. "You can't tell with all the blood on me? I don't know if you heard, but bloody guts are all the rage back at the capital."

A bark of surprised laughter escaped him, and he finally released me.

I clamored to my feet and spun around, my mates

fanning out around me protectively. Ryland's shadows curled around his upper arms and torso, and his blue eyes darkened significantly as he stared at the man I considered a friend, mentor, and father figure. Bash's hands still sparked with his powers, though he didn't lift them again to attack.

My mouth dropped open as I stared into B's familiar, arresting face. His hair was longer than I remembered, curling around his ears in brown, untamed curls interwoven with streaks of gray. He seemed to have lost weight as well, though no one with eyes would consider him lanky or thin. He had always been a large man, but his belly had been replaced by hard, defined muscle that hinted at just how much he had been through in the time I'd been away.

His sharp eyes landed on me and narrowed, studying me attentively. And then, he smiled. At first, it was the merest twitch of his lips in a mockery of a genuine smile, but the longer he stared at me, the wider it became until his entire face was cleaved in half. Laughter danced in his eyes as he held his arms out wide for a hug.

I didn't hesitate.

Despite the blood staining my skin and clothes, I rushed forward and wrapped my arms around his thick waist, burrowing my head into his chest.

"Fucking hell, Z," he murmured against the top of my head. He pushed me back an inch and placed his hands on my shoulders, studying me from head to toe. "What the fuck have you been up to since you've been away, girl? Becoming the Liberator? Mating the princes? Starting a rebellion?" He shook his head with a rueful grin. "Nothing is ever simple with you, now is it?"

"You should know by now that I prefer doing things the hard way," I responded with a slightly hysterical laugh. Fuck, seeing B was the balm to my tattered soul I didn't know I needed. "I'm so goddamn relieved you guys are all okay."

"We were able to make it out before the kings' armies attacked," B said seriously, his expression turning grim. "The shadow king brought us here to protect us, but we haven't heard from him in days."

"The other kings discovered he was a spy," Ryland interjected, taking a step forward so he was shoulder to shoulder with me. His glacial blue eyes burned a hole in B's hands on my shoulders, as if he wished to wrap his shadows around the older man's wrists and rip them off.

B's face twisted and distorted, sadness giving way to unreadability.

"I see," he said after a long moment of silence, finally pulling his gaze off of mine to face the other men present. A muscle in his jaw bunched up as he studied them. "And I'm assuming these are the mates I heard so much about?"

"They're good men, B," I assured him. "You don't have to trust them, but you should trust me. Haven't I proved that to you time and time again?"

He clenched his teeth but didn't argue, probably because he didn't know what to say. I was right, and we both knew it.

"I trust her, B," a quiet voice intoned from directly behind our group.

Bash jumped about a foot in the air, cursing up a storm, and Killian squealed like a little girl. I wasn't even surprised HH had snuck up on us—I swore the man was half shadow, despite knowing he was one-hundred-percent human.

"And believe it or not, I trust *them*." The tiny man glanced at my mates before immediately lowering his gaze to his feet.

HH looked better than the last time I'd seen him. Healthier. His tan skin seemed to glow beneath the harsh sun, and his dark hair had been combed and washed. His wire-framed glasses slipped down his nose, but he used the pad of his middle finger to push them back into place, all without blinking.

HH was a deadly fighter and a skilled sharpshooter... and he had also been mated to Diego, my best friend who had lost his life protecting me. Zack had placed a hex on Diego that prohibited the mage from using his magic, but that didn't stop Diego from charging into battle and sacrificing himself for me. He died in my arms, and I could never forgive Aaliyah for the role she played in his death.

Neither could HH.

The tiny, sinewy man shot sharp eyes at me and dipped his head in acknowledgement. He was a man of few words, but when he spoke, you better damn well listen.

B licked his upper lip as he volleyed his gaze between me and my mates. For a long moment, he didn't speak, simply regarded us with that canny, unfaltering intensity I had grown accustomed to over the years. The silence stretched between us like putty, and I shivered as the air became electrically charged.

Finally, he nodded, and that miniscule gesture seemed to say more than a thousand words. My lungs expanded as I greedily inhaled air, and beside me, my mates' shoulders sagged with relief.

"All right. We should get you guys back to the camp and cleaned up." He focused on me, and his nose wrinkled. "Z, no offense, but you're a little gross right now."

"And smelly," HH piped in quietly.

"You try fighting off a hoard of monsters and smelling like daisies afterwards," I retorted with a scoff before offering him a small smile. It was an olive branch if I ever saw one—he trusted me and my mates, at least to some extent, so I would extend him the same courtesy. "Lead the way."

THE NEW RESISTANCE CAMP WAS CARVED DEEP INTO the base of the mountain.

Killian's jaw turned slack as he marveled at the landscape, while Bash's clenched tightly.

"Don't like being underground?" I whispered to him as we traversed the winding caves.

"I don't like the thought of the ceiling collapsing on us and burying us alive," he retorted somewhat haughtily, jutting his chin up into the air.

"That won't happen," HH murmured from directly behind us, his voice a ghost in the breeze. And then, almost as an afterthought, he added, "Probably."

"That's reassuring," Ryland murmured.

I studied our surroundings as we ventured from one series of caves to the next, the pathway to the base purposely disorienting to stop intruders from finding it. Rocks jutted out of the walls, and the ground was made out of compacted black dirt that had hardened over time. No sunlight could breach this far into the mountain, so we were forced to rely on the torches positioned at intermittent intervals along the way.

B jerked his chin at one of the pathways. "Rooms are in that direction," he explained. "Girls to the right. Guys to the left. Over there, you'll have the cafeteria. We have a few mages who are able to transport food directly to the kitchen, so we don't have to risk showing our faces in town." We finally stopped at a long hall that branched outwards in both directions. "Bathroom's this way. Girls to the right. Guys to the left." He turned towards me. "There are showers in there as well, with soap and towels. I suggest you use them."

"Thanks, B." I placed a hand on his arm, overcome by the enormity of my emotions for this man.

He'd raised me after my parents and A died, and he trained me to become like him—a fierce fighter and an even fiercer friend. He reminded me time and time again that the possibilities were limitless, that I didn't need to be confined to one box because I was a human.

Though I wasn't sure if I even *was* human anymore, not after I'd brought Jax back to life.

But that was an issue for another day, another Z. This Z? She was determined to shower until her skin was raw and aching, until the events of the last few hours were wiped away from her body.

"My office is that way." He jerked his head in the direction of a lone hallway with a single door at the end. "Meet me there once you're done."

"I'm going to get some damn food." Bash rubbed his hands together excitedly. "I'm starving."

"I'll join you." Ryland clamped his hand down on Bash's shoulder and shifted his eyes to stare pointedly at Dair.

Dair regarded them with confusion in his glittery blue orbs before his lips popped open and he nodded sagely. "Me too."

"Why the fuck are you three acting so weird?" I demanded, but Bash was already walking away, dragging Ryland and Dair with him.

"We'll meet you guys in a half hour at B's office." He paused his hasty retreat and amended, "An hour."

"I don't need an hour to shower." I rolled my eyes at his antics.

"Not to shower," he said cryptically, practically dragging my mermaid and shadow mates around the corner.

When they disappeared from sight, I realized I was left alone with Killian and Jax, both of whom still appeared rather shaken from the events of the last few hours. Killian repeatedly raked his fingers through his garnet hair, disrupting the meticulous strands, and Jax stared vacantly at the wall in front of him, a million miles away.

Oh.

Ohhh.

"Do you guys...want to come with me?" I timidly asked, nodding towards the bathroom.

Killian blinked owlishly up at me. "But that's the girls' bathroom."

I had to bite down on my smirk. "I'll make sure it's empty," I assured him, and he nodded once in agreement.

My vampire mate continued to stare blankly ahead, not acknowledging my offer. But when I stepped into the bathroom, he was right behind me, his body coiled tighter than a cobra preparing to strike.

Fortunately, the bathroom was already empty and there was a lock on the main door. I felt a little bad for locking it, but I figured if someone had to take a shit that badly, they could use the men's room. Just for an hour.

Killian eyed the 'toilets' with unveiled disgust. "Do girls usually do their business in *those?*"

I snorted. "No, of course not, but I imagine they don't have a lot of resources this far underground in the mountains." I glanced absently at the deep holes dug into the dirt before turning away. "My guess is someone's job is to clean out the holes every night before bed."

"That's disgusting."

"Not everyone can be a pampered prince, Kill," I teased, interlocking my fingers with his and leading him towards the showers.

Jax continued to follow aimlessly behind, his gaze focusing on everything but me.

"If they don't have piping and plumbing this far underground, how do you suppose the showers work?" Kill mused, staring at the string that I supposed would allow water to fall once we pulled it.

"Magic?" I shrugged, not overly caring about the hows and whys. "Science?"

They didn't have individual stalls for the showers like they did with the makeshift toilets. Instead, we stood in a large room with numerous nozzles and strings dangling overhead. I supposed the humans here had more pressing things to worry about than modesty.

A long, wooden bench took up one side of the wall, and above it sat shelves of supplies. I grabbed a fluffy towel, a bar of soap, and a bottle of shampoo. After placing the items on the bench, I began the painstaking task of removing my blood-soaked clothes. Fuck, I should've asked B for something clean to wear after my shower.

Jax's eyes finally seemed to focus on my face as I pulled my shirt over my head and then shimmied down my pants. The heat in those vibrant green orbs nearly set me aflame, though I worked to keep my expression impassive.

I was absolutely disgusting at the moment, but both men stared at me as if I were the most beautiful and perfect woman alive. Ripples of pleasure skated across my skin as I removed my bra and panties, then chose a shower at random and pulled a string.

Warm water immediately cascaded through the showerhead, dousing me in its torrent. I squeezed my eyelids shut as I worked to wipe the blood, sweat, grime, and guts from my body. I could feel Killian's and Jax's gazes on me, but I didn't reopen my eyes as I scrubbed my body down with soap and then washed my hair. Three times. The whole process took over thirty minutes, but still, my two mates didn't move from their spot against the wall, content to watch me.

Killian slowly licked his lips, his eyes flaring with a wanton need that had my pussy clenching around air instinctively. I knew what they were doing, even if they didn't.

They were punishing themselves.

For some stupid reason, they blamed themselves for losing me in the Forest of Monsters and Beasts. It was utterly ridiculous, but I knew they wouldn't just take my word for it. I had to prove to them that it wasn't their fault, that I didn't blame them, that I'd made it back in one piece.

Once the disgusting slime had been completely removed from my body, I bit down on my lower lip and fluttered my lashes in the direction of my mates. Killian's eyes widened, as if he didn't quite know what to do with me, while Jax continued to stare straight ahead, his expression hewn from marble.

"You know," I began casually as I rubbed the bar of soap over my pebbled nipple, drawing their gazes to the tender flesh. "You guys probably need to shower too."

"Z..." Killian all but groaned, his cock tenting the front of his pants. "I know what you're doing."

"I don't know what you're talking about," I responded nonchalantly as I dragged the bar of soap down my toned belly and towards the dip between my thighs. As I expected, both men followed the pathway of my hand with their eyes.

I knew Killian could sense the lust wafting off of me in palpable waves, but he didn't take a step closer. He didn't give in to the desire coursing between all three of us, the desperate, aching need to claim one another.

I'd had sex with Jax before, but Killian? We hadn't ever taken that step. We had done other things, of course, but he had never been inside of me.

I wanted him. I wanted both of them so badly, it nearly killed me.

"I don't blame you for what happened in the forest." I dropped the hand holding the soap back to my side and met each of their stares. "And you shouldn't blame yourselves either."

"We let go of your hands, Z," Killian choked out. "You could've become lost in the forest forever because of us."

"But I didn't," I responded plainly. "And you want to know why?" I didn't wait for them to respond. "Because of the bond between all of us. It allowed me to find you in the darkness." Emotions bubbled up inside of my chest, squeezing my heart. "I'll always find you guys."

"You shouldn't have had to," Jax said, speaking for the first time since he'd entered the shower. He seemed to be struggling to focus on my face, as if his mind was being particularly brutal to him today, creating visions that didn't truly exist. "We should've held on to you tighter."

"There was nothing you could've done," I said softly. "I needed to fight, and—"

"We could've tried harder," Jax interrupted, his eyes darkening with some unnamed emotion. It prickled the skin of my neck before skating down my spine. "We *should've* tried harder."

"Come here," I demanded, crooking my finger in the universal come-hither gesture.

They hesitated, their expressions wary, but whatever they saw in my face had them removing their clothes and stepping beneath the warm spray of water.

My mouth watered at the sight of them—Jax, tall and lean, with light brown hair that was beginning to become just a little too long and striking green eyes. Killian, hewn out of hard stone with muscles most men would kill for and garnet hair speckled with gold and orange. Both so different from one another, and both so heartbreakingly beautiful that my chest felt too tight.

Even their cocks were different, though both were currently erect at the moment.

Jax's was long and slender, the mushroom head dripping with precum. Killian's was just as long but slightly wider, a splatter of red hair at the base and crawling up his toned stomach. My mouth watered as I took in his defined, delectable V.

Slowly, Jax stepped forward and gripped my hand holding the bar of soap. Without removing his eyes from mine, he spun me around and began to wash my back, making tender, careful strokes against my skin. My heart thrashed in my chest at the way he cared for me, at the tender way he washed me. I knew I wasn't made of glass, but sometimes... Sometimes it was nice to be treated as such.

Killian moved to stand in front of me, droplets of water rolling down his defined cheekbones and landing on his tattooed chest. His eyes shone with emotion as he cupped my cheeks.

"I'm so sorry, Z," he whispered breathlessly, his gaze dipping to my lips and sticking there.

"There's nothing to be sorry for."

I breached the distance between us and kissed him slowly, tenderly, allowing him to feel the sincerity of my words. His love for me felt like a javelin to the chest, but the pain it brought was beautiful and pure. I could die from it, from *him*.

His body trembled with the force of his emotions, the force of his feelings for me, and he took a step closer until his hard cock brushed against my stomach.

Jax continued to wash my back, the soap soothing against my suddenly overheated skin but not enough. I needed his hands on me.

"Jax," I whimpered, arching back against him until his dick lined up with my ass.

He planted a soft kiss on my shoulder a second before he dropped the bar of soap and began to use his hands to wash my body. I didn't know if it was because he'd heard my unspoken plea or if he simply wanted to touch me. Either way, my body burned beneath his ministrations, my heart racing faster with every stroke of his hands on my skin.

He reached between me and Killian to cup my breasts, his fingers gently squeezing my hard nipples. Killian's eyes flared hotly at the sight, and he began to kiss me even faster, his cock jerking against my stomach.

"We shouldn't have left you," he murmured, his lips finally leaving mine to travel down my neck.

I arched slightly to give him better access, putting my body flush against Jax's. "You didn't have a choice."

"We always have a choice, Z." For once, there was no nervousness in Killian's voice. No hesitancy. He sounded like an entirely different person, and I wasn't sure how I felt about that. "And we made the wrong one." He bent forward to kiss a fiery pathway down my chest, stopping only to capture one of my nipples in his mouth.

Jax continued to fondle the other one, twisting and pulling at the tight bud.

Killian's lips left my breast and descended down my stomach. His tongue snuck out to lick at my belly button, and I gasped at the intrusion.

In a lot of ways, Killian was inexperienced when it came to sex and pleasure, but no one could ever claim he didn't understand lust. When we were together like this, he transformed into a walking, talking sex god—one who took what he wanted, when he wanted, regardless of the consequences. He was in charge of my pleasure, and I greedily handed him the reins, allowing him to do what he saw fit.

He dropped to his knees before me, and my breath sharpened at the sight of the normally shy, arresting man kneeling at my feet. Only he no longer appeared timid. Lust blazed in his heavily hooded eyes as he stared at me.

"Fuck, you're so beautiful, Z. So damn beautiful." He eyed my pussy hungrily, as if he didn't quite know what to do but wanted to make me feel good.

I licked my lips instinctively as he stared at my wet heat like it was his next meal and he was absolutely famished for a taste.

Ever so slowly, he leaned forward and licked the

length of my slit, his eyes rolling to the back of his head in bliss.

"How does she taste?" Jax murmured from where his lips rested against the skin of my neck.

"Like heaven," Killian answered. As if he were in a trance, he ducked his head and licked my pussy again. "Fuck, I can't get enough."

"Eat her out, brother. Make her scream your name," Jax whispered as he pulled on my nipples, tugging them away from my chest and then letting them go.

I gasped at the sharp, blistering pain, but that pain was immediately overridden by the pleasure of Killian's mouth descending on my pussy. I moaned, the noise pulled from deep within my throat, and Jax tilted my head over my shoulder to swallow the noise with his mouth. His lips moved softly but very seriously against my own, and no matter how hard I tried to deepen the kiss, he refused.

I didn't know if he was punishing me or himself, but it was driving me mad.

"Jax," I whimpered against his lips.

He pulled away from me but kept my head twisted so I could meet his eyes. "I don't know what I'd do if I lost you."

"You won't lose me," I whispered.

"You can't promise that." A hint of desperation entered his tone, and his hands on my breasts turned almost punishingly tight.

"I can, and I will." Keeping my eyes on his, I tilted my head to the side, baring my neck to his hungry gaze. "Bite me, Jax."

Horror flared in his eyes, followed immediately by lust. Then the horror returned once more as he focused on my pulse beating rapidly.

"Z..."

"You need to drink, Jax." I gently reached above my head and raked my fingers through his brown hair before guiding his head to my neck. "This isn't healthy."

"I'm a murderer," he whispered as he began to kiss the skin there desperately.

At the same moment, Killian's lips tugged on my clit, eliciting a gasp of pleasure from my lips.

"You're Jax, and I love you."

"Z—"

"And I trust you," I said, knowing he needed to hear those words. "Drink, Jax. Take what you need from me."

He still seemed hesitant, his lips almost ravenous on my skin, before his fangs extended and I felt the sharp prick of them in my neck. I gasped at the initial stab of pain, but it was immediately eclipsed by the feeling of Killian's tongue still prodding my slick entrance. The pain in my neck turned into pure bliss when Jax's venom entered my bloodstream, washing away any and all discomfort and replacing it with pleasure.

I could feel my orgasm rapidly approaching, and my mates knew it. Jax's hands on my breasts turned almost brutal as he plucked, slapped, and twisted my sensitive nipples. Killian's teeth grazed my clit, the gentlest of burns, and I exploded, jerking my hips upwards to ride his face as I descended into a mind-blowing orgasm. Stars exploded across my vision and my legs shook violently, but my men didn't let me fall.

Droplets of blood merged with the clean water, providing a tantalizing pathway of pink that darkened my skin. Killian's eyes heated as he watched the blood-stained water cascade over my heaving breasts before landing at his feet.

Jax's lips moved against my neck as he drank deeply from me, and his hands finally left my breasts to settle between my thighs. I felt his fingers enter my soaking channel, running through the juices left behind from my orgasm. A second later, those same fingers caressed my ass crack, breaching the tight ring of muscles.

"Oh, fuck," I moaned as Killian watched the enticing, sensual scene from his knees before us.

"Do you like that, sweetheart?" he practically purred, licking his lips. "Do you want me to take your sweet little cunt while Jax pounds into your ass?"

"Since when did you get so good at dirty talk?" I panted, and my incubus's cheeks turned crimson, though that wicked smile never left his face.

"Since I tasted your perfect pussy and watched Jax fuck your ass with his fingers," he retorted, and I bit back on a chuckle—a chuckle that quickly turned into a moan of pleasure when Jax added a second finger to the first, preparing my ass.

"I want you to fuck me," I all but begged. "Both of you."

"Greedy girl," Killian teased as he gracefully moved to his feet and stood before me. He had to bend forward to capture my lips with his. His hands moved to fondle my breasts as he kissed me. "We're never letting you go, Z," he vowed, his voice slightly breathless.

With every slant of his lips against mine, I swore I could taste myself on him. My arousal heightened at the sensation.

"I'm never letting you go. Both of you. All of you."

Killian's entire face seemed to soften as he smiled at me, his eyes shimmering. "I love you, Z. So damn much. I know I said I wanted our first time to be special, with candles and flowers and all that shit, but I can't wait anymore. I need to be inside of you so damn badly. I need to feel you clench my cock and know that you're okay and here with me."

"I love you too." I paused and added, "But I'll love you even more if you fuck me."

"Did you hear that, Jax?" Killian smirked at the vampire. "She wants me to fuck her."

"She wants *us* to fuck her," Jax corrected, nibbling on my earlobe. "Isn't that right, sweetheart?"

I rested my head against his shoulder as I wiggled in his tight hold. "Yes."

Jax nipped my skin and finally removed his fingers from my ass. "I think she's ready for us, brother."

"Are you ready for us, sweetheart?" Killian crooned. "Are you ready for my cock in your pussy and Jax's cock in your ass?"

His dirty words had my pussy clenching and the butterflies in my stomach flapping their wings erratically. "Yes."

I practically mewled like a damn cat when Killian's huge, muscular arms banded beneath my ass and hoisted me off my feet. My legs instinctively twisted around his waist, my heels digging into his firm ass, as his cock settled against my slick folds. But he didn't immediately enter me. Instead, he rubbed his dick back and forth across my slit as his hooded eyes met my own.

"Are you sure about this, Z?" A hint of his familiar nervousness returned as he nibbled on his lower lip. "Because if you're not sure—"

"I'm more sure about this than anything else in my life," I assured him. "I love you, Kill. So damn much."

My words seemed to be exactly what he needed, because his lips devoured mine in a desperate frenzy as his cock slowly slid inside of me.

"Holy fuck!" His eyes widened. "Holy fuck. Is this what it always feels like?"

"It's what it'll feel like for the rest of your life," I huffed, cupping his jaw and kissing the corner of his mouth. "This is the only pussy you're allowed to touch."

"Agreed," he said instantly, his body trembling with the strain of holding himself still. His gaze flitted to Jax over my shoulder. "You ready?" My incubus's long, talented fingers caressed my ass cheeks before crudely opening up my back hole for Jax's inspection.

I flushed instinctively, not used to being put on display like that, but there was something extremely sexy about it too.

Jax stepped up behind me, his breath feathering against my neck, and slowly inched himself inside my tight hole. I felt too full, close to bursting, and it was fucking amazing.

"Move," I hissed out a breath, throwing my head back to once more rest on Jax's shoulder. "You guys need to move."

Killian's breath shuddered as he pistoned in and out of me almost instantly, and Jax did the same. It took them only a few seconds to find a rhythm—when Jax pulled out of me, Killian pushed in, and I found myself bouncing between the two men. The only things keeping me in the air were Killian's arms beneath my ass and Jax's hands on my hips.

I threw my head back in wanton pleasure as they fucked me within an inch of my life. I wasn't even being dramatic. I swore I wouldn't be able to move again once these two men were done ravaging my body and wringing out all of the pleasure it was capable of.

It felt as if lust was being pumped directly into my veins, swirling in my chest like a typhoon made of fire.

Killian leaned forward and pried my lips apart with his, his tongue darting in. Tasting me. Claiming me. Loving me.

"I want to try something," he murmured, and a split second later, my arousal intensified tenfold.

"What the fuck?" I rasped.

"Pheromones," Killian managed to say. "Incubus, remember?"

Killian sent out another wave of pheromones, and a throb pulsed deliciously between my thighs, forcing my pussy and ass to clench around the two cocks inside of me. My nipples tightened as I rubbed against Kill's chest, desperate for friction.

Pleasure filled me, and I knew I was seconds from unraveling, from falling apart in their arms and praying they held me up through the worst of the storm.

And when Killian's finger dropped to my clit, circling it in hurried strokes, I knew I was a goner.

"Come for us, Z," he whispered breathily.

And I did.

The force of my orgasm slashed me to ribbons, and I screamed my release to the heavens. My pussy clenched around Killian's hard length, and it wasn't long until he fell over the edge as well, joining me in blissful oblivion. Jax pounded into my ass a few more times before his cock jerked, squirting hot cum down my ass cheeks. My heart battered my ribs with a frightening speed as I leaned forward and rested my wet forehead against Killian's shoulder.

"Holy fuck," I breathed.

Killian laughed heartily as he kissed the top of my head. "Holy fuck indeed."

NINETEEN

Z

One of my other mates must've had the foresight to ask for clean clothes.

By the time we emerged from the shower wrapped in fluffy, white towels, there were three bundles of clothes just outside the bathroom door and a note with a winky face on it.

Fucking men. It didn't matter if they were nightmares or humans—they were all the same when it came to sex.

Still, I couldn't contain the giddy smile that erupted across my face as I dressed in the loose harem pants and silky blouse provided for me. Killian and Jax also put on a clean pair of trousers and button-down shirts that showed off their defined, rippling muscles. My mouth practically watered as I watched Killian button up his shirt, obscuring his tattoos from view, and he offered me a shy smile.

Something had shifted between the two of us, and I fucking loved it.

"We should go find B and the others," he murmured, stepping towards me and kissing my forehead.

I offered him a pout. "Can't we just hide in here for the rest of our lives?"

Jax chuckled from my other side. "Unfortunately, it'll become a little too stinky for that. But I wouldn't be against finding a nice, non-toilet home to hide away in..."

I chuckled and looped my arm through his.

"Wouldn't that be nice," I mused with a sad shake of my head, but we all knew that was nothing but a pipe dream. We had too many responsibilities, too many people who were relying on us. We couldn't just run away from our problems, no matter how much we might want to.

Curse being a responsible adult.

The three of us made our way down the hall B had indicated earlier, stopping when we reached the door at the very end. I knocked once, and B's familiar, gruff voice immediately exclaimed, "Come in."

I wasn't surprised to find Bash, Ryland, and Dair already seated around the huge desk taking up the majority of the small room. Bash smirked when he saw us, his vibrant green eyes glowing with wicked amuse-ment, and Ryland chuckled darkly, though it was impos-sible to see his expression with the shadows coalesced around him. Dair simply offered the three of us a kind, knowing smile before reaching forward to grab my waist and plop me onto his lap.

B's eyebrows rose at the blatant display of affection between us, but I refused to be self-conscious. Maybe the old Z would've been, but the new Z reveled in each and every touch her mates gave her.

She knew what it was like to be without them.

"I'm glad the three of you could join us." B's eyes narrowed suspiciously on Jax and Killian, and the incubus's cheeks turned crimson as he ducked his head.

"We were dirty," he muttered helplessly, and B's lips pursed.

Really, Killian? Really?

I resisted the urge to face-palm, even as Bash hid his chuckle in the sleeve of his shirt.

B's brows arched in a knowing way. "No matter." He cleared his throat and swept his gaze around the room, meeting each of our eyes before focusing on me. "Now that we're all here, we can discuss everything that happened over the last few weeks." A crease materialized in the center of his forehead as a frown tugged at his lips. "Where are your other two mates? The shifter and the genie?"

The chasm in my chest that had been fixed by my time with Killian and Jax returned with a vengeance. It took all of my willpower not to bring my hand up and rub at my breastbone.

Dair, sensing my pain, squeezed me even tighter and kissed my cheek.

"Away," he answered vaguely, apparently not willing to go any further than that in way of explanation.

If B was upset or even offended by Dair's lack of answer, he didn't show it. He simply nodded once before continuing on. "I wanted to say first and foremost that I'm so happy you're okay, Z." He swallowed heavily, his gaze dipping towards his bruised knuckles before focusing once more on me. "I knew what I asked of you when I made you join the Damning." Leaning forward in his seat, he dropped his elbows onto the desk and ran a hand down his face. "It was selfish of me to put you in harm's way."

"There wasn't anything you could do," I reminded him gently, feeling the surety of that statement in the hollow of my bones. "The magic chose me to compete."

"I should've done something—"

"You didn't have a choice," I repeated firmly, not allowing him to argue this a second longer. It would get us nowhere. Still, a pleasant ache spread through my chest at his words and at the knowledge that he cared about me. Truly cared about me. A part of me had always assumed I was nothing but a fun project to him, a pawn to utilize and then discard, but I now knew that wasn't the case.

B's jaw clenched tightly, but he managed a single nod of assent. "I suppose there's a lot we need to catch up on." He clasped his hands together on top of the desk. "HH told me everything he could, but I wanted to hear it from you as well."

I swallowed once before reciting everything that had happened since I first became a competitor of the Damning to now. I told him about Zack and how he killed Diego after poisoning me. I even brought up Mali's betrayal and how she had been trying to redeem herself when she could. My heart broke thinking of her, but I pushed it aside. It wouldn't do me any good to hold on to my hurt.

I told him the exact moment I realized I was mates with the seven princes and how they weren't the men we believed them to be. He already knew about the prophecy—the one that claimed they would either save the world or destroy it—but he still listened with rapt attention as I told him every detail I had learned. I kept out what Tavvy had said about my mates appearing out of thin air. I didn't know if I believed the sadistic mermaid prince, and I didn't want B to become more suspicious of my mates than he already was. Besides, that was a snippet of information I still had yet to share with my mates as it was. Not because I wanted to keep it from them or anything like that—there just hadn't been time.

I told him about Aaliyah and her monsters and about her claim that I was her sister. I even mentioned her ominous story about me being a fallen angel who fell in love with the Seven Deadly Sins...and about her being a demon who fell in love—and then killed—the Seven Heavenly Virtues.

B listened to it all without interruption, and by the time I was done, I was gasping for breath. Damn. I was pretty sure I hadn't breathed once during that entire speech. That truly was an accomplishment.

B reclined backwards, his fingers tapping against one another as he considered us with sharp eyes. After a prolonged moment of silence, he leaned forward once more and said, "I see."

"I see?" I parroted in disbelief, quirking an eyebrow. "After all that, you say, 'I see.'"

His lips curved upwards in the makings of a tentative smile as he bent down to grab something beneath his desk. After a moment, he reemerged with a bright red tome in his hands. It appeared to be ancient, the pages yellowing with time and the script faded. The title was written in a language I wasn't familiar with.

"What's that?"

"Everything you just told me," he replied ominously, opening up the book and twisting it to face us.

Most of the writing was in the same, unfamiliar language as the cover, but that wasn't what he wanted me to see. No, what he wanted me to pay attention to were the two illustrations in the book.

The first one depicted a woman with flaming red hair and dark horns protruding from her skull. A black dress hugged her curvy figure as she stood in a center of seven beings, their bodies seeming to radiate light. They stared at her with adoration and love, though her own expression was sly. Cunning.

The other picture showed a blonde-haired woman dressed in white, with brilliant, golden wings erupting from her back. Seven men circled her, just as they had with the red-haired woman, but if the demon woman's expression could best be described as snake-like, the angel's face was a picture of serenity.

"What am I looking at?" My voice barely rose above a whisper.

Around me, my mates had gone rigid, their muscles tense.

A strange roaring sound reverberated between my ears. It reminded me eerily of ferocious waves battering against the rocky shoreline, breaking apart and then returning back to sea in a plume of white lines.

"The history of nightmares," B responded, tapping the picture incessantly. "One of our mages was able to decipher the ancient language, and it basically reiterates everything Aaliyah told you. An angel"—he pointed to the angelic entity—"named Gabrielle was in charge of the humans on earth. She was supposed to look after them, care for them, protect them. The Seven Deadly Sins had been able to watch earth for years, but they never had any desire to visit it themselves...until they set eyes upon the angel and fell desperately in love. They traveled to earth in order to be with her, but their love was frowned upon by both heaven and hell. All eight of them were banished for their transgressions and forced to remain apart for all of eternity."

My brows drew together, even as sick panic welled up in me. A vicious pain burned a hole in my chest, searing my veins. "But aren't the nightmares descended from the Seven Deadly Sins? Aren't the royal families their direct relatives?"

Did that mean the Seven Deadly Sins had relations with other women as soon as the angel, Gabrielle, was banished? The thought made me queasy.

"That's the legend," B said cryptically, his fingers tapping against the picture with increasing speed. His gaze never wavered from my face. "But I don't believe that's the truth."

"What do you think happened?" Bash demanded, crossing his arms over his chest in a posture that almost looked defensive. The frost in his tone could rival that of a winter storm.

"According to this book, the Seven Deadly Sins

recognized how much Gabrielle loved the humans and wanted to protect them. So they each offered up a piece of themselves to make…evolved humans, so to speak. What we now call nightmares." B's finger drifted from the image of the angel to the demon, settling directly between the woman's sharp black horns. "This story… This story is the exact opposite." He swallowed heavily. "My mage wasn't able to interpret everything, so please bear with me as I try to explain what he found."

All six of us leaned forward, hanging on to every word. Dair's chest had gone completely still against my back. I wasn't even sure if he was breathing.

"Apparently, the angel had a sister who was born with a wicked soul. As such, the universe decided to keep her separate from Gabrielle. The demon was wicked and cunning, but she loved her sister more than anything and anyone, so when seven men fell in love with her, she saw her chance."

"What happened?" I whispered, though I had already heard the story from Aaliyah. Or at least, a version of it.

"She convinced the seven men—who the text refers to as the Seven Heavenly Virtues—to free her from hell and take her to heaven. She had hoped to reunite with her sister there, unaware that Gabrielle had been assigned to look after earth. The demon became enraged when she discovered her sister was missing and killed the men she claimed to love. However, before she could flee, she was captured and shoved back into hell, where she was forced to spend the rest of her days."

My hands trembled on my lap, my heart pounding erratically.

A part of me almost felt pity for the demon before that emotion was swept away in a tsunami of anger. Fire burned in my blood, scorching my veins.

What cold-hearted bitch could kill her mates? The men she claimed to love?

"What does any of this have to do with us?" Ryland demanded softly, the shadows writhing around his body.

"That's what I'm trying to figure out, kid," B said, though there was a cautious look in his eyes that said he had already reached some sort of conclusion and didn't wish to share it with us. The knowledge pumped adrenaline through my veins, a trill of sensation I felt along the length of my spine. My heartbeat echoed in my skull as I gulped convulsively.

"Spit it out, old man," I snapped. When he didn't speak right away, I decided to answer for him. "You think that Aaliyah is this demon, correct? And that this angel... this Gabrielle...is me? And my mates are the original Seven Deadly Sins?" My voice betrayed my incredulity, and I half wanted to break into hysterical laughter. Was he insane? Were they all insane?

But one glance at the somber faces of my men showed that I was the only one who found this even remotely funny.

A cold fist gripped my heart and gave it a tight squeeze.

"It seems as if I'm not the only one who has jumped to that conclusion," B said at last, his tone carefully guarded. His emotions were locked up tighter than a nun's asshole. Nothing I did would be able to penetrate his unflappable defenses.

"That's ridiculous. You know that, right? I'm not some fucking angel, and these men aren't the original Seven Deadly Sins." I shook my head in denial, refusing to believe it. It wasn't true, and the sooner they understood that, the sooner we could dismiss the outrageous theory and come up with our next step towards ending Aaliyah and the kings once and for all.

B continued on as if I hadn't spoken, his tone grim. "This textbook is old...hundreds and hundreds of years old. It took my men and women years to get it. We actually found it in the shifter king's castle, guarded by over a dozen shifters. Lost a lot of good men and women trying to retrieve it—Gerald, Ali, Brett..." He flipped a few pages forward in the book as I shifted uneasily on Dair's lap. "There's another passage that my translator found... alarming. A different variation of the story, so to speak."

"What does it say?" Bash gritted out.

B's lips pursed, almost as if he didn't want to confess the truth, before he relented with a heavy sigh. "That Gabrielle and the Seven Deadly Sins weren't merely banished. This section claimed that Gabrielle was killed by the angels for defying them and that her mates and her sister were forced to watch. Her mates, in order to avenge their lover, used their powers to create a subset of humans that could defy the natural order before killing themselves. And her sister? She murdered her own mates, believing them to have a part to play in her sister's death, and vowed to get revenge no matter the cost."

A low, guttural growl echoed from the corner of the

room, where the shadows had become so thick, I couldn't even see Ryland's eyes.

"You're saying they murdered Gabrielle for falling in love?" His voice could've cut glass.

B shifted uneasily. "Not just murdered. This particular passage suggested that they...tortured her. Raped her, even. I'm not going to go into details—"

Something shattered behind B's head, and it took me a moment to realize that Bash had unintentionally released a well of his power, exploding two bottles of bourbon that were resting on a shelf above the old assassin's head.

B didn't even jump as glass and brown liquid rained down around him.

"Tavvy..." I whispered, blinking away the tears that threatened to fall.

Dair stiffened at the name of his older brother, while my other four mates turned to stare at me.

"What about that fucker?" Bash demanded.

"He said... Fuck, I didn't believe him. I didn't think it was true..."

"What did he say?" Ryland asked dangerously.

"He said that we weren't born," Dair deadpanned, not a hint of inflection in his tone to suggest how he felt about that revelation. "That we just appeared out of thin air."

The silence that settled over our group was stifling. Cloying. I felt physically nauseous as I watched a myriad of emotions flicker over my men's faces. Shock, surprise, hurt that I kept it from them in the first place, fear, anger, and then, finally, suspicion.

"Tavvy is a compulsive liar," Killian pointed out, his voice small. "We can't believe a word he says."

"He's right," Bash agreed, though he didn't sound convinced. His eyes were faraway and dazed. I knew his words were meant to be comforting, but they did very little to stave off the fear percolating inside of my belly. "We can't believe a word he says."

Ryland leaned forward and rubbed his hands over his knees, his attention locked on B. "My father mentioned that you had a way to…"

I volleyed my gaze between the two of them in confusion. What was Ryland talking about?

B's jaw clenched before he nodded once, flipping through a few more pages in the book before he came to a picture of a jewel-encrusted dagger.

"What is that?" I whispered, resisting the urge to lean forward and outline the design with the tip of my finger. It was absolutely beautiful, the hilt decorated with various gemstones and the blade curved at the tip in a way I hadn't ever seen before.

"We've known about Aaliyah even before you said anything, Z," B confessed. "We didn't know her name, but we heard rumors of a demon-like woman slaughtering nightmares and humans alike. We also heard rumors that she had made a deal with the kings… That she granted them a little bit of her own power to give them immortality."

My heart thrashed in my chest, and I sucked in a sharp breath. "So you believe that's true?"

"I do." He nodded curtly. "We don't know what they offered her in return, but we do believe that the kings—

for all intents and purposes—made a deal with the devil."

"So we're fucked," Bash deadpanned.

"Not necessarily." B once again tapped his finger against the image etched onto the page of the book. The illustration was so realistic, I half wondered if I could reach forward and pluck it straight out of the paper. "We don't believe normal weapons can hurt the kings, but this right here?" A slow smile unfurled on his lips. "It's not a normal weapon."

"What is it?" Killian asked, stepping forward to get a closer look.

"An *infernum pugione*, roughly translated to a hell dagger."

"A hell dagger?" Both of Bash's eyebrows rose.

"A dagger that has been forged by hell's fires. It's believed to be able to...drain hellish energy," B explained.

A strange sensation began to bubble up inside of me, starting at my hands and then spreading to my feet. It was as if fire ants were crawling over my skin, scuttling across my arms and legs. My breathing turned shallow, ragged, and the conversation around me dimmed to a dull murmur.

"We believe that if we were to stab the kings with this weapon..."

"It would reverse whatever Aaliyah did to them. Drain the power she gave them," Killian breathed in awe.

"Exactly." B gave a decisive head bob. "It would make them normal nightmares again, and as you all know, normal nightmares can be killed just as easily as humans can."

My lungs expanded, greedily sucking in bucketfuls of air, as my hand curled into a tight fist.

What the fuck was happening to me?

"Where can we get the dagger?" Bash demanded. A hint of excitement seeped into his normal acerbic tone, and his green eyes flared with hope.

"You mentioned that Aaliyah has a portal to hell somewhere, did you not?" B quirked a single eyebrow as all of my mates began to talk at once.

"Absolutely not."

"You're not seriously suggesting we travel to hell, are you?"

"Fuck that shit."

B lifted both of his hands into the air, silencing them. "You don't need to travel to hell. You simply need to find an object that has been made in hell. You can forge the dagger from that."

"How—"

Bash cut off abruptly when I jumped to my feet, practically shoving Dair's arms away from me. I didn't know what had taken over me, but I knew I needed to stop B. I needed to kill him before he could kill my kings.

It was an animalistic type of need, something innately primal, and I was barely aware of what I was doing even as I jumped onto the desk.

"What the fuck?" Bash exclaimed.

"It's the damn spell! She sees B as a threat against the kings, so she's going to kill him." Dair's voice was rife with alarm and fear.

Ryland and Jax both rushed at me, but I ducked out of the way, continuing towards my target.

B didn't even blink at me as I swiped at him, prepared to end him once and for all—

Then he lifted his hand and stabbed me in the neck.

Shock widened my eyes and popped open my mouth, but I didn't have time to scream before darkness descended, taking me with it.

TWENTY

LUPE

Pacing. Pacing. Pacing.

That was all I could do, all I was aware of as I struggled to free myself from the cage crafted out of my own mind. Voices floated to my ears, but I couldn't understand a single word being said. Sometimes, I would see flashes of images—faces, shapes, colors—but most of the time, there was nothing but darkness as I paced, paced, paced.

Always fucking pacing.

I punched the malleable walls, desperate to break free, but nothing seemed to work. No matter how hard I tried, I couldn't escape. The cage would tremble beneath the force of my blows, caving in on itself like slime, but would remain intact.

One voice was louder than the others. Lyrical, almost, and so familiar, I felt physically ill whenever I heard it. Feminine. Soft. Sassy.

That voice alone conjured up images of a gorgeous, blonde-haired girl with rosy cheeks and a sharp-witted tongue. She was so close, I just had to stretch up and touch her...

And then the vision was swept away as I paced, paced, paced.

What had happened?

Where was I?

Why couldn't I remember anything?

I needed...

I needed to get back, but why? There was nothing but pain in the land of the living, nothing but darkness and despair more pronounced than the shadows closing in on either side of me ever could be.

There was something I was forgetting. *Someone* I was forgetting. Her name settled on the tip of my tongue, spicy yet sweet, but no matter how hard I tried, I couldn't remember it.

Think, Lupe, think.

Pacing. Pacing. Pacing.

There was nothing to disrupt the monotony of my routine, nothing to disturb the flow. All I knew was darkness, the brief flashes of my surroundings, and an emotion that curdled in my gut like sour milk.

Wrath.

So much fucking wrath, I feared I would drown under the onslaught of it all.

Where did that emotion come from? What had happened?

Once again, the memory eluded me, catching fire and turning to ash, so I did what I did best—paced.

And then suddenly, I felt it. It spread through my entire awareness like sticky peanut butter on bread. I gasped, my back arching, at the knowledge that something was inherently wrong. Someone was in trouble.

Someone needed me.

She needed me.

My pulse raced, my skin suddenly too tight to contain my muscles and bones, as that golden-haired woman made another reappearance in my mind's eye. Her gorgeous blue eyes were alight with amusement and a plethora of dirty secrets, all of which I yearned to know. Blonde hair framed a face angels dreamed of—a soft jawline juxtaposed by sharp cheekbones and a button nose.

Her name slammed into me like a hurricane, a swirling storm of heavy winds and pelting rain that threatened to carry me out to sea.

Z.

My mate.

The bond between us twisted and writhed, and I knew I needed to go to her, to save her. She was in trouble.

Distantly, I was aware of a roar tearing the world apart, but it was barely audible over the repetitive *thump-thump-thump* between my ears. Those strange flashes of awareness returned to me in rapid procession.

Flash—I saw the dark, iron bars of the cage I was kept in.

Flash—a familiar face stared back at me in shock. Axel, I thought his name was.

Flash—more darkness as my bear took over and shoved me to the side.

Metal twisted, and it occurred to me that I had

somehow opened the cage. Dented the metal. Twisted it beneath my huge paws.

No, not me.

My bear.

But that shouldn't be possible. Bash had managed to infuse his magic into the cell in order to contain me. I had gathered that much through the brief flashes allowing me to see into the land of the living.

Screams echoed around me, distant and slightly muted as if I were hearing them from underwater, but that didn't matter to me. None of those screams belonged to the one person who made up my entire world—Z.

I needed to get to her.

Another voice. Yelling. Calling my name. Cursing. "Lupe, you can't go in there! Goddammit!"

I felt as if I were flying, as if my paws didn't even touch the ground. Growls sounded from every direction, and keen teeth dug into the flesh of my neck. I swiped and bit and kicked at the beasts who wanted to keep me from my mate.

I needed to get to her.

A guttural roar escaped me when talons dug into my side, and I shook erratically, attempting to dislodge the monster. Like before, the images came to me one after another, so quick that I couldn't quite understand what I was seeing.

Darkness.

Glowing eyes.

More darkness.

Trees.

Darkness.

I needed to get to her.

My lungs struggled to take in air as I ran, ran, ran, no longer merely pacing. I was a man possessed—a beast in a forest of monsters, ready to reclaim his throne and become the king.

I needed to get to her.

I burst into the sunlight, just barely dodging a sword that had been aimed at my stomach. Pushing up onto my hind legs, I roared savagely, pawing at anyone who dared to get too close.

I needed to get to her.

Z.

My mate.

Her image haunted me, and I desperately clung to it with all of my might.

Z.

I needed to get to her.

My mate.

Words tumbled around in my skull, but I couldn't quite grasp their meaning. A part of me understood them, at least logistically, but the rest...

The rest couldn't quite understand how they fit together.

Who did I need to get to?

Wait...Z.

My mate.

I needed to get to her.

A second person ran at me with a dagger, and another roar ripped from my lips as I swiped at him. He staggered to the side, his eyes wild with fear, but before I could claim my kill, something heavy landed on my back.

Rope.

It twisted around me, prohibiting any movement, and my desperate roars turned to whimpers.

I needed to get to her.

I needed to get to her.

I needed to get to her.

Someone stepped closer, a sword held in his hand, and I saw my life flash before my eyes. I knew with unwavering certainty that I was going to die today, and I wouldn't be able to say goodbye to Z. I would just...end. And not as the man she had grown to love, but as a monster she was terrified of.

I needed to get to her.

Something clicked in my brain, though I wouldn't be able to tell you what. It was as if the rope tethering me to my animal snapped, providing me the coherence I so desperately craved.

Z.

My mate.

Needed me.

A shuddering exhale left my lungs as my body changed and distorted, my fur receding into my skin and my torso shrinking. Where there was once a beast, there was now a man.

Lupe.

My name was Lupe.

And Z...

My connection between her throbbed and jolted, and I knew she was near. Desperate tears welled in my eyes at the knowledge she was still alive, that she had been alive this entire time, that I was too late to save her from this unknown threat. Behind me, I could hear growls and roars of the monsters and beasts I'd just sliced through in order to reunite myself with my mate. And in front of me was an army of angry humans, all regarding me with unbridled rage and fear.

I saw the sword rushing towards my chest, and I braced myself for the pain.

"Z." Her name was a plea on my lips, a prayer, as I thanked whomever was listening for keeping her safe while I was lost to my sin.

The moment the sword would have breached my skin, a voice bellowed, "Wait! Fucking wait!"

The man holding the sword hesitated, his features pale and his eyes as wide as saucers in his face, but he didn't stab my chest the way I expected.

A small, lanky man—a few inches shorter than even Z—pushed through the crowd with a frown carved into his bronze face. His almond eyes widened marginally when he caught sight of me.

"Lupe?" His gaze flickered towards the forest I'd just emerged from while in my bear form, and his entire face drained of color.

"HH?" My voice was groggy, raspy from days of no use.

Z.

I needed to get to her.

Z...

TWENTY-ONE

KILLIAN

"What the fuck?" I jumped forward and just barely caught Z before she could topple over completely. Her head lolled to the side, her eyes fluttering closed, as her chest rose and fell with her shallow breaths. I desperately scanned her body for any injuries, but she appeared to be unharmed. Unease crept through my stomach like a cold frost. "Wh-what the fuck did you just do?"

"Settle down, incubus," the domineering man snapped out, still sitting calmly in the chair in front of his desk. He clasped his hands together and nodded towards the woman in my arms. "She'll be okay."

"What the hell did you inject her with?" Bash bellowed, his hands clenching into fists by his sides.

My gaze flitted to the syringe hanging loosely in B's hand, but if I thought the assassin would be ashamed of his actions or even terrified of the consequences, I was sorely mistaken. He merely opened his palm and allowed the syringe to fall onto the table with a barely audible clanking sound.

Bash lunged forward to inspect it while Ryland sent his shadows forward. Before they could connect with B's flesh, they dissipated in a cloud of black smoke.

"I told you, boy." B rolled his eyes as if we were idiots. "I have a charm made by a few very powerful mages." With steady hands, he pulled at the string tied around his neck, revealing a bright red gemstone dangling from the end.

"There are other ways we can kill you," Jax pointed out softly. Dispassionately. His gaze never wavered from Z's form in my arms.

"You should be thanking me," B exclaimed nonchalantly, leaning forward to rearrange some of the papers on his desk.

My teeth gritted together at his audacity. Just who did he think he was?

Besides, of course, a super-scary rebellion leader and one of the best assassins in all of the kingdoms.

Yeah...we might have been out of our depth here.

Still, I wouldn't leave until I got answers, dammit.

Z looked almost peaceful in my arms. Without the ornery, combative glint in her eyes I had grown to love and admire, she almost resembled a different person. There was a softness in her features I wasn't used to seeing, one that made me want to bend down and kiss her.

Memories of our time in the shower played on a loop in my head, and I could feel my cheeks involuntarily flame. Now was definitely not the time for my cock to get hard.

Be a good boy for Daddy Kill, okay? I mentally whispered to the disobeying organ. *You'll get a reward later if you do. You want a treat? Does my little Kill want a treat? Good boy. Good boy. Good—*

Oh dear fuck.

I really did talk to my cock like it was a sentient pet.

I shifted Z in my arms as Bash, Dair, and Ryland converged on the indolent assassin. Jax moved to stand beside me, one of his hands reaching forward to cup Z's unconscious face. She murmured something incoherent, twisting towards him, and both of them released a sigh simultaneously when they connected.

"Turn to page thirty-three in the book," B instructed, that lazy drawl of his making me want to stab him in the nut sack. And considering the fact I was the least violent person here, that was saying something. I would expect that type of behavior from Bash and Ryland, but definitely not me. I didn't even like nut sacks, for Pete's sake, yet I really wanted to knife B's.

"Is this some fucking joke to you?" Bash hissed the words in a single breath.

"Does it look like I'm laughing?" B blinked at the mage once before heaving out a sigh. "I fixed Z, if you were wondering."

"What?" Ryland bit out scathingly.

"The spell the kings placed on her... The one prohibiting her from harming them... The one making her attack anyone who she perceives as a threat to their rule..." He swiveled his chair back and forth, back and forth, his gaze flickering towards the girl still in my arms.

I didn't like that, not one bit. I knew, logically, that he saw her as a daughter and she, in turn, regarded him as a father figure, but the incubus inside of me went a little crazy whenever any male stared at her too long. Apparently, my sin made me a tiny bit stabby when it came to my mate. Who would've thought?

Never mind the fact that I didn't feel a single puff of lust emitting from his pores. That didn't seem to matter to my incubus. He didn't like any male staring at her—father figure or not.

I filed it neatly away to analyze later. Or never. Never was good too.

"How the fuck did you do that?" Bash's voice turned high-pitched in shock.

"Page thirty-three," B repeated, and Bash practically tripped over his own two feet in his haste to grab the book.

"You know I don't fucking read this language," he murmured as he scanned the page. But then his eyes widened, and he swallowed heavily. "Is that... Is that what I think it is?"

"What the fuck are you looking at?" Ryland didn't wait for Bash to answer, simply reaching forward to pluck the book out of his arms. He scanned the book quickly, and even with the shadows shrouding most of his features from view, I could still see the imperceptible widening of his eyes.

My curiosity got the better of me, and I awkwardly waddled towards where Ryland stood, making sure not to jostle Z too badly. What I saw had my mouth popping open as shock pierced me in the heart.

Out of context, the page wouldn't mean anything to me. The words were nothing but gibberish, though there were a few annotations scribbled in English, but the picture...

The picture showed seven skeletons, each one bedecked in robes signifying their sin. Golden crowns rested on top of their skulls, tilted slightly to the side.

"There are a lot of reasons the shifter king would want to keep this book hidden away, but this passage right here..." B's lips curled upwards in a wary smile. "He probably never expected for this to see the light of day."

"What the fuck am I looking at?" Ryland demanded, his shadows coiling up his arms and biceps before snapping back into his chest.

"A way to stop the kings' magic."

B's words didn't just slap me in the face. They beat the ever-loving shit out of me and fucked my asshole while I was forced to take the abuse like a good little slut.

Oh. My. Fuck.

"We were taught to believe the kings were all powerful, even before they made that deal with Aaliyah." B tentatively ran his finger over the skeleton of the mage king. "But that's a lie. Sure, they may be some of the most powerful nightmares in existence, but the world was created with a system of checks and balances in place. The kings wanted to play god." A humorless laugh escaped him as he pulled his hand away from the page. "So I suppose that makes us heretics."

"What does it say?" Bash breathed almost reverently.

"It's quite simple, actually—to counter the kings' spells, you need the bones of the past kings. Dig them up, ground them up, and inject them into your bloodstream. The deceased carcasses are capable of wiping away any and all lingering traces of the kings' current magic." He jerked his chin towards a still sleeping Z. "It's what's happening to her right now. When she wakes up, the spell the mage king placed on her will no longer be in effect."

Dair had gone perfectly still in front of me, his shoulders so tense they physically spasmed. I knew what he was thinking about—the same thing we all were.

The potion his father continually gave him to make it so he was confined to a wheelchair.

Right now, he had enough left of Paco's brew to remain on his own two feet, but it wouldn't be too long until he ran out and would be forced back into the chair.

"Do you...?" Dair's voice broke, and he was forced to clear his throat and begin again. "Do you have any more of that?"

B's face tightened with what looked like sympathy. It wasn't surprising that B knew about, or at least suspected, Dair's predicament.

"Unfortunately, that's the last syringe we have available at this time." Dair's face immediately fell, but B forged on ahead. "However, we do have more bones left. It's a lengthy process—our mages have to grind the bones a certain way, perform a specific spell, and then allow it to settle. I'm sure we can find a way to get you a vial."

Dair's throat bobbed as he swallowed. "And how long

will this last? Will Z wake up one day and want to protect the kings again? What if they put another spell on her?"

"That we don't have an answer to," B confessed. "Z could live her entire life free of the kings' influence. Perhaps the potion even remains dormant in her blood in case they ever try to bewitch her again. But it also could only last a few days. This is all trial and error, son. We know as much as you do."

Dair nodded, though I could tell by the stubborn set of his jaw he was determined to get his hands on a vial... no matter the cost. And I would help him get it, if only to free him of that wretched wheelchair once and for all.

"So for all we know, Z could wake up tomorrow and be back under their spell?" Bash demanded bitterly, and B's eyes narrowed.

"Yes, but she could also step on a nail, get an infection, and die before the sun even sets." All of us growled at the possibility, and B held his hands up in a placating manner. "I'm not saying it's going to happen, but I'm saying it's possible. Everything is possible in the world we live in. Is it likely? I can't tell you. I've only had this book in my possession for a few weeks, and I'm still reeling from everything I learned. But at least it's better than nothing."

"Better than nothing," a drowsy voice parroted, and my head snapped down, my eyes colliding with a pair so blue, they reminded me of the pond behind the capital. Z blinked warily up at me, as if trying to get my features into focus, and then managed a tiny smile.

"Hey. What did I miss?" Her words slurred together, but she was talking, which was better than a few minutes earlier.

"Um...B might've cured you from the spell the mage king placed on you. Or he might have placed a temporary bandage over it and you'll be back to protecting the kings by tomorrow. Or you might be permanently free of their influence. Or—" I realized I was rambling and smashed my lips together.

Z blinked at me. "Are you kidding?"

"Um...no?"

Why the fuck did I phrase that as a question?

Before Z could respond, a shout sounded from directly outside the office. All seven of us tensed, and B immediately pulled a sword out of who the fuck knew where. His ass? It wouldn't surprise me. He seemed like the type of man who loved hiding shit up there—pun unintended.

Ryland's shadows coiled around his fists, and Bash's magic flared to life, as bright green as his glowing eyes. Dair and Jax moved to stand in front of me and Z, though the damn woman in my arms kept wiggling, as if demanding that I put her down.

"Killian..." she growled out.

"Hush. You just passed out, and you still look seconds away from collapsing again. I'm not letting you go until I know you won't fall over and die on a nail."

"Die on a nail?" She stared at me incredulously, but I blamed B for putting that suggestion in my head in the first place.

The door to the office was thrown open, careening off the wall, as a large, naked man stepped forward.

A *familiar* large, naked man.

"Lupe," Z whispered, and his head snapped towards her.

TWENTY-TWO

Z

Lupe was here.

In the office.

As a human.

Here.

My heart thundered in my chest as I met his eyes, his unruly brown hair pushed away from his face. Dark stubble coated his jaw, but it only added to his allure. He was without his reading glasses, but somehow, that drew attention to the few freckles that dotted his nose and cheeks. He was enormous—a mountain of a man that looked as if he could crush me with one squeeze. However, he had never been anything but gentle with me, regarding me as if I were fine glass he yearned to treasure and protect.

Lupe.

I wiggled in Killian's arms, and he obediently set me on my feet, seemingly in a daze.

I didn't know how it happened—if he ran towards me or if I ran towards him—but the next thing I knew, I was in his arms, my legs wrapped around his waist as I kissed him desperately.

Bash cleared his throat obnoxiously. "Um...perhaps we should give you two a moment?"

"Not in my office," B grumbled irritatedly, but I barely heard him. I barely heard anything over the pounding in my ears and the sloshing of blood in my head.

Lupe was here. Human. Here. Human.

A giddy laugh fled my lips as I continued to kiss him senseless, distantly aware of my mates and a disgruntled B exiting the office.

"It's good to have you back, man."

"Fuck, it's so good to see you, Lupe."

"Glad you're home."

I didn't know who said what, too consumed by my mate to focus.

Something wet touched my cheek, but I didn't know if it was my tear or his. Perhaps it was both of ours, merging together and becoming one, just like our souls. His glossy eyes met my own as our kisses slowed down, becoming less urgent.

"I didn't know..." He took a shallow breath. "I didn't know you were still alive. I felt you die, Z, and I thought —" He broke off on a choked sob, and my arms tightened around his neck.

"I'm still here, Lupe. Fuck, I missed you so much. Don't you ever do that to me again." I didn't know if I wanted to kiss him or slap him, so I settled for sloppily kissing away his tears as I attempted to meld my body against his. I didn't want anyone to be able to tell where he ended and I began.

"Never again," he vowed adamantly, tilting my chin up to claim my lips. "I'm so sorry I put you through that, Z. I don't even remember what happened when I was in my bear form, but I know that I must've hurt you—"

"You weren't yourself," I said, hating the space between us. Hating the layer of clothes that separated my flesh from his.

"You needed me, and I wasn't there." Melancholy laced every word, and he tore his lips away from mine, his eyes glimmering with guilt and shame. "I thought you were dead, and I hid behind my sin like a damn coward—"

"Don't," I warned fiercely, clutching his chin and forcing his gaze to rest on mine. "Don't you dare drown in self-pity, Lupe Shifter."

A growl tore itself from his throat, vibrating through his massive body. "I deserve to hate myself, Z. I gave up. I allowed my wrath to—"

I cut off his pity party with another toe-curling kiss, one I could feel in the mushy center of my heart. Kissing Lupe was never just a clashing of lips; it was an explosion of feelings and emotions that rippled through my bloodstream like molten magma. It burned everywhere it touched, but the sensation was oh-so-delicious. I would gladly burn in the fires of hell for this man.

"I missed you," I murmured against his lips as he stumbled backwards, switching our positions at the last moment so I was sitting on the edge of the desk and he was between my legs. "How did you come back?"

"I knew that you needed me," he answered, and I hated the unfettered guilt that emanated from his eyes. It tore at something vital inside of me, shredding it to ribbons. "But I should've come sooner. I should've been strong enough to—"

Once again, I interrupted his pity party with another kiss.

My hands roamed his bare back as my knees rested on either side of his hips. I could feel his cock press against the fabric of my harem pants, already hard for me.

At one point, I feared his cock—no lie. I'd had my fair share of dicks over the years, but his was by far the biggest I had ever taken. It was even larger than Killian's, which was saying something because incubi were known for having massive penises. But Lupe's? I once described it as fitting a bazooka through a donut hole, and I still felt that was an adequate description. Or maybe a semitruck through a hula hoop. I truly believed the only way he fit inside of me was because we were mates or else he would have torn me in half and made it so I could never have kids. That fucker could probably touch my reproductive organs if he wanted to and rearrange them.

I reached between our bodies to palm his huge dick, stroking it in tandem to our hungry kisses.

"I need your clothes off," he practically growled, his hips jerking forward instinctively. "Now."

"Then take them off," I purred, lying down on the table and releasing his dick. "You're a big boy."

He growled, though I didn't know if it was because I stopped stroking him or if he was mad I insulted him. Fuck, I loved it when he got like that—possessive, growly, and fucking insane with his need for me. It was sexy as fuck.

Lupe moved to rip my clothes straight off my body, but I stopped him with a warning look. "Wait. These clothes don't belong to me, so we need to make sure we don't destroy them."

He rolled his eyes, even as a tentative smile danced on his luscious lips. "Do you want me to fold them for you, too, baby?" he teased.

I nodded seriously. "Yes, that would be amazing. Thank you."

He didn't fold them for me...but he also didn't rip them off, either. His huge, towering frame belied the gentleness he always exuded when he was with me. He pulled the shirt over my head, being extra careful not to get it stuck in my hair, and then shimmied the harem pants down my legs. When I was naked before him, he stood back and regarded me with heavily hooded eyes, his tongue darting out to lick his lips.

"Fuck, I can't decide what I want to do to you first. Eat your sweet pussy or fuck it."

"Fuck it. Definitely fuck it." My chest heaved as I greedily spread my legs as far as they could go, hoping to accommodate his massive frame.

He tsked his tongue. "Sweetheart, I've been away from you for too damn long. I didn't even realize what I'd been missing, but now that I'm here, now that I'm inhaling your sweet aroma..." He dramatically flared his nostrils, and a blush rose to my cheeks before I could mask my instinctive reaction.

"You can't smell me...can you?"

"You know I can, baby." He tapped his nose with a smirk. "Shifter senses, remember?"

I made a face at him but refused to be embarrassed. "So are you going to do something, or am I just going to lie here with my legs spread like an idiot?" I drawled.

"I rather like the view..." He rubbed at the stubble on his chin contemplatively, and I growled.

"Lupe!"

His huge hand wrapped around the base of his cock, and he jerked it a few times.

"A part of me wants to eat you out until you forget your name, until you're screaming to the heavens, but a larger part of me can't wait to be inside of you again. I need to feel your pussy squeezing my huge cock."

His dirty words sent lightning skirting through my veins, and I could barely breathe through the sudden tightness in my throat.

"Lupe?"

"Yes, my love?"

"Fuck me, please."

He grinned—a smile so predatorily lethal that I felt like a tiny mouse caught in the eye of an eagle, or a bear, as the case may be—and then prowled forward. His huge hands landed on my thighs and hoisted me up, so my ankles could rest on his shoulders. This new position put me halfway in the air, most of my weight resting on my shoulders and head. At first, it was slightly uncomfortable, but when Lupe's massive cock began to prod the entrance of my pussy, that thought fled as quickly as it arrived.

Because when he finally entered me, inch by painful inch, I. Felt. Everything.

I swore he hit areas I'd never known existed before, and stars danced across my vision.

"Holy fuck," I panted as he began to pound into me, his hands tightening around my ankles on his shoulders. My tits bounced with every thrust of his hips, and from the way his eyes lit up and smoldered, he seemed to like that.

"My cock was made for your pussy," he growled out, leaning forward slightly to enter me at a new angle. The bond between us thrummed in agreement, and I managed an articulate gasp in response. "You're so fucking tight, Z. So perfect. Fuck, I missed you. I'm so sorry for leaving, baby. So sorry. I love you. Fuck."

At this point, I wasn't even sure he knew what he was saying. His features were slack with pleasure, his eyes glazed.

I sucked my bottom lip as he released one of my ankles and began rubbing gentle circles on my throbbing clit. Jolts of lightning zapped through my nerves, and I gasped his name. At least, I thought it was his name. It honestly sounded like a random string of syllables haphazardly jammed together.

Small moans escaped me as the friction between us built. Lupe pounded into me faster and faster, his hand moving across my clit in tandem to his thrusts. Our eyes collided, and the love in his nearly made my heart stutter to a stop. This man...

I thought I would never see him again, and he thought the same about me. We were two souls who had found each other after what felt like an eternity apart, and I knew this was where we belonged. Together.

My eyelids fluttered shut as bursts of light danced across my vision. I could feel my skin buzzing with energy, even as my muscles shook.

"Oh, fuck!" I screamed as tremors of pleasure wracked through my body.

Lupe pounded into me two more times before his moans turned into a primitive roar.

When he came back down from his orgasm, he collapsed on top of me on the desk, his head nuzzled beneath my chin.

"I can't believe you're here," he whispered against my sweat-soaked skin.

I rubbed a hand up and down his back, across the width of his broad shoulders, and then through his dark brown hair.

"I can't believe you're here," I said softly.

Lupe had found his way back to us, and as soon as Devlin did as well...

I would be whole.

Not even the kings could take that away from me.

TWENTY-THREE

JAX

B's thin lips pursed as he rifled through one of the drawers in the surprisingly expansive library, located on the opposite end of the hall that housed his office. Shelf after shelf stood proudly in the center of the room, each one full to the brim with dusty, old books. It seemed as if B was creating an arsenal of knowledge instead of just weapons, and I respected him for that.

Even if he seemed oblivious to the monster attempting to chew on one of the archaic tomes.

Of course, I was beginning to believe the monster wasn't actually real—no one seemed to notice it except for me—but it claimed my complete and utter attention nonetheless. I blinked my eyes, and still it remained, a figure plucked straight out of my nightmares.

From far away, you might've believed it to be a normal man—notwithstanding the fact he was over seven feet tall and the width of a toothpick. But the more you looked at him, the more you began to see the things that were inherently wrong, the things that set him apart from a nightmare or human.

Instead of skin, his body was hewn from nothing but bright pink and red muscle—sinewy, pulsating muscles that wept blood. When he noticed me staring at him, his razor-sharp teeth curled upwards in a mockery of a smile, and a tiny bit of saliva drizzled down the flesh of his chin.

I simply nodded my head in greeting before focusing once more on B as he finally found what he was looking for.

"This will help you return." He triumphantly held up a pink tablet and swung it back and forth. Bash reached for it expectantly, but B stealthily stepped out of his way before his hand could connect.

"What the fuck is that?" my mage brother demanded with a tight frown.

"It creates a portal that will place you on the opposite side of the Forest of Monsters and Beasts," B explained. "Our team of mages and the shadow king created it for us to allow easy access back and forth."

Ryland's shadows withered around him as his icy-blue eyes narrowed into slits. "That would've been rather helpful when we were trying to come here."

An amused smirk played on B's lips. "That would've been too easy, don't you think?" Before Ryland could retort, he continued on with a resigned sigh. "Besides, I'm the only one who has access to these tablets, boy. Your father helped to make them, yes, but do you really think we would trust the king with such an easy way to access all of our people?" He clicked his tongue once.

Ryland huffed out a harsh breath but didn't refute B's reasoning.

"So we have to find Aaliyah...or at the very least, the hell portal...and figure out how to make that damn dagger that will siphon the kings' unnatural magic that makes them immortal?" Bash demanded, scrubbing a hand through his ash-blond hair. "Am I hearing that right?"

B's lips twitched. "Did you think this would be easy?"

"I thought it would be possible," he countered with a snort. "What you're suggesting is rather...unimpossible."

"Impossible," Killian corrected, and when Bash threw him a withering glare, the incubus squeaked. "Or unimpossible. That works too. Definitely works."

Over Killian's shoulder, the seven-foot monster began to glide forward on silent feet. He almost reminded me of Ryland, the way he seemed to fly through the air, his feet not touching the ground. He wore a fine-threaded tunic and pants, and a cape was clasped around his neck, billowing out behind him. A golden crown rested snugly on his red and pink head, tilted slightly to the side. He almost reminded me...

Of the kings we saw in the old book. At least, a version of the kings. The ones in the book had been skeletal, nothing but jaundiced bones and empty eye sockets, but this one was something else entirely.

And he was coming right towards us.

Fear pumped into my veins and rattled my lungs. Swirling, swirling, swirling through my chest like a tornado.

Why couldn't anyone see the monster except me?

Because it's not real, you dumbass, I told myself snidely, squeezing my eyelids shut. *It's not real. It's not real. It's not real—*

Something cold touched my cheek and then caressed the skin of my neck. That splinter of fear turned into an entire sword that jammed itself blade-first into my gut. Panic crawled up my throat.

"Open your eyes, Jax," a rattling voice whispered. "Open your eyes."

"There you guys are! We've been looking everywhere for you!"

Z.

Her sweet voice slid over me like honey, and when her fingers laced with mine, the pain in my soul abated. She always seemed to bring with her a soft, comforting presence that slid over me like a warm winter jacket.

And when my eyes reopened, the monster was no longer with us. It was just me, my brothers, B, and my sweet, perfect mate...who was currently staring at me with a furrow between her brows.

"You okay?" she whispered, her voice too low for the others to hear.

Love for her licked up my spine as I focused on the feel of her soft palm in mine. All I wanted to do was drag her farther into my arms and bury my face in her pomegranate-scented hair. The compulsion to hold her was undeniable.

"I am now," I assured her, resisting the urge to just scoop her up and never let her go.

"You guys were gone a while," Bash teased with a pointed look at a still naked and unashamed Lupe. "Glad to have you back, buddy." He reached upwards to clap his hand on Lupe's shoulder, and a blush tinted the bear shifter's face.

"Glad to be back. I...I just wanted to apologize—"

"No reason to apologize," Dair assured him softly. "You're back now, and that's all that matters."

"And naked," B growled out, his face pinched. "Put some damn clothes on."

Lupe's blush deepened, color migrating from his cheeks to the tips of his ears. "I don't really have clothes, sir. I'm Lupe, by the way." He stalked forward with his hand extended and his cock swinging in the breeze. All of us fixated on that huge appendage as he waited for B to take his proffered hand.

"That actually fits inside of you," Killian whispered in horror, whipping his head to the side to stare at Z.

Z snorted, twisting in my arms to face the incubus. "Yours is almost as big, Kill."

"It is?" His brows drew together. "And that's...a good thing? Because it looks painful."

"Is it weird that I want to touch it?" Bash murmured, eliciting a surprised laugh from Z. "Just to know if my hand can fit around that mammoth thing?"

"If you touch it, just let me watch," Z responded, still chuckling.

B's right eye began to twitch erratically, and his face had turned a little green. "I'm going to need to cut off my ears. No... I'm going to need to first burn my office to the ground, then cut off my ears, and finally kill myself so I can forget this ever happened."

Lupe, who still had his hand extended, slowly

dropped it to his side with a sheepish smile. "I...um...am sorry about your office. We didn't...um...destroy anything. We just...you know...on the desk."

"Shut up before I stab you."

"Noted." Lupe took a huge step back until he was shoulder to shoulder with Killian, who was still ogling the shifter's cock as if he were trying to figure the ins and outs of it. Or just the ins...like how that thing could fit in a vagina.

I snorted at my own joke and wrapped my arms around Z's waist, resting my chin on her head.

B murmured something inarticulate as he stalked out of the library and reappeared a second later with a pair of trousers. They were slightly too small for Lupe's massive frame, but at least they covered up everything. Mostly. I was pretty sure we all could see the outline of his erection through the fabric.

"Now,"—B clapped his hands together, apparently determined to get the conversation back on track—"I'll send you guys off with all of the research I've gathered. Keep in mind, it's not much, and I don't feel comfortable sending the actual book back with you guys, but here are the loose translations and replicas of the images in the book." He handed Z a stack of papers, which she took immediately.

"Thank you, B." Her voice turned small. "I mean it. Thank you for everything."

For the first time since I knew him, the scary assassin's face softened, drawing attention to the lines carved into his cheeks and around his eyes, belying his true age.

"Be careful, Z. Three of you went to the capital, and

so far..." He ran a shaky hand through his gray-streaked hair. "And so far, only one of you has returned to me."

"Mali isn't dead yet," Z pointed out, and I thought she sounded a little defensive on behalf of her ex-best friend and the woman who betrayed her. But then again, this was Z, and she had the greatest capacity for love than anyone I had ever met.

"No." B's lips compressed into a grim line. "But if she's working for Aaliyah, she may as well be."

Z looked as if she wanted to argue, but one squeeze from me relaxed her back into my embrace.

"We should go," Bash told us all. "We don't know how long it'll take us to find Aaliyah's home, and we need to get back to the capital before the kings get suspicious."

"They're already suspicious," Ryland interjected with a snort of derision. "They just don't believe we're truly a threat."

"We also need to find Devlin," Killian piped up. "That is, if he's not already waiting for us at the edge of the forest."

Lupe's eyes bulged, and he glanced desperately from side to side, as if only now realizing that the genie wasn't with us. "What about Devlin? What do you mean? Why do you need to find him?"

"There's a lot we need to catch you up on, brother," Dair said gently.

The huge shifter lowered his head in what almost appeared like shame.

Did he really blame himself for what happened?

Z left my embrace to step towards B and hug him tightly. He went rigid as her tiny arms twined around his waist before he held her back, lowering his cheek to her head.

"Take care of yourself, old man." Her voice was muffled from speaking into his shirt.

A low chuckle left his lips as he gripped her shoulders and pushed her back a step. "You too, kid." He looked as if he wanted to say more—his lips opening and then immediately smashing together—before he eventually sighed and placed the tiny pink pill into Z's hands. "I told your mates, but I'll tell you as well. This tablet will bring you to the edge of the forest, so you won't need to go through it twice."

"Thank you, B." Z's hand slowly closed over the tablet as she took a shuddering breath, one that sounded as if it were being processed through mutilated lungs. "May we see each other again."

A soft smile carved itself into his haggard face. "We will."

Z turned away quickly, as if overcome by a strong emotion, and I wasted no time pulling her into my arms once more. Bash placed his hand on her shoulder, while Killian gripped her hand. Dair and Lupe both touched her waist, and Ryland practically draped himself over her back.

"You guys ready?" she asked.

Without waiting for us to respond, she dropped the tablet onto the ground. Immediately, a cloud of pink smoke erupted around us, swirling through the air like a typhoon. Killian coughed and twisted his head to the side as the smoke curled up my nostrils and tightened around my throat like a noose.

One second we were in the makeshift library, deep within the mountain, and the next...

The next we were standing directly before a startled Axel, with the Forest of Monsters and Beasts looming maliciously behind us.

All of us staggered away from each other as we struggled to replenish our lungs with fresh, untainted air. Fuck, I hated portal traveling.

My stomach rebelled painfully as I squeezed my eyelids shut, a reminder to myself to breathe through the pain searing apart my flesh.

"What the fuck?" Axel exclaimed, his eyes wide with alarm. He focused on Z. "What's going on, little sister?"

Z slowly straightened from her half bent-over position and smoothed back a strand of golden hair that had fallen forward.

"We got what we needed," she responded evasively, her eyes shifting over the crowd of humans surrounding us.

And then she froze, her muscles going rigid and horror splaying across her face. I immediately followed the direction of her gaze, and my own body locked tight at what I saw.

Standing on the outskirts of the crowd was my brother—dark, curly hair brushed away from his face, olive-toned skin slick with sweat, and violet eyes flaring with hatred and anger. Behind him, smiling smugly, was—

"Aaliyah," Z breathed.

Z

"Aaliyah," I breathed in horror, my gaze latching on to the woman who claimed to be my sister before immediately flickering towards the man directly in front of her.

Devlin.

My genie.

My mate.

His violet eyes widened when he caught sight of me, the anger draining from them like water in a strainer. Emotions tightened his features as he took a desperate step towards me, his arms extended, before immediately jerking to an abrupt stop. His body seized, his teeth gritting together as if to hold in a scream, and then he dropped to his knees at Aaliyah's feet.

"What the fuck did you do to him?" I screamed, reaching automatically for my dagger...before remembering I hadn't placed it back on after my shower.

Fuck.

"He's fine, sister." Aaliyah waved her hand in the air

as if she could somehow swat away my ire. "I just wanted to talk to you."

"Let him go." I ground my jaw tightly and curled my hands into fists at my sides.

This woman...

I hated her.

I hated her with every fiber of my being.

It was the type of hatred that twisted up my insides and sent my world careening off its axis. It was potent and acidic, caustic and bitter, and it flowed through my veins like a damn toxin. Even staring into her smug, beautiful face had black spots erupting across my vision, distorting the scene before me.

"Z..." Devlin struggled to get to his feet. "You're alive. You're alive." He seemed to be repeating those two words over and over again, disbelief lacing his tone.

And despite everything in my body screaming at me to look at him, to free him, I kept my attention fixed pointedly on the she-bitch herself.

Aaliyah had always been beautiful, but the hard jawline she'd been blessed with had never looked so sharp before. Her reddish-orange hair cascaded around her shoulders in loose curls, the color accentuated by the glittering green gown she wore. The smile adorning her face was a direct contrast to the glare marring my own.

What the fuck did she want?

To kill me?

To kill my mates?

I wouldn't let that happen.

B's story played on a continuous loop in my mind.

Was it true?

Was Aaliyah truly the demon who had murdered her seven mates in order to avenge her sister? Be with her sister? Something about the story didn't sit right with me. It percolated in my stomach like the rising and falling of a wave, destroying everything it came into contact with under a torrent of ice-cold water.

"Don't look at me like that, Gabrielle," Aaliyah mused, stepping around Devlin and sashaying towards me.

The humans had gone very, very still, and I spotted Davia near the front of the crowd, her sword raised hesitantly. One glance at my stricken expression made her quickly lower it.

I didn't know Davia or any of these humans that well, but I definitely didn't want them to die. And I had no doubt that if they tried attacking Aaliyah, they would. She was nothing if not volatile, prone to violence and anger if she didn't get her way, and I couldn't help but compare her to a child throwing a tantrum.

"How should I look at you, Aaliyah, when you just harmed my mate?" I hissed out.

A frown tugged at her ruby-red lips as she stopped directly in front of me. All six of my mates tensed, inching a step closer as if they wished to put themselves between me and her.

Could we take her on?

Could we end this right now?

The thought crossed my mind before I immediately dismissed it.

I didn't know the extent of Aaliyah's powers, but I did know with unwavering certainty that she wasn't like anyone in all the lands. She had more danger in the tip of her pinkie finger than we could even comprehend. She practically screamed violence, and my body cautioned me to heed the warning emanating off of her in palpable waves.

"Your mate is alive, isn't he?" She took another step closer. "I just wished to speak with you."

"And you couldn't have sent a letter?" I asked dryly, trying to hide how fast my heart was pounding.

Fear was a funny, insidious thing, just like hatred was. If hatred was the boulder sitting on your chest, then fear was the spider crawling up your throat, making speech virtually impossible. All I could focus on was the press of my nails against my palms and the tightness of my chest where my heart raced.

"I actually have a present for you," Aaliyah said with a jovial smile, pulling up the skirt of her dress to reveal the skin of her thigh. She sent a wink at Killian—who merely glared in response—before removing what appeared to be a dagger from her thigh sheath and presenting it to me.

My breath siphoned from my lungs as I regarded the familiar blade in her hands.

What had B called it?

Infernum pugione.

The hell dagger.

It was exactly like the one illustrated in the book, right down to the gemstones adorning the handle and the slightly curled blade.

"I heard you've been looking for this," Aaliyah said in

a sing-song voice, dangling the dagger in front of my face like a pendulum.

"Where did you get that?" I could barely ask the question through the sudden tightness in my lungs.

Aaliyah's smirk broadened, revealing a flash of shiny white teeth. "You know the answer to that, Gabrielle."

"How did you...?"

"Know that you'd need it?" she finished for me. When I didn't immediately respond, she offered a negligent shrug of her dainty shoulder. "Call it a...sister's intuition."

"Or she has a spy in the resistance," Bash growled, and the glare Aaliyah cast his way could wilt flowers.

"It's rude to speak when you're not being spoken to," she huffed out, and that lick of danger I felt before returned with a vengeance. It burned through my skin and bones until it felt as if all of my nerve endings were awash with fire.

Bash gritted his teeth and took a threatening step forward, but Lupe quickly grabbed his arm and pulled him back before his impulsiveness could get him into trouble.

"You know what this dagger can do," I bit out.

"Of course I do." She rolled her emerald green eyes with a sigh of irritation. "It can remove hell's magic from nightmares and humans." She twirled the dagger around and around in her fingers, the way I'd sometimes see Axel do. "All you need to do is stab one of the kings, and..." She lunged forward with the blade extended, stopping when the dagger was a mere inch from Killian's chest. Panic spiked my bloodstream, and it took every ounce of willpower not to run forward, grab the bitch, and pull her away from my mate. I didn't dare even breathe, afraid I would startle her into piercing his skin with the blade. "It's a one-and-done type of deal. You stab one, you'll remove the magic from all."

"How would that work?" Dair demanded.

Aaliyah finally removed the dagger from near Killian's chest, and all of us released a heavy sigh of relief. She spun it expertly around a few times before lowering her hand back to her side.

"Because the magic is the same in all kings." A cunning smile tugged up her lips. "I granted them immortality by placing a tiny piece of myself in all seven of them. The *same* piece. You kill the magic in one, the magic in the others will die as well."

"Why the fuck would you give this to us?" I blurted out, unable to bite my tongue a second longer. "You gave the kings immortality in the first place. Why would you be so happy to take it away?"

Aaliyah released a long-suffering sigh, as if my constant barrage of questions was beginning to irritate her. Still, the smile she flashed my way was indulgent, albeit a little condescending.

"There are reasons for everything I do. Haven't you figured that out already, little sister?" She pushed out her lips in a mockery of a pout. "You don't trust me. I understand that, but don't you wanna..." She pantomimed slicing her own throat. "Don't you wanna kill the kings? Or at the very least, take away their immortality?"

"This is a trap, Z," Ryland whispered in my ear, his hot breath feathering across the back of my neck.

"I know," I responded. I didn't allow my eyes to waver from Aaliyah's face.

Aaliyah shrugged nonchalantly. "It may be a trap...or it may be your only chance at stopping the kings."

With another flip of her wrist, the dagger soared into the air before landing blade down in the dirt at our feet. Not one of us made a move to grab it, our eyes intent on her.

"I'll just be leaving that here for you...if you want it, of course" she mock-whispered. "I'll be seeing you real soon, Z." She winked in my direction, and then in a flash of wispy black and red smoke, she disappeared from view.

TWENTY-FIVE

Z

I didn't care about Aaliyah's words or the dagger sticking up from the ground.

I didn't care about anything except for my genie mate, still kneeling on the ground a few feet away from me.

"Devlin!" I all but screamed, launching myself at him. He caught me instantly, and we fell to the ground, kissing and touching each other wherever we could reach.

"I didn't think I would ever see your face again," he murmured against my lips as his fingers tangled in my hair.

"What the fuck did that bitch do to you?" I demanded, sitting upright until I was straddling his lean hips. I was distantly aware of Axel screaming at everyone to "mind their own business and not ogle," but I didn't peel my gaze away from Devlin's arresting, violet eyes.

"I'm okay, Z. She didn't hurt me. I promise." His fingers dug into my hips through the fabric of my borrowed pants.

"And I swear I didn't tell her where she could find you." A hint of urgency and desperation leaked into his voice as his fingers tightened against me. "She already knew where you would be, though I don't know how. She just wanted me to come along as a 'gesture of good faith.' Her words."

"We know, man." Bash extended a hand for me to take, but I wasn't quite ready to get off of Devlin just yet. When it became apparent I had no intentions of moving, he heaved out a breath and dropped his hand back to his side. "You wouldn't have sold Z out like that."

"Do you think there's a spy in the resistance like you said?" Killian asked shakily. All of my mates had clustered in behind me, varying expressions of distaste and horror on their faces.

Lupe folded his massive arms over his chest and scowled. "How else would she know about the dagger and where we'd be?"

"Her super evil demon powers?" Killian suggested in a timid voice. When all of us stared at him dubiously, he threw his hands up into the air with a resigned sigh. "I'm just throwing out suggestions."

"What the fuck are we going to do about the dagger?" Ryland jerked his chin towards where the jewel-encrusted hilt seemed to vibrate where it stuck out of the ground. Axel was guarding it from the way-too-curious humans with a fierce expression on his face.

"What does that dagger even do?" Devlin's brows tugged together as he flicked his gaze from me to his brothers.

All at once, immense irritation and anger flooded me.

I had to curl my hands into fists to keep from doing something stupid. "You would know if you didn't decide to run off on a stupid suicide mission!" I barked out, desperate to release some of the unfettered rage percolating inside of me.

Devlin's violet eyes shuttered closed. "I thought you were dead, Z. What the fuck was I supposed to—"

"You could've stayed with your brothers. Helped them. Been with them," I snapped back. "Not become some sort of martyr!"

"So you're allowed to be a martyr, but I'm not?" A hint of Devlin's familiar fire appeared in his tone, and it only served to raise my hackles. I loved the man fiercely, but fuck...I was so pissed at him.

"I'm mad at you, Devlin," I hissed out, even as I practically threw my body on top of his still on the ground and rested my head just beneath his chin. His arms came around my waist to hold me to him, iron shackles that I couldn't remove even if I wanted to. His cinnamon scent surrounded me, cocooning me in warmth, and delicious goose bumps pebbled on my skin at his proximity. "I'm so, so mad."

"I know." His arms tightened around me as his body gave a painful shudder.

Something wet touched my skin, but I didn't look up to see the tears I knew were in his eyes. A breath of warm air fanned over the back of my neck as we held each other.

For a brief moment, the rest of the world faded away. There were no kings we needed to stop. No Aaliyah and her ominous threats. No dagger that could potentially end this once and for all.

With all of my mates surrounding me, and sparks of lightning shooting through my body, I felt safe and loved in a way I hadn't felt in years. I had all of my men back, and I would be damned if I let anyone take them from me again. We were inevitable, them and I. There was no ending to something that I knew to be infinite. I didn't know if I believed B's theory about the eight of us being the reincarnations of the original angel and sins, but I did know that what we had was special—a love that transcended mere logic.

"What the fuck are we going to do about the dagger?" Bash demanded—because trust my impatient mage to not allow us to have a few moments of peace and quiet.

"We can't use it," Ryland replied immediately. "It's a trap."

"We don't know that," I pointed out, nuzzling my cheek against Devlin's chest. I didn't give a damn that some of the humans were staring on. Let them look. I had nothing to be ashamed about.

"Z, you're not fucking using the dagger," Bash growled at me.

"You're not the boss of me, Bash-hole." I felt tired all of a sudden, as if my eyelids were made out of concrete. They fluttered against my cheekbones like the wings of a butterfly attempting to take flight.

"We need to destroy the dagger," Ryland decided.

"Um...I don't know if that's a good idea." I knew, without even opening my eyes, that Killian would be nibbling on his lower lip anxiously.

"Why the fuck not?" Bash demanded.

"Because what if B was telling the truth? What if the dagger is the only thing capable of stopping our fathers?"

"Then why would Aaliyah give it to us?" Dair asked, but not as if he was arguing with Killian. More like he was trying to assemble a puzzle that was missing more than a few of its pieces.

That was the question, wasn't it?

What was Aaliyah's angle? Why would she give us a dagger that could destroy the magic she offered the kings? What was she after?

Was it a trick? A way to put me in harm's way?

No, that didn't seem right. Aaliyah was hostile, yes, and certifiably insane, but she seemed almost...protective of me. I couldn't see my death benefiting her.

What she wanted was me ruling at her side, which would never fucking happen.

"We don't need to decide now," Lupe grunted out. "Though if someone could please fill me in..."

The murmured voices of my mates provided a metronome I could easily fall asleep to. That, and the repetitive thump of Devlin's heart beneath my ear and his hands lazily running through my wild blonde curls.

My eyes fluttered open and almost immediately clashed with a pair of brown ones standing at the edge of the forest.

S?

What the fuck? Was I hallucinating?

My heartbeat echoed in my skull as I shut my eyes again.

When I reopened them, he was gone.

It felt like we took hours to reach the Forest of Monsters and Beasts when we left a day ago. However, it seemed as if only a few minutes had passed by the time we pulled up to the familiar, towering building located in the center of a mountain range.

I sat in the back of the truck between Lupe and Devlin, both of their hands clamped down on my thighs.

The dagger rested in my backpack, and it almost seemed as if it were burning a hole through the fabric. Or at least, that was what it felt like. I was acutely aware of its presence the entire drive and the ramifications of using it.

My mates and I were all divided on what to do with it. Bash and Ryland, predictably, believed it to be a trap and wanted to see it destroyed. Dair and Killian pointed out the fact that B claimed we needed the dagger to kill the kings—and even if Aaliyah had an angle, there was no downside in potentially eliminating seven major threats. Lupe wanted to gather more information on both the dagger and Aaliyah, as well as read through the papers B had given us. Devlin agreed that we couldn't move forward until we knew everything. And Jax? I was pretty sure he didn't care either way, just as long as we all remained safe.

I knew all eight of us needed to find time to talk and dissect everything we'd learned at the resistance camp and decide what to do about the dagger, but apparently, fate had other plans.

The moment we entered the front doors of the capital, two human servants ran forward and grabbed my arms.

"Hey!" I jerked back instinctively, and Ryland's shadows coiled around their waists, pulling them away from me.

"Don't touch her," he hissed out.

Wide, terrified eyes flickered from my face to the princes' before the smaller one—the girl who had led me to the shifter king's office the other day—said helplessly, "You need to come to your room. Now."

The steel in her voice surprised me, especially since her features were still enveloped by fear.

My heart squeezed in my chest, even as my brows arrowed downwards. "What's the meaning of all of this?"

In lieu of an answer, the woman grabbed my arm and practically dragged me down the hall towards the room designated as my own. My mates followed closely behind us, their own curiosity flowing through the bond and exacerbating mine.

The servant girl gestured for me to enter ahead of her, and I did so with a tight frown. That frown turned into a scowl when I saw what was waiting for me. Or who was waiting for me, to be more precise.

Ester, the woman who had fitted my wedding gown, stood in the center of the room, a bundle of white fabric draped over her arm. She smiled brightly when she caught sight of me and beckoned me forward.

"Z! Perfect timing!"

"What the bloody fuck is going on?" Devlin demanded, his violet eyes blazing brightly.

"Did no one tell him about the engagement?" Killian whispered to the group at large.

"Engagement?" both Lupe and Devlin growled out.

Bash's lips pursed. "I take that as a no."

"Who the fuck is Z engaged to?" Lupe demanded. His huge hands curled into fists by his sides, and I swore I saw a couple of sharp talons cut through his skin as his bear threatened to take over. "I thought we agreed she would marry all of us or none of us?"

"Wait...hold on. Back up. What?" I waved my hands in the air erratically in a futile attempt to capture their attention, even as Ester dragged me towards a raised podium she had already set up in the center of the room.

"She's not engaged to any of us," Ryland bit out. Shadows skirted up and down his arms, wrapping around his wrists like iron shackles before dissipating in a blaze of smoke.

Ester tugged at my pants and shirt, and with a scowl, I removed the garments until I was standing naked before her. She held open the dress for me to step into.

"Then who the fuck is she engaged to?" Devlin hissed.

"Axel." Bash's voice was practically a snarl, his lips pulling away from his teeth and his eyes flaring with haughty disdain. "That fucking bastard."

"Axel?" Lupe asked incredulously. "What the fuck?"

"Where did that sly bastard even go?" Devlin demanded. "Wasn't he just with us, like, five seconds ago?"

"I think he separated from us when we entered the capital," Dair said calmly.

With sure, unhurried fingers, Ester zipped up the dress and then stepped back to admire her work. Her thin lips pursed thoughtfully as she studied me from head to toe. I squirmed under her scrutiny.

Seeming to come to some unknown conclusion, she clapped her hands together loud enough to startle all of my mates, who immediately stopped their conversation and turned towards us.

"You look beautiful, Z," she gushed empathetically. "Definitely an ethereal bride-to-be."

"A bride-not-to-be," I murmured. After everything that had happened—and after finally getting all of my mates back—I had no intentions of going through with this sham of a marriage.

"Are you getting cold feet?" Ester cocked her head to the side with an amused smile lighting up her face. "Because it's awfully close to your wedding to be having second thoughts."

My feet were fucking ice cubes at this point, but semantics.

"Z." Dair's breathless, reverent voice pulled my attention off of Ester and onto my mates.

My throat closed and my breath sped up at the look in their eyes. They stared at me...

They stared at me as if they had never seen anyone more beautiful. As if they wanted to lunge forward and tear the white dress straight off my body. As if they wanted to prove to me again and again and again that they were the only men for me, just as I was the only girl for them.

My lungs released the air they'd been holding hostage

as lust traveled south down my body. The longing in their eyes was a sucker punch to my stomach, because I knew it stemmed from more than just mere desire.

They wanted to be the ones who married me some day. I could see it in their eyes, in the way they looked at me with unfettered desire. The thought burned a vicious pain through my chest.

I wanted that future, too, more than they could possibly know, but it wasn't possible. Not yet. Not with the kings breathing down our necks and Aaliyah planning who the fuck knew what.

But one day...

One day, that dream would become reality.

"Z..." Killian repeated, and that single word came out on a whoosh of air. "You look..."

"Radiant," Lupe finished for him.

"Beautiful," Ryland added.

"Fucking perfect," Bash inputted. His hungry green gaze raked over me.

I sucked in a sharp breath, but the air felt like it was made out of razor blades. My heart was doing acrobatics as I bit down on my lower lip.

"I...um...thank you." I still wasn't used to compliments, and as I turned back towards the mirror, I tried to envision what they saw.

The dress was gorgeous, there was no denying that, with a V-neck that emphasized the swell of my breasts. The top of the gown was embellished with lace that zigzagged across my chest. When I twisted back and forth, the long, white skirt swished around me in a barrage of satiny silk.

"Um..." I turned towards Ester. "Can I ask what the rush is? Did we have an appointment scheduled that I forgot about?"

Ester blinked at me, her brows scrunching together. "Do you know what day it is today?"

"What do you mean?"

"Z..." She took a step closer and nervously tugged at her fingers. "It's the end of the week. You understand what I mean, right?" She paused when I gasped sharply, and something akin to pity emerged in her eyes. "Today's your wedding day."

TWENTY-SIX

Z

The only sound in the hall was the poignant clap of my shoes against the meticulously polished tiles as I prowled forward like a panther stalking its prey. And this time around, the kings were my goddamn prey. I refused to be theirs a second longer.

My mates fanned out around me, their jaws clenched tightly and their hands balled into fists by their sides. I could practically feel the tension radiating from their pores in tangible waves, so pronounced that it made me choke on nothing but air.

What the fuck were the kings doing? What was their goal? What was their endgame? To ruin our lives?

The white dress swished around my ankles as I stalked forward, feeling every bit the avenging angel B believed me to be at that moment. Maybe the legends were right. Maybe I truly was Gabrielle reincarnated—though I definitely felt more devilish than angelic as icy tendrils of anger skittered down my arms and legs in a mockery of a caress. Perhaps they got the stories wrong.

Perhaps Gabrielle was the one seeking revenge on those who had wronged her, not the Seven Deadly Sins. It certainly felt as if I had nothing but acidic hatred and vengeance in my heart, threatening to burst free of my rib cage at any moment.

My breaths escaped me in shallow pants as I struggled to hold on to my anger. It wanted to slither out of me like a venomous snake, hell-bent on sinking its fangs into anyone and everyone it came into contact with. That caustic hatred and anger only intensified when I pushed open the doors to the throne room and saw exactly what the kings had in mind.

The thrones were still there, resting on a raised pedestal on the opposite end of the room, but they weren't the only furniture in the once sparse ballroom. Row after row of pews lined the center walkway, each one filled to the brim with smirking nightmares, all bedecked in fine dresses and intricate ensembles.

The kings were also dressed to the nines in elaborately tailored suits, with colored cloaks representing their individual sins cascading around them. The incubus king smirked when he saw the eight of us in the entryway, leaning forward to whisper something in the sloth king's ear. Both men fixed their eyes on us as we stormed forward, down the long aisle decorated with flower petals and bouquets.

At the very end of the aisle, directly in front of the kings, stood Axel. His sharp, angular jaw was bunched up as he took in my white dress and my mates spread out behind me. Something akin to shame distorted his features as he dipped his head, focusing his attention on his polished loafers.

Anger wracked through me, but I knew I couldn't point all of my ire at the ex-assassin. He was just as much a pawn as the rest of us, but that didn't mean he had to sit idly by and allow this sham of a wedding to happen. I knew, logically, that nothing would change even if I did marry Axel. He would allow me to remain with my mates, and despite being husband and wife, our relationship would never turn romantic, no matter what the kings decreed. But...fuck. This couldn't be happening. I wasn't going to marry Axel, of all people, and then consummate our 'marriage' in front of the princes and kings.

Axel released a discreet sigh and stealthily shifted to the side to allow me to pass. I purposely rammed my shoulder into his as I stomped up onto the stage, where the grinning kings regarded me with hungry, ravenous eyes.

"You clean up well, assassin," the incubus king purred, then his tongue darted out to lick his lips salaciously. His gaze dipped to my cleavage, and I resisted the urge to shudder in disgust.

"What are you doing, Father?" Killian demanded. One glance over my shoulder confirmed he was hurling daggers with his eyes at the six grinning kings, his teeth gritted together. There was no hesitation in his voice or glare, no wariness or anxiety. His body trembled with barely restrained tension and righteous fury.

"Do you boys not know what a wedding is?" the mage king asked in a lazy drawl, his head lolling to the side as he struggled to remain awake.

"We're not in the mood to play these fucking games," Bash practically snarled. Wisps of green magic circled around his wrists like shackles before crawling upwards, dominating the length of his arms. His ash-blond hair stood erect on his head from the force of his magic as he struggled to rein it in.

"Don't worry, kids." The genie king waved his hand in the air, and a second later, seven women stepped forward, fanning out around us. "Z isn't the only one getting married today."

My blood scorched my veins, and bile inched up my throat. Anger licked up my spine as understanding dawned, and with it came a tsunami of jealousy so strong and potent, it sent me staggering back a step.

These women...

These beautiful, nightmare women...

They were all wearing white wedding dresses.

I recognized one of them as Lupe's sister, Atta, her face a picture of melancholy and shame as she fidgeted with a strand of her light red hair. The other six, however, were unfamiliar to me, but they all smiled wickedly, *hungrily*, as their eyes devoured my mates.

As if propelled by some unseen force, or maybe because they'd rehearsed this ahead of time, the seven of them stepped forward until they were directly in front of my mates.

The gorgeous blonde attempting to place her fingers on Killian's arm was definitely an incubus like him. She fluttered her eyelashes seductively, purposely leaning forward to give him a view of her cleavage, and he jumped away as if her touch repulsed him.

The brunette standing before Bash? A mage, just like him, with sparkling green eyes and a dewy complexion.

The only coupling that was mixed species was Jax and Atta, both of whom looked so miserable, I wanted to wrap them in my arms and take their pain away.

"This isn't fucking happening," Bash bit out, attempting to dislodge the claw-like nails digging into his arm.

The brunette pouted, casually bringing a finger to her cleavage and tracing the skin visible there. "Sebastian—"

"Don't call me that," he snapped.

Her pout deepened. "Bash," she corrected, leaning in close enough so her breasts grazed his arm. Dark, insidious jealousy gripped my heart and gave it a tight squeeze. "You father told us—"

"My father is a piece of shit who is already fast asleep," Bash countered, finally able to shake her off of him. He nodded towards the mage king, who sure enough, was sleeping soundly, his ear resting on his shoulder.

"We're not marrying these women." Dair twisted to face his sadistic father, whose smile only broadened, displaying razor-sharp incisors more befitting of a monster than a mermaid.

"Do you really think you have a choice in the matter, son?" He tilted his head to the side, a strand of golden hair slinking forward to obscure one of his eyes from view. "We own you. *I* own you." Briefly, he lowered his gaze to Dair's legs, and I felt my blood go cold. "Unless you want to face the consequences..."

"Don't fucking threaten him," I bit out, taking an

automatic step forward to hide Dair from view. Not that it did a lot of good, considering he was twice the size of me, but I would do anything to keep the mermaid king's attention off of my sweet mate.

"Z." The mermaid king clicked his tongue with a condescending shake of his head. "You shouldn't get involved in family affairs."

"And you shouldn't be a fucking asshole who tortures his son for fun," I retorted, venturing even closer with every word. "I won't let you hurt my mate again." I swept my gaze across the six kings present, making sure they all understood the sincerity of my next words. The promise of retribution in them. "My *mates* again."

It was the first time I had publicly claimed all seven of my men. We were all sure that the kings knew the truth about our mating bond, but no one had explicitly said it outright. But I was done playing their deranged games. They wanted me to be demure and obedient, but they were about to see what happened when they pushed me too far. When they shattered what little control I had over my emotions.

The mermaid king stood, his blue cloak fanning out around him, and took a single step closer, forcing me to crane my head back to meet his glittering, cerulean gaze.

"You're nothing, Z." His voice was low, a hushed murmur that swirled around me like a tornado, pulling me deeper and deeper into the windy gales.

I clenched my jaw but refused to back down. Refused to look away. He would *not* win this round.

"You're just a toy we like to play with. Do you really think we trust you?" A bark of dry, humorless laughter escaped him. "We're not fucking idiots, child. We know you work for the resistance. We know you went to visit them when you claimed you were looking for Devlin. You honestly thought you could get one over on us?" His hand clamped down on my shoulder hard enough to bruise. "And here's the thing... By the end of today, you're going to be married to a man you don't love, and we're all going to watch your sweet little cunt getting fucked in a million different ways. And afterwards..." His lips stretched upwards in a malicious grin, one that had bumps pebbling along my arms. "Maybe we'll have a turn with you. After all, we all know you're capable of handling more than one nightmare."

Chuckles reverberated through the throne room, but I didn't look away from the mermaid king's eyes to see who was laughing. My guess? The kings, the brides-to-be, and the disgusting men and women watching the spectacle with rapt fascination.

A guttural growl vibrated Dair's chest, a sensation I felt from how close we were together.

"Don't fucking threaten her, Father," he bit out angrily.

The mermaid king's smile sharpened, a shark sensing blood in the water, and he focused his gaze over my shoulder.

Darkness coiled inside of me, thick and sinister, and I curled my hands into claws by my sides.

"And your mates..." The mermaid king's fingers clenched around my shoulder, and I had to stifle the gasp of pain that wanted to escape at the pressure. "Your mates will be married to women of our choosing. High-society, respectable women. And they will fuck these women because we won't give them a choice. They'll know that if they refuse, we'll slice your pretty little neck." His free hand crept up my waist, caressing the side of my breast, before reaching the hollow of my throat. He used one pointer finger to make a macabre line from ear to ear as I watched him with a scowl. "You're nothing but a little bitch, Z, and it's about time you learned that."

I dug my hands into the fabric of my dress and inched it upwards.

"After today's wedding, I will take my son back to his room and show him exactly what happens when he defies me. I won't just take his legs." He stepped so close, I could taste his putrid-smelling breath on my tongue. Bile churned in my stomach, but still, I didn't remove my gaze from his.

My dress had finally lifted enough that I could reach the hilt of my dagger.

"I'll torture my pathetic excuse for a son until he's begging for mercy, until he's screaming for me to end his life. But I won't. You want to know why?" He grinned tauntingly down at me, and I slowly slid the dagger from the sheath on my thigh. "Because his life will be so miserable that he'll do whatever I say. He'll forget about his feelings for you. Hell, he might be willing to torture you himself, just so the pain will end."

"That will never fucking happen," Dair growled out from behind me.

A roaring sound echoed between my ears. It grew and grew and grew, like a tsunami collecting more and more water as it raced to shore. Dark spots danced across my vision, and my pulse thudded in a rapid rhythm against my skull. Anger spread through my veins like a disease.

"I've been going easy on you, boy." The mermaid king's gaze flicked to me before focusing once more on his son. His expression could be hewn from stone. "But I won't any longer. You're a disrespectful little punk who—"

With a roar of rage, I slammed the dagger into the mermaid king's heart. There was no hesitation. No guilt or second-guessing. All I knew was that I needed to end him before he could harm my mates—before any of these sadistic assholes could harm my mates. It was an innate need inside of me, a fight-or-flight response tuned in to my mates' needs and wishes. But flight wasn't an option for us, which meant I had to fight.

For a moment, there was nothing but silence, thick and cloying, and then the screaming began.

TWENTY-SEVEN

DAIR

"Z!" I yelled as the room exploded into chaos.

All I could see was the gemstone-encrusted dagger protruding out of my father's chest as his face turned slack with shock and horror. Around him, the other kings gasped and brought their own hands to their chests, as if they could feel the pain of the dagger as well. Blood oozed from between their fingers, the dark red liquid dripping onto the floor at their feet.

"Z!" Devlin shouted, but his voice was far away and distant.

At first, I thought it was because my heart was pounding too loudly, that too much blood was sluicing between my ears, but then I realized it was because a goddamn windstorm was blowing through the throne room. A strange roaring sound reverberated through my head as the force of the wind pushed me onto my ass. My golden blond hair flew in front of my face, momentarily obscuring everything from view.

"What the fuck is happening?" Killian had to scream

to be heard over the storm. His red hair was sticking out in all directions, and his shirt was halfway over his head, revealing the hard lines of his abs. He awkwardly tried to press his clothing back down as he attempted to stumble to his feet. He couldn't even make it to his knees before the wind blew him back to the ground.

Lupe roared, the sound so innately lethal and predatory that I felt it in the hollow of my bones. It took monumental effort, but I was able to swivel my head to see him trudging forward through the typhoon of air, his brown hair blowing around him and his shirt clinging to his hard pectorals.

"I told Z not to use the goddamn dagger!" Bash bellowed in rage, though I couldn't see where he was as a chair flew through the air directly over my head and connected with the wall behind us.

I squinted through the storm, desperately trying to set eyes upon Z. At first, she was impossible to see amidst the flurry of wind and miscellaneous items billowing around us, but the more I focused, the more she came into view.

Horror lit a thousand fires in my veins, and I once again attempted to climb to my feet. I needed to get to her, to save her.

"Z!" I screamed in anguish.

"What the fuck is happening, Dair?" Devlin demanded from somewhere to the right of me. "What do you see?"

"I see..."

I didn't even know what I was seeing, which terrified me more than anything else.

All six kings were slumped over on their thrones,

their eyelids shut and their breathing even. Z remained standing over my father, her hand an iron vise around the hilt of the dagger. Preternatural black wisps of smoke seemed to be emitting from the kings' bodies. It almost reminded me of shadow magic, though I spotted rivulets of red and even purple circulating amidst the smoke.

The smoke...

Horror numbed my every thought as I watched it funnel into her nostrils, mouth, and ears. Her skin crawled as the strange, indecipherable magic cascaded through her veins.

"Dark magic," Bash breathed from beside me. I hadn't even heard him approach, too horrified by the scene before me. When I glanced at him in alarm, he swallowed. "Aaliyah's magic... The power she gave the kings... It was dark magic."

"And now it's entering Z," I whispered in under-standing. Fear lanced my heart at the revelation of what was happening to the woman I loved.

I desperately tried to get to her, tried to take a single step through the sludge-like air, but it proved to be futile. I screamed her name mindlessly, but she never turned to stare at me.

She never removed her hand from the damn dagger still sticking out of my dad's chest.

And then...

Everything stopped.

The wind snapped back into Z like a rubber band being pulled too taut, though she still didn't move to face us. Her head was lowered, golden curls concealing her face from view, but her body trembled with unfettered energy.

Shocked gasps and murmurs rippled through the crowd, and one of the 'brides' began to sob from where she sat curled on the ground, her arms above her head. Lupe was holding his sister protectively, his light blue eyes trained on Z's back, just like mine were.

"Z?" he rasped out.

Slowly, mechanically almost, Z lifted a single hand into the air. Silence descended as we all watched with bated breath, wondering what she was about to do.

And then, she snapped her fingers, and everyone around us dropped to the ground, dead.

The guards. The women our fathers told us to marry. The crowd of onlookers.

Dead.

There was nothing dramatic about their deaths—no blood oozing from their eyes or leaking from their mouths. No heads bent at unnatural angles or bodies grotesquely deformed. They simply fell over, their expressions perpetually fixed in ones of fear, horror, and shock.

Axel spun around in a wide circle, seemingly surprised he had been spared, and Lupe's grip on a still trembling Atta tightened almost imperceptibly.

"Z?" Devlin took a tentative step closer.

Z slowly turned around.

I sucked in a sharp breath, a noise that was echoed by all of us who were still alive.

My mate's eyes were normally a shade of light blue, a striking contrast to her fair skin and golden ringlets. But just then, they were pitch-black, as if the pupils had swallowed the irises and sclerae.

Her wedding dress fanned out around her, and she tilted her head to the side as she studied us. There was no recognition in her gaze, no spark of love. Nothing but an apathetic mask peered back at me from the face of the woman I loved more than life itself.

"Z?" Killian trembled beside me, and my mate's lips stretched into a snake-like grin. Poisonous. Deadly. Unforgiving.

"What's the matter, Kill?" she asked in a singsong, mocking voice. She absently touched a red smear on the front of her wedding dress. "Afraid of a little blood?"

TWENTY-EIGHT

KILLIAN

This woman was not my mate.

Not my Z.

Sure, she had the same face, the same blonde hair, the same crooked smile, but everything about her was all wrong. Z's smile usually expanded towards her eyes, causing the blue to sparkle like water in sunlight. But this Z's smile? It was forced, a mockery of the grin I had come to know and love. And her eyes...

Her sweet, beautiful eyes...

Staring into them now reminded me of the ocean—dark, fathomless, and full of monsters you couldn't even begin to comprehend.

"You killed all of those people," Ryland murmured, his shadows twitching around his broad form as he hovered in the corner of the room.

"Are you suggesting I let them live?" Once again, Z canted her head slightly to the side, an expression of genuine disbelief marring her perfect features. "That's silly of you, Ryland." She heaved out a prolonged breath and descended the last few steps of the raised platform, stopping when she was before us. "You're lucky I let you guys live."

"Z, this isn't you—" Bash's heartfelt plea was interrupted by a dark portal manifesting in the center of the throne room.

I spun around, my heart in my throat, to see a familiar red-haired woman step through the swirling vortex of smoke.

Aaliyah.

She appeared positively giddy as she studied the room and the dead bodies littering it.

"You..." Ryland growled threateningly, his shadows propelling him forward in a blur of darkness. "You did this."

Aaliyah placed a hand over her chest in mock surprise. "I have no idea what you mean, shadow. I simply helped you guys defeat the kings, did I not?"

"Y-you did something to Z," I stammered out, hating how small I suddenly felt. How useless. Where did all my strength and courage go when I needed it? "What did you do?"

"Nothing." Aaliyah pushed her lips out into a pout. "I mean, it's not my fault that she was the one who used the dagger on the kings. If one of you had used it, it would've happened to you..." She feigned a sigh, studying her nails without a care in the world.

"What the fuck did you do?" Lupe growled out.

"You probably should've read the entire text of that

little book B found before you did anything rash," Aaliyah remarked, amusement obvious in the tilt of her lips.

"The dagger..." Bash scrubbed a hand through his ash-blond hair. "It took the magic away from the kings, just as you promised." He swallowed. "But it also placed that dark magic inside of Z."

Looking into Aaliyah's ineffably smug stare made me want to lunge forward and slap her. The intensity of my hatred towards her took me by surprise. I'd never wanted to hit a female as badly as I did her.

"The world is nothing if not a dangerous spider web, Sebastian," Aaliyah cooed with a saccharine-sweet grin. "The second you become trapped in it, it's impossible to free yourself. You just have to wait until the spider comes and eats you." She playfully gnashed her teeth together and then giggled. The noise clawed at my back and sliced open my skin. "You're all nothing but pathetic, little flies. But Z? Z's a spider." Her smile softened when she flicked her gaze towards my mate.

Struggling to keep my expression placid, to not allow her to see how rattled I was by this entire situation, I snapped out, "You mean nothing to Z. You may as well be a damn candle next to the brilliance of the sun. You can't compare to her."

I didn't know where that burst of courage came from, but it was damn worth it, especially when Aaliyah's face darkened.

"Watch your mouth, incubus," she hissed.

"Enough with the dramatics." Z rolled her black eyes

as she sashayed forward, her white wedding dress cascading over the faces of the men and women she'd killed. She didn't give their dead bodies more than a passing stare, utterly indifferent to the carnage she'd caused.

Fuck, this wasn't Z. This wasn't the woman I loved.

How the hell were we supposed to get her back?

"You can't seriously be thinking of going with her?" Ryland's voice was incredulous and maybe even a little desperate.

"She's my sister, Ryland." Z waved a hand in the air dismissively before shifting her gaze towards mine. Our eyes met, and a bolt of ice slashed through my chest. "I'm keeping you alive because of...sentimentality's sake, but don't think I'll extend the courtesy again if you try to stop me or my sister."

"Z, don't do this," Jax all but begged. He stumbled forward and dropped to his knees at her feet. "You promised you wouldn't leave me. Please."

Z's eyes shone like flinty chips in the darkness. "That was the old Z, Jax. The new Z..." She pursed her lips and shrugged. "She honestly doesn't give a damn."

Her words were like a garrote, digging into me so deep, they drew blood.

"Z..." Jax pleaded.

"Grow the fuck up, Jax." She leaned down and patted his cheek condescendingly. "Maybe you wouldn't be so reliant on me if you actually grew a pair and drank some blood."

I felt the breath being siphoned from my body when

she laughed, the dark, husky sound curling around me like smoke.

"Wait!" Like before, my mouth moved away from me before my brain could catch up. I stumbled forward a few steps as Z's lips curled into a frown and Aaliyah's eyebrows bunched together. "Take me with you."

"Killian—" Bash hissed, but I ignored him.

"Why the fuck would we do that, incubus?" Aaliyah rolled her eyes, but I could see Z wavering. She considered me with a tiny frown.

My heart stuttered and got caught in my throat as I held my mate's stare, begging her to see me, to remember me. Her face was so pinched, you'd think she'd just swallowed a lemon, but she didn't immediately deny my request.

I continued on before I could lose my nerve. "I'm an incubus, so I'm really good at the...errr...the sexy stuff. Really, really good. Z knows." I swallowed heavily. "Z, you could keep me with you so I could pleasure you and...um...do sexy stuff to you."

Fuck, Killian, you really suck at selling yourself.

"I see." Z's lips pursed further.

"I'll be, like, an incubus on tap," I continued desperately. "My entire purpose will be all about your pleasure."

Aaliyah scoffed haughtily. "If it's pleasure you want, sister, I can find you a thousand incubi who actually know how to use their cocks."

No fucking way in hell would I allow that to happen.

"Z, you know me. You know that I'm good." I attempted to stand straighter and puff out my chest, emulating a confidence I didn't truly feel. "Take me with you."

"You'll only be allowed to touch me, incubus." Z stepped forward and grabbed a hold of my wrist, giving it a squeeze. "No one else."

"I don't want anyone else," I answered honestly.

A muscle in her cheek fluttered, and her grip around my wrist tightened. "All right. I suppose it wouldn't hurt."

"Killian," Devlin hissed, his voice rife with alarm and fear.

I tried to send my brothers a reassuring smile over my shoulder, though I knew it was slightly wobbly and off-kilter.

What was the saying?

Fake it till you make it?

I definitely was faking the shit out of this right now.

"I'll be okay," I assured them, praying it was the truth. "I'll look after our girl."

Z gave my wrist a small tug, and I was helpless to do anything but stumble forward. Aaliyah continued to watch me with a pinched face, her eyes narrowing in suspicion, but I simply offered her a tentative smile and wave.

Please, please don't kill me. Pretty please with sugar on top.

Please give me the strength to be brave and smart enough to save our mate.

"Kill! Z! Don't do this," one of my brothers implored, but I didn't look over my shoulder to see which one. At the moment, their voices all sounded the same—muted and distant through the waves of blood cresting against my skull. My heart pounded erratically, and I knew Z could feel it where her fingers dug into my wrist.

And then we stepped through the churning portal, and the world around me faded in a burst of dark ink.

EPILOGUE

S

"Quit pacing, brother," T hissed, but his words barely registered as I forked my fingers through my light brown hair.

Where the fuck were they?

Aaliyah promised they would be here soon, so what was taking them so long?

My thoughts swirled rapidly as my feet ate up the distance from one wall to the other in the ostentatious mansion Aaliyah had claimed for herself.

From the corner of the room, Mali watched on with wide, terrified eyes. Her vampire fangs lengthened as she nibbled on her lower lip, and I flashed her a wide, toothy smile. She blanched, seeming to curl in on herself like old, brittle paper, and I scoffed at how ridiculous she was behaving.

Sure, she had believed me to be dead, but I was the same man I had been when those shifters tore me apart and Devlin made a deal with me to save my soul. The exact. Same. Man.

I rubbed my hand through my disheveled brown curls again and frowned when a strand got tangled in my fingers. Was I...? Was I losing hair? I swallowed heavily as I stared at the innocent brown curl tangled between my fingers before immediately shoving it into my pocket. I didn't want T to see, to know how...dysfunctional I was becoming. How broken.

The prospect of my imminent hair loss faded when a portal materialized in the center of the living room and three figures stepped out. Aaliyah, looking as radiant and pretentious as always in a frilly green dress that hugged her curves. The fucking incubus, who swallowed convulsively as he glanced around the room, stark fear splayed across his features.

And then...

Z.

My heart rate elevated when I took sight of her slender frame outfitted in a white wedding dress. Her golden curls tumbled loose around her shoulders, and I had to rein in the impulse to grab a strand of that gorgeous blonde hair, tilt her face upwards, and kiss that pink, pouty mouth. My cock stirred to life in my pants as lust barraged me from every direction, blowing air into my lungs and breathing life into a body I'd long thought dead.

"Did it work?" T's face had drained of all color, his eyes haunted as he stared at Z. No, not at Z...

At her pitch-black eyes.

I bit my lower lip at the thought of gazing into those gorgeous, onyx gemstones as I fucked her tight little cunt. Would she still be as wet for me as she had been years ago, before her bastard of a boyfriend stole me away? Or would her pussy be used up from all of her so-called mates? The thought unfurled wrath in my stomach, along with a healthy dose of envy. It exploded in every direction, coursing through my veins like molten magma.

Unwittingly, my gaze slid to that damn incubus. What the fuck was he doing here? Aaliyah promised me Z if T utilized his contacts in the Alphabet Resistance to figure out her exact location. This incubus fucker was never supposed to be in the equation.

I was a greedy, selfish fucker, and I didn't want to share. At all. Z was fucking mine.

My girl glanced dismissively around the room, her eyes sweeping over me but never sticking. I noticed her tiny hand was gripping the incubus's wrist like a life raft, and the jealousy that curdled in my bloodstream was acidic. It burned everything it came into contact with in a torrent of white-hot fire.

Mali cowered in the corner of the room, her large eyes wide and terrified as she stared at what remained of her best friend.

"Z..." she whimpered helplessly, and the incubus's head whipped in her direction. The two of them exchanged a wordless conversation, and the redheaded fucker's jaw clenched, his eyes narrowing to slits.

"It worked," Aaliyah said triumphantly, gesturing towards an impassive Z.

I wanted her to look at me, to notice me, but instead, her attention remained riveted on my brother.

"Z, I don't know—" T began, and Z finally released the incubus's wrist to take a step in our direction.

"I know you sold me out to Hans at the Bloody Carnival," Z hissed.

If it were possible, T's face turned even paler. It was as if all the color dissipated with that one sentence.

"I don't know what you mean—"

"You allowed me to be taken and sold," she growled out. "You knew what could've happened to me but didn't care."

T glanced desperately in my direction, but I simply regarded him with cold indifference.

What the fuck was Z talking about? T would never have betrayed her like that. He knew how much she meant to me, how much I loved her. He wouldn't—

T swallowed and took an automatic step backwards, and it was then that I saw the guilt in his eyes. It stabbed at something already bleeding inside of me, something broken beyond repair. Every muscle in my body locked tight as the full truth of T's betrayal washed over me in a crushing tsunami.

T betrayed Z.

He sold her to the fucking vampires.

And for what?

Memories momentarily pierced the wrath percolating in my heart.

My soul. Yes, that was it.

He traded Z...for my soul.

And I fucking hated him for that.

My breathing was stuttered, a noisy exhale followed by an equally noisy inhale, and it took every ounce of willpower I possessed to not teach my damn brother a lesson. To tear him apart with my bare hands. How could he? What the fuck was he thinking?

"I-I saved you," T stuttered, still shuffling backwards as Z advanced. "When the gorgon attacked you, I saved you—"

"Do you really think that makes up for the fact that you goddamn sold me?" she hissed, and I swore her veins pulsated and writhed, the color more black than blue beneath her porcelain skin. "That you left me to die?"

Fuck, she looked so beautiful like that—full of wrath and fury, vengeance and death. Full of *life*. With her golden hair and flowing white dress, she truly looked like an angel.

My angel.

Only mine.

I absently scratched at the skin on my wrist, feeling blood well and then cascade onto the carpet in rivulets of red. One glance down confirmed a chunk of skin had fallen onto the floor at my feet. I quickly placed my hands behind my back before anyone could notice and comment on it.

My angel wouldn't love me anymore if she knew I was falling apart, and I *needed* her to love me.

Z continued to advance on a rapidly retreating T, her features twisted in anger.

"There will be no forgiveness, T," she bit out. Before I could even blink, she was directly in front of my brother with her hands around his neck. One twist, and his body fell to the ground, his eyes vacant and unseeing.

Mali shrieked from her corner of the room, and the incubus's eyes widened in surprise and fear.

I knew what emotions I was supposed to feel after seeing my brother get murdered—horror, surprise, anger, maybe even a little guilt—but not one of them managed to breach my defenses. They couldn't slice through the walls of wrath, lust, pride, envy, greed, sloth, and gluttony I had erected around myself. Those emotions... Those emotions I understood. They enveloped me in a warm embrace, and I couldn't differentiate where I ended and they began.

But the other emotions? The ones that made me weak?

They were nothing but a distant memory.

I couldn't even remember what horror or sadness felt like.

Lust stirred in my bones as Z stared dispassionately at T's dead body and Aaliyah began to laugh jovially.

My brother was dead, murdered by the woman I loved, and I had never been more turned on in my life.

"Z," I murmured, and her head snapped in my direction.

For a brief, brief moment, her apathetic veneer crumbled and brilliant blue eyes peered back at me. Shock splayed across her face, and her pink lips parted. Just as quickly, her mask slammed down into place and ink seeped back into her eyes, overtaking the blue. Anger hammered off her like a malevolent energy, even as a lazy, indolent smile curled up her lips.

My heart thundered at her proximity, and goose bumps skittered up and down my skin. Sparks of excitement and arousal shot through my body, crackling through my nerve endings.

"S." My name was a breathy exhale on her lips.

"Z." I took a step towards her. There were so many things I wanted to say to her, so many things I wanted her to know, but all I said was, "I came back for you. We can be together now."

"I suppose we can." That perpetual smirk didn't leave her face as she tilted her head slightly to the side.

"We just have to take care of the incubus." I slid my gaze towards the red-haired man, who watched the two of us with blatant horror splayed across his face.

He took an automatic step backwards, a muscle in his throat bobbing, and Z shifted slightly to follow the direction of my gaze.

Her smile sharpened as she stared into the incubus's glittering emerald eyes. "This should be fun."

And then, Z advanced on him.

AFTERWORD

On a scale of one to ten, how bad was that cliffhanger? A solid eight, perhaps? A nine? Or maybe it was only a five on your scale.

Either way, thank you so much for reading the next installment of The Damning! I hope you enjoyed revisiting Z's world as much as I enjoyed writing it. I plan to write the next two books—Lust and Wrath—this year! Make sure to join my group to see my official release schedule. My group members will be the first to know if anything changes.

ACKNOWLEDGMENTS

Thank you to my incredible alphas, Ellen, Ash, and Kelly, for helping me make this the best book possible.

Thank you to my amazing editor, Lindsey, and my cover designer, Melody.

And finally, I would like to thank you, the reader, for loving Z and her mates as much as I do. I know it can get irritating when an author doesn't release as rapidly as you would like them to, but I appreciate you guys sticking with me regardless! If you know me at all, you know that I pour my blood, sweat, and tears into all of my books, and this one is no different. So thank you for reading this series, for loving these characters, and for supporting me unconditionally. I love you all!

ABOUT THE AUTHOR

Katie May is a reverse harem author, a KDP All-Star winner, and an *USA Today* Bestselling Author. She lives in West Michigan with her family, cat, and adorable puppy. When not writing, she can be found reading a good book, listening to broadway musicals, or playing games. Join Katie's Gang to stay updated on all her releases! And did you know she has a TikTok? Yeah, me neither. Follow her here! But be warned...she's an awkward noodle.

ALSO BY KATIE MAY

Together We Fall (Apocalyptic Reverse Harem, COMPLETED)

1. The Darkness We Crave

2. The Light We Seek

3. The Storm We Face

4. The Monsters We Hunt

Beyond the Shadows (Horror Reverse Harem, COMPLETED)

1. Gangs and Ghosts

2. Guns and Graveyards

3. Gallows and Ghouls

Out of Sight (Prison Reverse Harem, COMPLETED)

1. Blindly Indicted

2. Blindly Acquitted

Kingdom of Wolves (Shifter Reverse Harem Duet, COMPLETED)

1. Torn to Bits

2. Ripped to Shreds

The Damning (Fantasy Paranormal Reverse Harem)

1. Greed

2. Envy

3. Gluttony

4. Sloth

5. Pride

Prodigium Academy (Horror Comedy Academy Reverse Harem)

1. Monsters

2. Roaring

3. Venom

Tory's School for the Trouble (Bully Horror Academy Reverse Harem)

1. Between

2. Beyond

3. Beneath

Kings of Grove Academy (Contemporary Academy Reverse Harem)

1. Mania

2. Psychotic

3. Pandemonium

Supernaturalette (Interactive Reverse Harem)

1. Introductions

2. First Dates

3. Group Outing

4. Game Night

5. Exes

6. Truth or Dare

7. Scavenger Hunt

CO-WRITES

Afterworld Academy with Loxley Savage (Academy Fantasy Reverse Harem, COMPLETED)

1. Dearly Departed

2. Darkness Deceives

3. Defying Destiny

Darkest Flames with Ann Denton (Paranormal Reverse Harem, COMPLETED)

1. Demon Kissed

1.5. Demon Stalked

2. Demon Loved

3. Demon Sworn

Darkest Queen with Ann Denton (Paranormal Reverse Harem)

1. For Whom the Bell Tolls

Fae Revealed with Quinn Arthurs (Paranormal Reverse Harem)

1. Courting Darkness

2. Seducing Shadows

STAND-ALONES

Toxicity (Contemporary Reverse Harem)

Not All Heroes Wear Capes (Just Dresses) (Short Comedic Reverse Harem)

Charming Devils (Bully/Revenge Reverse Harem)

Goddess of Pain (Fantasy Reverse Harem)

Demon's Joy (Holiday Reverse Harem)

Broken Howl (Wolf Shifter Reverse Harem)

BOXSETS

Together We Fall

9 798890 640161